PUFFIN BOOKS

QUEST FOR THE SUN

V. M. Jones lives in Christchurch, New Zealand, with her husband and two sons. Her previous novels are *Buddy*, which won the Junior Fiction and Best First Book Awards in the 2003 New Zealand Post Children's Book Awards, and *Juggling with Mandarins*, winner of the 2004 Junior Fiction Award. *The Serpents of Arakesh*, the first book in The Karazan Quartet, was shortlisted for both the 2004 New Zealand Post Junior Fiction Award and the 2004 LIANZA Esther Glen Medal. *Quest for the Sun* is the final book in The Karazan Quartet.

karazan.co.uk

D1291541

QUEST FOR THE SUN

KARAZAN
The Fourth

V. M. JONES

PUFFIN

I would like to acknowledge my editor, Lorain Day:
For your wisdom, guidance and endless patience;
For your rare gift of always being right, yet somehow never annoying;
For being there every time I needed you,
And above all, for your friendship –
Thank you.

PUFFIN BOOKS

Published by the Penguin Group
Penguin Books Ltd, 80 Strand, London WC2R 0RL, England
Penguin Group (USA) Inc., 375 Hudson Street, New York, New York 10014, USA
Penguin Group (Canada), 90 Eglinton Avenue East, Suite 700, Toronto, Ontario, Canada M4P 2Y3
(a division of Pearson Penguin Canada Inc.)
Penguin Ireland, 25 St Stephen's Green, Dublin 2, Ireland (a division of Penguin Books Ltd)
Penguin Group (Australia), 250 Camberwell Road, Camberwell, Victoria 3124, Australia
(a division of Pearson Australia Group Pty Ltd)
Penguin Books India Pvt Ltd, 11 Community Centre, Panchsheel Park, New Delhi – 110 017, India
Penguin Group (NZ), cnr Airborne and Rosedale Roads, Albany, Auckland 1310, New Zealand
(a division of Pearson New Zealand Ltd)
Penguin Books (South Africa) (Pty) Ltd, 24 Sturdee Avenue, Rosebank, Johannesburg 2196, South Africa

Penguin Books Ltd, Registered Offices: 80 Strand, London WC2R 0RL, England

www.penguin.com

First published in New Zealand by HarperCollins Publishers (New Zealand) Ltd 2005
First published in Great Britain in Puffin Books 2006
1

Text copyright © V. M. Jones, 2005
Illustrations copyright © Christopher Downes, 2005

The moral right of the author and illustrator has been asserted

Set in 11.5/15.5 pt Monotype Plantin
Typeset by Rowland Phototypesetting Ltd, Bury St Edmunds, Suffolk
Made and printed in England by Clays Ltd, St Ives plc

British Library Cataloguing in Publication Data
A CIP catalogue record for this book is available from the British Library

ISBN-13: 978-0-141-31945-2
ISBN-10: 0-141-31945-3

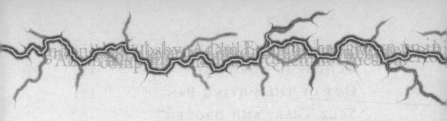

CONTENTS

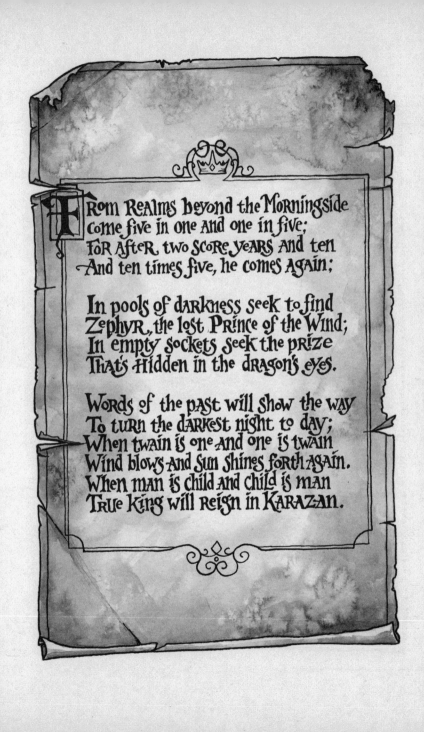

From Realms beyond the Morningside
come five in one and one in five;
For after, two score years and ten
And ten times five, he comes again;

In pools of darkness seek to find
Zephyr, the lost Prince of the Wind;
In empty sockets seek the prize
That's hidden in the dragon's eyes.

Words of the past will show the way
To turn the darkest night to day;
When twain is one and one is twain
Wind blows and sun shines forth again.
When man is child and child is man
True King will reign in Karazan.

PROLOGUE

Twin moons hang low over the treetops, their light a burnished barrier between the shadows of the forest and the sleeping city walls. High above the forest floor the old owl roosts on his favourite perch. The downy feathers of his breast stir in the night air. He has hunted well, but something keeps him here, his talons locked on the rough bark, his gaze fixed on the spill of moonlight below. There is a movement in the wall. Quicker than thought the owl's head turns, his eyes snapping into focus. His grip tightens.

A dark outline traces itself on the stone. A rectangular section of wall shifts and swings outwards. The owl stares, unblinking. Two plumes of mist breathe themselves at man-height into the brittle air. For an instant they mingle in murmured words, whisper-soft; then part.

The owl's night vision is keener than any living creature's, but even he can see nothing other than two rhythmic gusts of vapour, one moving soundlessly eastwards, towards the sea, the other into the clutching shadows of the forest.

The radar-dish of feathers rimming the owl's face catches faint ripples of sound, channelling it into ears that can hear and interpret a mouse stepping on a twig at thirty metres. His three-dimensional hearing builds up a sound picture of the creature moving cautiously towards him over the icy ground. A man, carrying a heavy, inert bundle.

A sense separate from sight or hearing tells the owl he is in no danger: the man's attention is focused elsewhere. The heart-shaped face tilts downwards, then swivels to follow as the man passes beneath the tree. The owl's brain processes the changing frequency of sound waves as the crunch of frost gives way to the rustle of leaves . . . and the man begins to run.

The owl turns to face forward again. Now the first groping tentacles of shadow are touching the city walls; the moons will soon be gone and the sun will rise . . .

A fleeting after-image of the sounds he has seen echoes in the owl's mind. 'Whooo,' he hoots softly. 'Whooooo?' He ruffles his feathers, spreads his wings and floats silently away into the darkness.

To the east the first light of the new morning streaks the sky with violet, the sea with gold. The bulk of the city walls and the pinnacles of the palace take shape against the lightening horizon.

In the heart of the palace a private garden rings with

the clamour of waking birds. Abruptly their song is silenced. A purple-cloaked figure is hurrying towards the royal apartments at a hitching shuffle.

The soldier stationed at the entrance snaps to attention. He might not exist. Eagerly the misshapen figure hobbles up the stairway to the bedchamber. At the top he pauses, cracks his knuckles, tilts his head to listen.

The landing is lit by burning brands in brackets at either side of the arched doorway. A rug of royal scarlet rests on the floor; beside the door a pedestal holds a delicately painted porcelain urn. Grey light drifts up from below as morning steals softly through the narrow windows that light the stairwell.

Two soldiers guard the door, swords crossed. The sorcerer approaches. The torches flicker as the swirl of his cloak disturbs the still air; reflections of flame spill scarlet stains down the razor edges of the swords. Dark eyes burn from a nest of hair. 'Well? Has it come – the cry of the newborn?'

Before the guards can reply, there is the sound of booted feet on the stairs. They move with a heavy, deliberate tread. 'Stand aside. The King approaches. The hour is come.'

To the west, in the depths of the forest, night is dissolving into the gossamer greyness of dawn. The man runs uphill. His lungs are on fire; his breath comes in harsh gasps. His shoulders burn with the weight he cradles tenderly.

He stops to check that the sound of the stream is

still within hearing, as he was told he must. He cannot see his feet on the forest floor; cannot see the familiar face nestled within the soft fur. His fingers feel for the silken cascade of hair, the smoothness of the cheek . . . but it is cold as marble. He can see nothing; hear nothing. Fear twists his heart. He bends closer. '*Zaronel?*' he whispers. '*Ronel . . .*'

A tiny mewling comes from deep within the mantle, and he feels an answering sigh, the caress of a breath on his skin. His soul lifts. He runs on, the air lightening around him with every stride. At last the trees begin to thin. Ahead he sees pale sky and looming rock; a standing stone, tall as a man.

This is the place.

Gently he lowers his burden to the ground. A tangle of young ferns cushions and conceals it, but as he withdraws his hand he sees her face at last. It is bloodless and still. He steels himself for what he knows he must do. His hand reaches out; by touch he finds the tiny bundle.

'*No . . .*' A low cry of anguish, as if it is her heart he is taking.

'*Yes. Strength and courage, Zaronel of Karazan. I will return.*'

The red rim of the rising sun bleeds over the horizon. A shadow grows on the rose-washed surface of the cliff, faint at first, stretching tall as the sky. The sun drags itself up from the sea; the shadow strengthens and begins to shrink.

Now there is another shadow on the cliff face: the ghost of a man. The shadow-figure blends into the shadow of the standing stone, merges with it, and is gone.

The dead of night. A white gate creaks open of its own accord. Soft footfalls crunch on gravel . . . then move soundlessly over grass. Up the red steps . . . *one, two, three* . . . into the deep shadows of the porch.

There is the soft *tap* of something solid being set down with infinite care; a scrape as it is pushed into the furthest corner, out of the wind. A pause as two objects are snuggled into the lacy folds of a shawl. The outline of a box appears and disappears as clumsy, gentle hands tuck and rearrange, resting one last time on the swaddled bundle in a silent blessing.

Invisible footsteps pad across grass; crunch on gravel. The gate snicks shut.

In the dark stillness of the porch, snug as a caterpillar in a cocoon, a tufty-haired baby blinks and yawns. He chews sleepily on his fist, finds his thumb and starts to suck.

It is a long time till dawn.

PROMISES

'I sort of thought I saw a reflection of myself – a kind of wavery splodge –'

'Get real, Jamie,' interrupted Richard. 'If you saw anything fat and round it was probably the moon.'

'It couldn't have been the moon,' said Gen. 'There were no reflections in the pool: not the clouds, not the moon, not our faces. Only Adam.'

Kenta spoke softly, quoting from the poem on the magical parchment:

'In pools of darkness seek to find
Zephyr, the lost Prince of the Wind;
In empty sockets seek the prize
That's hidden in the dragon's eyes.'

'I still don't get it,' said Richard. 'We're saying it's Adam? That Adam is him – Zephyr, the Prince of the Wind? But that's crazy. Adam's just an ordinary kid.'

'I dunno . . .' Jamie lowered his voice. 'There's a lot about Adam we don't know. Things he's kept . . . well . . . private. The whole orphanage thing, that silver flute . . . he even looks different, with his dark

7

skin. There's always been something . . . look at him now, for instance.'

Though they were speaking quietly, their voices carried across to where I was sitting, staring at the retreating storm. All my life there'd been so much I didn't know, so many questions I'd dreamed of one day finding answers to. Now I knew. And I'd never felt so alone.

'If it was me,' Jamie went on, 'I'd be excited. I'd be busy figuring out what must have happened, and what to do next . . .'

'Exactly.' Kenta's voice was very low. '*What to do next*. How do you think *Adam* feels? We were all expecting some kind of grown-up super-hero on a winged horse to magically swoop down and solve all our problems –'

'With an army to help him,' chipped in Rich.

'– and now what do we discover? There's no super-hero . . .'

'No winged horse . . .'

'No army . . .'

'Only Adam.'

'And us,' said Kenta fiercely. 'His friends.'

And suddenly, with those two words, everything changed. The others were all around me, the girls hugging me and crying, Rich giving me a clap on the back that practically busted my spine, Jamie shaking my hand and saying, 'Congratulations, Adam; you really deserve it,' as if I'd been made a prefect or picked for a sports team or something.

8

Rich conjured up some dry wood and soon we were huddled round a roaring fire. Gen unearthed a bag of marshmallows from her pack and we toasted them, squishing them between chocolate biscuits. 'I was saving the biscuits for a special occasion,' Jamie told us with his mouth full, a strand of marshmallow dangling from his chin, 'but I don't reckon any occasion could be more special than this!'

Gradually the cold numbness inside me started to thaw. Frowning down at the pink marshmallow on the end of my stick, turning it slowly over the flames, I watched it darken and bulge, then sprout shiny caramel bubbles and collapse into squishy gloop I only just managed to catch on my biscuit.

That was what seemed to be happening to me inside: a swelling warmth. Part of me wanted to capture it before it escaped forever, but another part of me – a deep-rooted, certain part that was new and strange – knew it would still be there when I crept into my sleeping bag and turned my back to the others and slipped my thumb into my mouth . . . still there when I woke in the morning and saw the first light brush the sky of Karazan with gold.

A wish had come true and a prayer had been answered, and the wonder of it would be with me forever.

'So,' said Rich cheerfully once the last crumbs had disappeared, 'what next? I guess we should start thinking how the five of us are going to sneak into the

Stronghold of Arraz . . . and what the heck to do when we get there.'

But there was something he was forgetting. For a while I'd almost managed to forget it too – or at least pretend I had. I took a deep breath. I expected the words to come out in a kind of strangled croak, or maybe not find their way out at all, but my voice sounded steady and matter-of-fact. 'Not us. Me.'

Four pairs of eyes stared at me across the fire. 'What d'you mean, you?' squeaked Jamie.

'We made a promise, remember? A promise to Q . . .'

It seemed like a lifetime ago. We'd been huddled in the library at Quested Court on what should have been a day of celebration, the last game in Q's fantasy computer-game series finally finished. How long had it taken for it to turn into a nightmare?

As long as it took words to appear on a computer screen.

If I closed my eyes I could still see them scrolling down as if they were imprinted on my retina:

| *stand* | *take* | *to* | *King* |
| *we* | *you* | *throw* | *Karazeel* |

We understand you undertake to overthrow King Karazeel. A message from another world: Karazeel and Evor's twisted interpretation of Q's last computer game, *Power Quest to Karazan.*

It didn't take us long to figure out what must have

10

happened. Using the microcomputer Jamie had left in Shakesh, they'd somehow hooked into the VRE Interface on the Quested Court computer system. Q had tried to explain how, but all the jargon had formed a log-jam in my brain and I hadn't understood half of it. But one thing had been horrifyingly clear to all of us, even Q's five-year-old daughter Hannah: King Karazeel and his evil sorcerer Evor now had direct access to every computer belonging to every kid who'd ever bought a Karazan computer game.

In the space of half an hour, an innocent computer game had changed into a war game – from fantasy to reality. Because Karazeel and Evor believed the best form of defence was attack: an attack that would unleash hordes of computer-generated monsters into our world.

Unless we could stop them.

That's what we'd come to Karazan to do: on a desperate mission to find the one person with the power to overthrow King Karazeel. Zephyr, Prince of the Wind, vanished into legend fifty long years before.

Q hadn't wanted to let us come, but in the end he'd agreed – on one condition. As soon as we found Zephyr we'd leave him to deal with Karazeel and come straight home. And we'd all promised, with varying degrees of reluctance; but the promises had been made. Now, finally, after days of blundering round Karazan, we'd accomplished our mission. Zephyr had been found. It was home time.

There was a slight complication . . . but only for one of us.

Me, Adam Equinox: Zephyr. The guy holding the entire future of Karazan – not to mention our own world – in his ham-fisted hands.

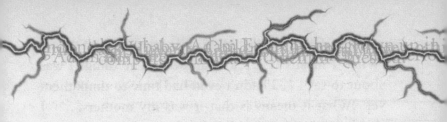

AN ARMY OF FIVE

'But . . .' said Richard.

'But what?' Jamie looked at him. From his expression it was impossible to tell whether he was hoping Rich would manage to find a way out of the promise, or not.

'But Q didn't know it would turn out to be Adam,' said Gen.

There was silence while we all tried to imagine what Q's reaction would have been if he *had* somehow known. Thinking of him, in his frayed old jersey and smeary specs, I suddenly wanted him there. I wanted to be held close, to see the smile in his kind blue eyes, to hand over the burden I suddenly found myself carrying and leave him to sort it out. Except he wouldn't be able to. Only one person could. It kept coming back to that.

Then I was talking slowly, finding the words as I went along. 'I feel so weird about this. I can't believe it . . . and at the same time it's almost as if I've always known.' I risked a quick glance to see if they were laughing. They weren't. Rich was scowling at the ground; Gen was listening, her eyes full of tears. 'What it means is . . .' I swallowed. The things I was about to say . . . I hadn't even had time to think them yet. 'What it means is that it was my mother . . . ' I shook my head, searching for the words. 'It was my father . . . ' My voice cracked. The shadowy image I'd kept tucked away in a corner of my mind had a face now: a strong profile, etched in gold. 'I've always wondered where I belong. Now I know. This is mine to do; it's my . . .'

'Destiny,' offered Jamie helpfully. 'But you don't need to get all starry-eyed, Adam. We understand how you feel. When you think about it, we have destinies too. Smaller ones maybe, but destinies just the same. Remember the poem? *Five in one and one in five . . .*'

I glanced up at him. He met my gaze, bug-eyed with sincerity.

'Jamie's right,' said Gen. 'Don't forget you also made a promise to Q – and you don't seem to have a problem breaking it.'

I opened my mouth, realised I had no idea what to say, and shut it again.

'Q would never want us to leave you on your own,' said Kenta.

'Of course he wouldn't,' agreed Rich. 'And anyhow, the whole point of promises is to be broken – or at least bent.'

'But it will be dangerous! I don't have the least idea what I'm supposed to do. I just know I have to try. I can't let you put yourselves in danger for me –'

'Zip it right now, Adam Equinox!' Jamie was on his feet, his face bright pink and his hands clenched. 'We're not doing it for you! We're doing it for . . . for the Future of Mankind, and if helps you as well, then great. We're coming with you, and nothing you can say is going to stop us!'

There was a startled silence.

'So you have an army after all, Adam,' grinned Rich. 'An army of four – whether you want it or not.'

'Five,' corrected Kenta, 'counting Blue-bum.'

Blue-bum. I hadn't given him a thought, and by the looks on the others' faces they hadn't either. Jamie glanced guiltily at the marshmallow packet, lying empty beside the fire. The rest of us peered round the circle of firelight, looking for the little chatterbot's familiar, hunched form.

Then Kenta was on her feet, moving quickly into the darkness of the rocky overhang where we'd dumped our bags. 'There you are! Had you fallen asleep? Come and join us. We've discovered the most amazing thing . . .'

But one look at Blue-bum's face as she carried him into the firelight told me he already knew. His eyes were bright, burning like coals in his wrinkled little face. They were fixed on me with a peculiar intensity, and there was an odd, unsettling stillness about him. Slowly he wriggled out of Kenta's arms and clambered onto the ground; hitched himself towards me with his awkward, crab-like shuffle. Stopped just out of reach, watching me.

I felt the hairs on the back of my neck rise. Forced myself to remember him the way he used to be – after he changed from Weevil to Blue-bum the chatterbot; before whatever had been done to him in the depths of Shakesh. 'What is it, Blue-bum?' I asked gently. 'What d'you want?'

His gaze moved from my face to my chest. He hitched himself closer, and pulled his scraggy little body onto my knee. He lifted one leathery paw – the paws that had been smooth and nimble, and were now so cruelly bent and twisted. At first I thought he was going to touch my face, and steeled myself not to flinch. But he wasn't.

His fingers scrabbled at my chest, patting at the outline of my ring. He gripped it under the fabric of my shirt, looked up into my face, and chittered.

I felt myself flush. The ring – along with my penny whistle – was the only thing I had from what I'd always thought of as 'before' . . . and now knew was Karazan. The penny whistle was no secret; Weevil himself had stolen it from my bedside drawer when we'd both lived in the orphanage, and the others had often heard me play it.

Now I knew it wasn't a penny whistle: it was a larigot. And the ring . . . I knew what that was too. Jamie was right: it was one of the many things I'd kept private. Long years of orphanage life had taught me that *secret* meant *safe*. But if the others were going to help me there was no place for secrets.

Feeling their eyes on me, I slowly drew the ring out from beneath my shirt, slipped the bootlace over my head, and held it up.

'I was left on the porch of Highgate when I was a newborn baby, in the early morning of 22 September thirteen years ago,' I said, keeping my voice level and expressionless. 'The day of the equinox, when day and night are equal lengths . . . the day that's called Sunbalance in Karazan.'

'The one day in the year the magic portal opens . . .' murmured Gen.

'Thirteen years?' repeated Rich, looking confused. 'Then how . . .'

But Jamie was on to it. 'Time's different in Karazan, remember? Say one of our years equals four Karazan ones: that'd fit with the fifty years of the prophecy: *After two score years and ten and ten times five, he comes again*. Go on, Adam.'

'I was wrapped in a shawl. Tucked in beside me were my penny whistle . . .'

'Larigot . . .' breathed Jamie.

'. . . and this.'

'Is it magical?' asked Gen. 'What happens if you put it on?'

'Nothing. I don't think it's magical – or not in the way you mean. Though there was a keyhole in the Summer Palace, hidden in the panelling . . . I never

17

got round to telling you, but I used the ring to open it . . .'

Jamie gave the others an *I told you so* glance: *more secret stuff from Adam.* But the more I thought, the more fell into place. 'At the time, I thought it was coincidence,' I said slowly; 'but now . . .'

'Now it makes perfect sense!' squawked Jamie. 'It's obvious! What would be more logical than for that ring to be the key to the hidden door in the royal chamber? Because –'

'Because what?' grumbled Rich. 'What's so obvious?'

'Because that's what Adam's ring *is*! Not a key; not just some random ring. It's King Zane's ring: the Sign of Sovereignty.'

Rich's eyes grew very round. 'Honest? Can I see it?' he croaked, holding out his hand.

'D'you mind, Adam?' Kenta gave me a doubtful glance.

'No, of course not . . .' But I did. Deep in my heart lay the knowledge that my ring was the Ring of Kings, not some trinket to be passed from hand to hand. I hesitated.

I'd been half-conscious of Blue-bum crouched on my knee, still and silent. Unlike Kenta, I didn't feel comfortable about having him close; now I realised I was holding my left hand against his chest in a not-very-subtle attempt to ward him off. Under my palm I could feel his heart racing, fast and excited.

In the same instant he reached up and snatched the

18

ring out of my hand, poking a twisted finger through it and holding it up to his face to peer at it, jibbering.

'Uh . . . Blue-bum . . . I really don't think you should do that,' said Jamie. 'It's not just any old ring. It's the Sign of Sovereignty, and only the true King of Karazan –'

He was cut short by a rapid warning chatter like the sound of a rattlesnake. I shoved Blue-bum to the ground and was on my feet. There was a strange heat in my face, a hot swelling in my chest. My heart was beating in a slow, heavy roll, as if in slow motion . . . and in the same slow motion, the ring dropped from Blue-bum's finger, rolled in a crooked crescent, and lay gleaming in the firelight.

The others stared up at me for a long moment.

Richard scrambled across and picked up the ring, holding it carefully in the palm of his hand. There was an odd expression on his face – one I'd never seen before and didn't recognise.

'I'm sorry, Adam,' he said in a low voice. 'Here it is. Jamie's right: I shouldn't have asked.'

Somehow that small incident seemed to put a damper on the evening. As we snuggled down in our sleeping bags the thought of what lay ahead weighed on my spirits, heavy and suffocating. I lay staring up at the stars, two words repeating endlessly. *Overthrow Zeel . . . overthrow Zeel . . .*

Before, I'd had a vague image of armoured men on horseback storming the ramparts of a castle; of clashing steel and distant thunder; a bright clarion-call of trumpets; then victory, glorious and abstract – all happening while we were snug in front of the fire in Quested Court.

It wasn't going to be like that. There were no horses in Karazan. No army. Only the five of us. *Overthrow Zeel* . . . I forced myself to focus on the thought, hardening my mind to what it had to mean.

There would be only one way to overthrow the man who had murdered my father and stolen the kingdom. I was going to have to kill him. Get close to him, and somehow kill him . . . just like he'd killed my father; just like he'd tried to kill me, a helpless baby.

Deep inside something trembled and quaked. I closed my eyes, pushing it down, into the darkness. Justice, that's what it would be.

Revenge.

An eye for an eye and a tooth for a tooth, just like Matron said when she punished us for doing something wrong.

A life for a life.

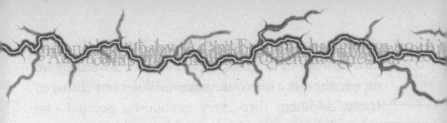

THE PUZZLE OF THE RING

In the morning, after a rather subdued breakfast, Kenta came up to me with Blue-bum perched on her shoulder.

'Adam,' she said, 'there's something Blue-bum wants to say.'

By now, like the others, I was used to Kenta's self-appointed role of chatterbot interpreter. 'Yeah?' I grunted, not altogether enthusiastically. 'What?'

Blue-bum peered up and chittered softly, then cringed and looked down, hang-dog. 'You see? He's sorry. He knows snatching your ring was wrong. So now he's come to apologise.'

Blue-bum slid a sly little glance at my face . . . but then I couldn't help noticing his gaze slip downwards to the bump of the ring under my shirt. I stretched my mouth into a stiff, phoney smile. 'That's OK, Blue-bum. Let's forget it, huh?'

I was turning away when Kenta spoke again. 'I think there's something worrying him about the ring. That's why he wanted a closer look at it last night.'

I turned back slowly.

21

Kenta shrugged apologetically. 'Something both-ered him about it.' She glanced at the hunched figure on her shoulder for confirmation. Blue-bum chittered softly, nodding; then, very cautiously, pointed one crooked finger at the bump under my shirt, snatching it away again quickly as if it might be slapped.

He wanted another look. Why? He sat silently on Kenta's shoulder, head sunk, eyes lowered. I saw the others had gathered round expectantly. With an inward sigh, I drew the ring out into the slanting sunlight, but this time I kept the bootlace round my neck, holding the ring out for them to see.

The circle of faces gazed at it respectfully. All except Blue-bum. He was off again, pointing, pulling at Kenta's hair and jabbering in her ear, making chopping motions with his hand and scratching at his head in an elaborate pantomime of puzzlement. Perplexed, I found my own gaze drawn to the ring – the silver circlet whose contours I knew as well as the features of my own face. 'I think he's trying to say that it looks . . . incomplete. Almost as if there's part of it missing . . .' said Kenta. But how could it be? It was the same as it had always been.

I stared at it, turning it in my fingers, seeing it for the first time through the eyes of other people. It was a man's ring, heavy and solid, cast from what I'd always imagined was pure silver. Plain, with no stones or decoration of any kind, no inscription, nothing. In cross-section, the back was similar to the curved D-shape of a man's wedding ring, but with two flat planes instead of one: the shape of a quarter circle, instead of half. At the front the silver thickened into an odd, angular design: a smooth, curved surface bisected by a deeply grooved angular channel.

'I know what it reminds me of,' said Jamie. 'A puzzle ring. I got one once in a Christmas cracker – sorry, Adam, I didn't mean it like that.'

'You're right, Jamie,' said Gen. 'They're made in two separate parts, but when you fit them together a certain way they interlock to form a single ring.'

Interlock . . . where had I heard that word before? Spoken in Gen's soft voice, in bright moonlight on the fringes of Chattering Wood. She'd been reading from Queen Zaronel's diary . . . *on a velvet cushion tasselled with gold rested the Twisted Crown of Karazan – plain gold and silver interlocking bands, unadorned with gems of any kind – and the Sign of Sovereignty.*

Zaronel hadn't described the Sign of Sovereignty, and at the time I'd wondered why. Now I knew. She hadn't needed to – the description of the crown applied to them both. The Sign of Sovereignty was the Crown of Karazan in miniature: *plain gold and silver interlocking bands, unadorned with gems of any kind.*

I stared down at my ring. Blue-bum was right. Part of it *was* missing. How hadn't I see it before? I had the silver half . . . so where was the golden one?

THE STRONGHOLD OF ARRAZ

*M*atron.

I could imagine the scene as clearly as if it was an actual memory – and for all I knew it might be, seen through the misty eyes of the tiny baby I would have been when it happened, and locked away in my subconscious mind.

Matron's sharp eyes catching the gleam of the larigot in the folds of the shawl; her cold, bony fingers groping for it. The furtive light in her eyes as her hand encounters something else, even more unexpected . . . draws it out, turning away to shield her find from Cook. Prises the two halves apart, the golden one disappearing into the starched pocket of her apron, the other – the worthless half, in her eyes – poked back into the shawl, just in case the abandoned baby is ever claimed . . .

There could be no hope of getting it back. It wasn't the only thing Matron had stolen while she'd been at Highgate; her years of criminal activity had finally caught up with her, and now she was in prison. As for Cookie, even if she had known – which I doubted – she'd left Highgate and gone to work at a girls'

24

reformatory school. I had no idea where and knew I'd never see her again. Even Highgate probably no longer existed . . . not that any of it mattered. The ring would have been sold off years ago.

I might as well face it: it was gone. I knew it was crazy to feel such a sense of loss for something I'd never even known about till a few moments ago.

But crazy or not, I did.

With breakfast over and the issue of my ring resolved as far as it was ever going to be, Richard turned to me, hands stuck deep in his pockets, and said bluntly, 'So, *Zephyr*: what's the plan?'

He put a deliberate emphasis on the name. I shot him a sidelong glance, but his face didn't tell me whether he meant it as an acknowledgement, a joke . . . or a challenge. Feeling my cheeks burn, I opted to ignore it. 'We need to find the Stronghold of Arraz. And once we've found it, we need to sneak in and get close to Zeel . . .'

'And then what?' Jamie was looking dubious – and who could blame him?

Yes . . . then what? It was a good question, and one I didn't feel ready to answer. 'Then we see what happens,' I told him, trying to sound confident.

The first part of the plan was unexpectedly simple. Out came the map, and there it was: the Stronghold of Arraz, complete with a picture of a castle with strange, twisted turrets and even what looked like some kind of drawbridge. It looked closer than any of us had dared hope: we just needed to make our way over the low ridge that formed the side of the dragon's head, then southwards round the edge of the valley.

We'd be there by nightfall. My stomach turned at the thought, but I gave the others a cheery grin. 'Simple, huh? What are we waiting for?'

They hoisted their packs, Blue-bum scrambling into Kenta's for his usual free ride. 'Want to lead, Rich?' Rich swaggered to the front of the line, the others taking up their positions behind him: Jamie, Gen, Kenta, then me, tagging along at the rear, thinking my own uncomfortable thoughts . . . and keeping a watchful eye on Blue-bum.

By mid-morning we were working our way along a narrow goat track on the western side of the main Draken range. Striding along behind Kenta, I could see Blue-bum's wizened monkey-face peering out of the top of her pack, gazing left and right at the unfolding view. Not that there was much to see: the eastern side of the mountain range was called Morningside, I remembered; this was Dark Face, and it was well named. To our left the bare slopes of the mountains reared above us into a thick pall of cloud, the only sign of life occasional glimpses of the shaggy-coated mountain goats who'd made the track; on our right the ground fell away in a tumble of loose scree and jagged rock, losing itself in a haze of darkness and distance far below.

The others struggled and stumbled on, occasionally almost losing their footing on the narrow path. Every now and then Kenta's face would turn towards the abyss, then quickly away; and when it did, I could read the pale, tense expression on it more clearly than words. It was full of dread.

She wasn't the only one who was afraid of what we'd find at the end of our journey. And yet . . . I thought back to Blue-bum's behaviour when we'd found him close to death at the edge of Chattering Wood, when any mention of Karazeel or Evor had sent him into a jibbering frenzy of terror. But now, with every step taking us closer to Karazeel's stronghold, he seemed as relaxed as a tourist on a bus trip.

And I wondered why.

As the day wore on the air thickened and darkened and our progress slowed. It had been a long time since I'd seen the last pale smudge of life on the mountainside; the track had long since disappeared. We'd been picking our way behind Richard along a contour line for what seemed an eternity, and now, with visibility at a few metres, had finally come to a stop.

I edged my way past the others to join Rich. His face grim, he pointed out over the well of blackness at our feet. I followed his gaze, space tipping beneath me in a wave of vertigo, groping behind me for the steadying solidity of rock.

At first I thought it was the storm he was showing me. It had been building for hours, and now the bank of cloud hung so close I could almost reach out and touch it – a low black ceiling illuminated by irregular flashes of white light and jagged javelins of purple. Then one bolt more violent than the rest lit the cauldron of the valley in a blue flare and I saw it far below us, swimming in a soup of swirling mist.

The Stronghold of Arraz: a crippled insect rearing skyward.

The flash was gone; dark descended. But the burning after-image of the shattered shape with its splintered tentacles remained stamped on my mind, black on blinding white, all stark angles and silent pain.

If you drew a picture of a scream, that's how it would look.

THE CAULDRON OF ZEEL

We slid and scrambled down the mountainside, zigzagging to lessen the steepness of the slope. The sense of height and nothingness below us was dizzying, and it wasn't long before I threw pride to the winds and lowered myself to my bum, using hands and feet to feel my way down, and the seat of my pants as an emergency braking system.

A stream of loose stones skittered around me as I descended, larger rocks bouncing past every now and then as one of the others momentarily lost their footing behind me – along with a frightened gasp and the slithering rush of a body temporarily out of control. I'd hang on to whatever I could find and brace myself for the impact of a sliding body; if one person lost control, they could easily take all of us with them.

At the steepest parts I waited, anchoring myself as securely as I could and giving the others a hand down. Jamie and the girls were pale, their faces set and stony with determination. Blue-bum had either taken pity on Kenta or decided he'd be safer under his own steam: he was picking his way downwards at the back of the group, using his tail for balance and muttering to himself. For once I was glad I didn't understand Chatterbot.

Slow though our progress was, with every flash of lightning our destination grew closer. At last we were level with the topmost pinnacles of the castle, then below them; and finally we were just above what I'd thought was the drawbridge.

What had looked like a narrow gangway from high above was a steep-sided ridge of natural rock: a long spur linking the western flank of Dark Face to the isolated crag on which the Stronghold of Arraz was built.

We were huddled on a small platform of rock slightly above the ridge, tucked behind a rocky buttress. Here, lower on the mountainside, there were vestiges of vegetation: dry tufts of grass; stunted thorn bushes; even an old tree with a few crumpled grey-green leaves clinging to its branches, its trunk gnarled and bent, twisted roots like arthritic fingers holding grimly to cracks in the rock.

At the edge of our platform the ground fell away in a perpendicular cliff face, curving round as far as the eye could see in both directions. This must be the Cauldron of Zeel, I realised; and like Dark Face the name was no accident: it was a steep-sided witch's cauldron with no way down that I could see . . . and the Stronghold of Arraz as its centre-point.

Above us to our left a dark ribbon of track wound

down from the mountains to join the ridge. I couldn't follow it far: it climbed steeply southeast, narrowing into distance and darkness before being swallowed by the cleft of the mountains.

This would be the link between Morningside and Dark Face used by King Karazeel's men – the route Danon of Drakendale had warned us to stay well clear of. I could see why. Even in the poor light it had the look of a well-used thoroughfare . . . and as we watched, a straggling caravan of dark, shambling shapes appeared in the gloom and wound its way slowly towards the ridge. Glonks, bound for Arraz.

The caravan was lit by flickering torches, the clank of armour and the scrape of hooves carrying across the darkness between us. We watched its progress in silence – if we could hear them, they would hear us if we made the slightest sound. I found myself checking the direction of the wind like an animal sensing the hunt; the air had the heavy stillness that comes before a storm, but the faint stirring of a breeze was on my face, bringing with it the scent of hot animal hide and leather. And something else . . .

The rotting, maggoty reek of *them* – the Faceless. I saw them, almost invisible in the darkness, drifting alongside the solid, clanking figures of the soldiers. A greasy sheen of sweat broke out on my skin. I glanced at the others – a warning glance I knew wasn't needed.

In absolute silence, hardly daring to breathe, we watched as the convoy made its slow progress along

31

the ridge. The rock, wider than a road at first, gradually narrowed to a slim finger that fell away steeply on either side like a knife edge. Illuminated by the flickering light of the torches, the track hung in the air like a tightrope of light suspended over a chasm of swirling darkness. The animals, forced into single file, plodded stoically forward, the shadowy shapes of the Faceless between them.

At last, when the shuffling figures were dwarfed by the towering darkness of the fortress, the natural rock gave way to a bridge of stone, lights set at intervals into its balustrade. We saw the flash of steel as their pale glow played over the armour of the guards flanking the bastions, two by two. The convoy crawled to a halt. There was a distant whirring as the drawbridge was lowered, any sound its landing might have made drowned by a crack of thunder as lightning split the sky.

For an instant, the castle seemed to blaze an impossible, fluorescent blue; instinctively, I flung up one hand to shield my face. Head ringing, dazzled, I lowered my hand and blinked into the darkness, trying to focus.

The convoy was gone. All that was left was the swimming emptiness of the chasm, the black bulk of the castle almost invisible above. The lights lining the bridge were pinpricks, tiny glow-worms in the vast darkness.

We had a problem.

The only way to get to the Stronghold of Arraz was

the one we'd just seen – and crossing the narrow, heavily guarded link between the mountains and the fortress would be suicide.

THE MYSTERIOUS CYLINDER

The first drops of rain splashed down on our perch, exploding on impact like miniature bombs. The others huddled together against the rock wall as far from the edge as possible, taking what little shelter they could from the twisted tree. Three miserable faces peered from beneath their hoods, another, smaller one peeking out at me from the folds of Kenta's cloak. It seemed as if they were all looking to me for answers . . . and I had none. My heart, already close to rock bottom, clunked down another notch.

I couldn't see a way forward. Even under cover of darkness, and assuming the rain continued, there was no way we could get across to the castle unseen. And even if we did, the guards weren't about to open the gates and lower the drawbridge for five strangers, no matter how bedraggled and harmless they might look.

Richard was beside me; I slid a glance at his face. Deep in the shadow of his hood it looked stern and grown-up . . . and something about the determined set of his mouth gave me courage. We might look like five helpless kids, but we were much more than that. We'd come this far, and nothing was going to stop us now. Like Hannah always said, there had to be a way. It was just a question of finding it.

The thought of Hannah with her sparkly confidence put a smile into my mind, and with it came another thought – Jamie's watchword, and one that finally got me moving: *When in doubt, eat.*

I shuffled cautiously over to the others and reached for my pack. Dug inside, feeling for the packet of energy bars I knew was in there somewhere. My fingers brushed the softness of leather – Zaronel's diary – and the smooth surface of the mysterious cylinder I'd found with it. Below it I could feel the crinkle of cellophane . . . impatiently I pulled the cylinder out and set it to one side.

I'd forgotten about the slope. The second I let go, it began to roll . . . and everything sped up like a movie on fast forward. I grabbed at the moving blur, but it hit a bump and twisted away from my clutching fingers; another flash of lightning blinded me and I spun round, off balance, one hand still jammed into the neck of my pack. As I turned I caught a flash of the others' faces, mouths open in shock, eyes staring . . . then I was throwing myself forward in a desperate lunge, fingers scrabbling for the tube before it vanished over the drop. Too late. Time crunched from super-fast-forward into slow motion; spread-eagled on the brink of the void I watched the shining shape slowly spinning as it fell.

Then the flickering flare that had lit the disaster was doused in darkness. I lay staring uselessly downwards, cursing my clumsiness, listening for the distant crash of the cylinder shattering on the rocks below.

None of us had the faintest clue what the cylinder was – I'd come across it by chance, hidden in the wall of the exit from the Summer Palace – but the simple fact that it had been there, secret and safe, told us it was precious.

Squeezing my eyes tight shut I could picture it as clearly as if it wasn't in a zillion pieces on the valley floor below: bluish grey, with a strange metallic lustre; as thick as my thumb, and rounded at both ends. Like a test tube at school . . . And suddenly I knew. It hadn't seemed heavy enough to be solid because it wasn't. It wasn't a cylinder, it was a tube. It was hollow, and it held something.

We'd been blind not to see it before. It had been right there in front of us; I'd read the words myself, written in Zagros' bold handwriting.

. . . *a secret passageway through the wall of the palace . . . a hidden store of potion that will render us invisible as we make our way to the forbidden depths of Shadowwood . . .*

The cylinder had held the potion of invisibility. The one thing that might have got us into the Stronghold of Arraz. And now it was gone, thanks to me. The old Adam Equinox stirred and shuffled shamefacedly in the dark recesses of my mind. *My fault – again. But*

one good thing: the others don't know what we've lost . . .
and if I don't tell them, they never will.

Slowly, stiffly, I peeled myself off the rock, turned
my back on the abyss and shuffled back to where
the others were waiting. 'That's it, guys – it's gone.' I
shrugged. Took a deep breath. 'It gets worse. I've just
realised what it was: invisibility potion. Zagros told
about it in the diary. Would've been pretty useful,
huh?' I looked from one face to the next, meeting their
eyes, and saw nothing there but sympathy. What was
there to say? 'I'm sorry.'

I shared out the energy bars and we munched in
gloomy silence. Everyone kept well away from the
edge of the platform – except Blue-bum. I watched
as he sidled to the edge and peered over, bum in the
air, tail twisted tight round a protruding knob of rock
for safety.

'Do be careful . . .' cautioned Kenta.

There was a brilliant flash of lightning right above
us, along with an explosive crack of thunder that
made us all jump. Blue-bum jumped highest, giving a
shrill chitter of fright and landing perilously close to
the edge. 'Come back here *right now*!' Kenta yipped
in alarm.

I couldn't help agreeing: the sight of him so close to
the drop was making me dizzy. 'Kenta's right, Blue-
bum – it's a long way down, and it's not as if there's
anything to see.'

I was wrong. Blue-bum was chittering and capering

and pointing downwards . . . he *had* seen something. I crawled to the edge, lowered myself gingerly beside him, and waited for the next flash. It wasn't long coming – and then I saw it too, caught in the tangled branches of a thorn bush way down out of reach, almost hidden by the overhang of the cliff.

The cylinder of potion, safe and sound. My first thought was that it might as well have been on the moon. But then I had an idea . . . and I felt myself begin to smile.

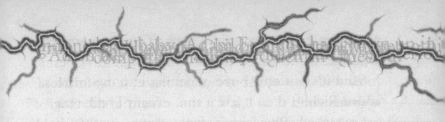

A VANISHING ACT

'I've made up my mind.' I'd never thought Kenta would remind me of the dreaded Miss McCracken, but now she did – right down to the thin line of a mouth and flashing eyes. I felt a familiar urge to back off, the only thing stopping me the sheer drop two paces behind.

'But –'

'*Adam Equinox . . .*'

I looked helplessly at Rich, who gave a resigned shrug. 'Kenta has a point, I guess. She's the littlest and lightest . . . and if anyone can be guaranteed not to let Blue-bum fall, she can.'

So the only person left to convince was Blue-bum, the reluctant hero of the rescue mission. Hunched in Kenta's arms he looked anything but keen, and who could blame him – I'd have had doubts myself about being lowered by my tail over a bottomless chasm. But Blue-bum was the only one with a built-in rope, and none of us were happy to rely on Jamie's scout knots.

'Adam will be holding on to my legs, and I won't let

go of you, I promise,' said Kenta. 'You know you can trust me.'

'And it's our only hope of getting into the fortress,' added Rich. 'I'd do it like a shot, if only I had a tail.'

I watched Blue-bum's face. I was betting he'd refuse. It wasn't easy to read his expression, but it wasn't enthusiastic. Yet it didn't seem to be fear tightening the little monkey-face ... he looked almost insulted, as if he was being asked to do something totally beneath his dignity. Yeah, that was it: the kind of expression a school principal would have if he was asked to strip to his boxers in front of the entire school ...

I shook my head impatiently. I was imagining things. Since when did a chatterbot worry about dignity? It was a waste of time trying to guess what was going on in Blue-bum's furry head ... and we weren't at school now: we were dithering on the edge of a cliff in the rain.

Just as I was about to step forward and try my hand at persuading him, Blue-bum did something that took me completely by surprise. He shrugged his skinny shoulders, stretched his slit mouth into a determined line, pulled up his dangling tail like someone hauling a bucket out of a well ... and solemnly wound the end of it tightly round Kenta's hand. And then he gave me a sly little glimmer of a glance that said louder than a chitter – or even real words – could ever have done: *You see, Adam? You've misjudged me again.*

*

Five minutes later the precious cylinder was safe in Kenta's pocket and we were edging our way along the crumbling ledge that linked our platform to the ridge.

We'd checked the contents of the tube, and as far as we could tell I was right: the two halves unscrewed to reveal a crystal phial containing a familiar-looking milky-blue liquid that glowed with a pale fluorescence in the darkness. It looked identical to the potion of invisibility we'd drunk in the Temple so long ago – but there was more of it. 'We shouldn't use it before we really need to,' said Jamie. 'We don't want to suddenly become visible again right in front of the sentries.'

'And whatever happens once we're inside, no one must tell about Adam being Zephyr. Even if we get caught . . .' Gen gulped.

'*Especially* if we get caught,' growled Rich. 'We tell no one – and I mean *no one*. A long time's passed since Shakesh, especially in Karazan years, and we don't know who we can trust.'

Though he didn't say so, I knew he meant Kai, the oldest and best friend we had in Karazan. *Friends forever* . . . Kai had insisted we leave him behind when we'd made our escape from the dungeons of Shakesh. Despite the danger, he was determined to continue his undercover work for the Believers, to gain the trust of King Karazeel and work towards his downfall from within the walls of the Stronghold of Arraz. *They say it will be mightier even than Shakesh, and that none – not even the True King – will be able to storm it . . .*

41

Part of me couldn't suppress an ironic smile at the memory. But another part, new and strange, seemed to stir inside me like an invisible muscle flexing and feeling its strength. *Oh yeah?* that part said. *We'll see . . .*

We were prepared to wait hours for the next convoy – the whole night if necessary. None of us liked the idea of camping out in full view of whoever – or whatever – might appear round the bend of the track, but we had no choice: even invisible, tagging onto a party of Karazeel's stooges was our only hope of getting across the drawbridge and through the gate, so we needed to be close enough to join the rear of the next caravan.

But we were lucky. A rocky outcrop at the side of the road gave us cover, and almost as soon as we settled ourselves behind it we heard a low rumbling I thought at first was thunder, and a span of glonks appeared out of the gloom with a covered wagon behind them. It must be part of the previous convoy, I realised – heavy and slow, it had lagged behind.

It was better than we could have hoped for. Not only was it drawn by glonks, whose smell would cover our scent, but the rumble of its steel-rimmed wheels was loud enough to mask any sound. Out of the corner of my eye I saw first Blue-bum, then Kenta, then Gen, sip from the phial and vanish. Jamie was next; then Rich. An invisible hand groped for mine and pressed the cool smoothness of crystal into my palm, alive with the prickle of magic.

I lifted the phial to my lips and sipped, feeling a tingling nothing-taste on my tongue . . . swallowed. A flickering chill rippled through me. I held one hand in front of my face to double-check it had worked, though I knew it had. The transparent double-outline of my nose, the shadow of my cheekbones, the curve of my lashes were all gone; the friendly bulk of my body below, so familiar I wasn't usually aware of it. Everything looked different, as if my eyeballs were floating in space. I closed my eyes, and could still see the wagon trundling towards me.

Kenta's slim hand felt for mine and gripped it tight. I gave an answering squeeze: we'd agreed that holding hands was the only sure way of staying together. In complete silence, ghosts floating weightlessly in the nothingness of our bodies, we crept to the edge of the track and watched the cart rumble towards us.

Then it was on us: hot-horse smell, the creak of leather harness, the scrunch of hooves on the wet track, a huffing snort and the jangle of a bit. A whip snaked out and cracked over the glonks' backs. I caught a flash of a swarthy face shadowed with stubble, of rheumy eyes staring straight through me; the driver hawked and spat, the glob of phlegm missing me by millimetres.

Then they were past and we were hustling after them, keeping as close as we dared to the swaying tailgate of the cart.

★

It was just as well the cart was so noisy – a herd of elephants would have moved more quietly than we did. Stumbling along in the dark was hard enough, but when the track began to narrow things got really tricky. Someone kept standing on my heels; someone else was constantly moving in front of me and then slowing down so I cannoned into them. But at last we sorted ourselves out into single file and shuffled along in the wake of the cart with me in the lead, still holding tight to Kenta's hand. I focused on the creaking wood and rattling chains of the tailgate, trying not to think about the sheer drop on either side.

At last a low stone balustrade appeared beside us and the track widened. We were on the bridge. The first pair of lights came into view – not the burning brands I'd imagined but pale glowing lamps set behind curved transparent covers. Two sentries loomed out of the darkness, so still they might have been made of stone: armoured figures in black cloaks, cruel faces impassive as masks under gleaming helms, only their eyes moving as they followed the slow progress of the cart.

There was a shouted challenge and the cart creaked to a standstill. This was it: the moment of truth.

The high canvas canopy hid the gate from view, but we could hear the growl of the guards and the snarl of the driver's reply. *Just lower the drawbridge and let him through*, I willed them.

A dark figure was striding past the cart straight for me. I recoiled, stumbling backwards into Richard, hearing the huff of his breath and the scuffle of a booted foot on wet gravel as the others stepped instinctively backwards. My heart jerked painfully as adrenaline kicked in, every instinct screaming at me to run. For what seemed an age the guard was staring straight at me, scowling. His skin gleamed in the rain; I could see the hairs in his nostrils, the raindrop trembling on the rim of his helmet, the wart on his eyelid. He burped, a hot blast of half-digested onions hitting me in the face; then turned towards the back of the cart. His wet cloak swung and stuck to my arm, hanging crazily in mid-air. If he turned his head a fraction he'd see it . . . I twitched it away and froze, the stench of his stale sweat catching in my throat as I struggled not to gag.

The guard unlaced the leather thong holding the canopy closed, yanked the two flaps apart and leaned in. There was a waft of wheat and old sacks; the startled cackle of a chicken. A mumble, the scrape of something heavy being pushed to one side . . . then the canvas was flipped back in place and the guard moved away, slapping the tailgate with the palm of his hand and shouting at the driver to move on.

As he stepped back his boot landed on my foot. I bit back a yelp of pain as I felt the bones crunch: the guard staggered and almost fell, his flailing arms missing my face by a whisker. 'What in the name of the Faceless . . .' he growled, wheeling round to glare down at my invisible foot.

I held my breath, every fibre in my body tensed to bolt.

'You should drink less mead with your dinner, or you'll be over the drop,' growled a second voice. 'That, or the Captain will hear of it – and that would be worse. Now take up your post before you fall – or I push you.'

The guard's lips curled in a snarl as he turned away. My heart gave an agonising twist and started beating again; I took a slow breath of fresh, rain-washed air.

The bridge shuddered as the gangplank crashed into place; the wagon rumbled forward, the cold shadow of the vaulted gateway fell over us . . . and we were in the Stronghold of Arraz.

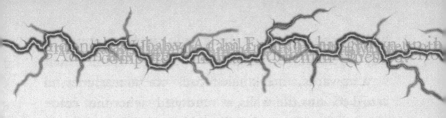

BLUE-BUM LEADS THE WAY

It was more of a gigantic tunnel than a gateway. Creeping behind the wagon in almost total darkness, I had the claustrophobic feeling of being swallowed by some colossal beast; and with it came the uncomfortable knowledge that while getting in had been hard, finding our way out again . . . well, that would be pretty much impossible.

The entrance tunnel opened onto a courtyard, stark black walls rearing up on every side. The wagon would be headed towards the stables, which was no good to us, and I watched it disappear into the gloom with a twinge of regret. It had been comforting having something to follow, but now we were on our own, and I hadn't a clue what to do or where to go next.

I stared around me. It seemed as if we were in the middle of a maze – or a nightmare. The courtyard was a jumble of angles, alleys and archways leading away in all directions . . . but none of the corners were right angles and no two walls seemed the same height. Nothing matched: walls reared up haphazardly and then leaned away into nowhere; there were doorways high in the middle of sheer walls, with no apparent way of reaching them. Narrow stairways wormed their way upwards, then angled back on themselves and vanished into the walls at random heights that made me wonder where they could possibly lead. Others zigzagged pointlessly upwards only to end in a blank wall. The treads of the steps tilted wildly, yet none of them had a handrail. I followed the progress of one up the far wall: it turned this way and that before jutting away from the wall and breaking off in mid-air. Even the walls themselves seemed to slant at impossible angles ... tilting my head, I followed them up to the crooked spires that reached like clawing fingers towards the tattered sky.

The storm was over. The moon was struggling to break through the clouds, but some strange trick of light had turned its pale glow red as blood, as if the pinnacles of Arraz were jagged shards that had pierced the sky.

'Well, that wasn't so hard,' Rich whispered. 'Now all we have to do is find our way to wherever Karazeel and Evor are hiding in this rats' nest.'

But which way?

I didn't realise I'd spoken aloud till I heard Gen's whispered reply. 'Even if we knew where we were headed, we'd never be able to find the way – not in a million years.'

'True enough,' agreed Rich cheerfully. 'This place is a disaster. It must have been designed by a total nutcase.'

'It gives me the creeps.' There was an ominous wobble in Jamie's voice. 'I wish we could go home.'

'Well, we can't –' Rich's answering growl broke off.

'What is it, Richard?' Kenta, close to panic. 'What's happened?'

'Something *bit* me, just above my boot. A . . . rat, maybe . . .'

'No rat could reach that high,' whispered Gen.

'An invisible *giant* rat . . .' quavered Jamie.

'. . . with teeth like razors,' finished Rich through gritted teeth. 'It's bleeding. I can feel it trickling down my leg.'

The thought that we might not be the only invisible creatures in the darkness sent an icy chill down my spine. There was a soft hiss, and something scrabbled at my arm. My blood froze. Something way bigger than a rat was scrambling up my arm, its claws snagging on the rough cloth of my cloak.

I stumbled away from the others, letting go of Kenta's hand and raising my arm to swat the *thing* off me. It tilted and pitched, clutching at my shoulder . . . then bony fingers twisted into my hair and I heard a familiar chitter in my ear. '*Blue-bum!*' I growled. 'Next time give me some warning!' The grip on my hair tightened, and his leathery little face pressed against my ear. He chittered softly, then tugged, then chittered again, more of a vibration than a sound.

I groped for the invisible forms of the others, drawing them into a damp, trembling huddle, the feel of them solid and wonderfully real. We hugged tight.

'Guys, Blue-bum's up on my shoulder, and – *ouch*! I think he's trying to tell us something.'

There was a lurch and a scrabble, and Blue-bum was clambering down my arm. I felt scrawny little fingers twine themselves round mine; then a series of insistent tugs. Blue-bum's message couldn't have been clearer. 'He wants us to go with him,' I whispered.

'That's dumb,' retorted Rich. 'How would *he* know which tunnel to take?'

'Unless . . .' Gen's voice had an edge of excitement. 'We've been assuming Blue-bum was kept prisoner in Shakesh. But what if he was brought here, to Arraz? That'd mean he's been here before, and managed to escape. And if he found his way out . . .'

'Then maybe he can find his way back in,' finished Jamie.

There was a long pause. At last Kenta spoke, very gently. 'Are we right, Blue-bum? Have you been here before? Can you help us get close to Karazeel and Evor without being seen?'

There was another tug on my hand. 'Looks like he thinks he can.'

'What d'you say?' whispered Rich. 'Do we give it a go?'

The way I saw it, we didn't have many other options. But I found myself wishing Blue-bum wasn't invisible – that I could see his face and look into his eyes. Could we really trust him? It was Blue-bum who had spotted the cylinder we'd thought was gone forever, I reminded myself; Blue-bum who had allowed himself to be dangled by his tail to retrieve it. It was Blue-bum who had got us into Arraz. And it was Blue-bum who had been tortured by Karazeel and Evor – and if that wasn't a cast-iron reason for him to be on our side, nothing was.

I didn't need to see his face to remember that strange glitter in his eyes. It hadn't been there before . . . but just because he'd changed, it didn't mean he wasn't on our side. It might mean he *was* – more so than ever.

'Go on then, Blue-bum: lead the way.'

There was no doubt Blue-bum knew where he was headed. Across the courtyard we shuffled, hand in invisible hand, Blue-bum in the lead with me right behind, terrified of standing on him by mistake.

Past a crumbling stairway leading to nowhere . . . past the crooked rectangle of darkness that had swallowed the cart . . . past the archway I'd earmarked as the most likely way in. At the far side we stopped, waiting for Blue-bum to get his bearings – because wherever the entrance to the castle was, it couldn't be here. We were standing under the one wall with no openings at all, the one with the zigzag stairway. From across the courtyard I'd thought the wall seemed to tilt, and now, staring upwards, I saw I'd been right. It hung over us, what we could see of the sky bisected by the sawn-off stub of stairway jutting out into nothingness way above. For a crazy moment I thought it was falling, the wall starting to topple . . . a wash of dizziness swept over me. I felt myself stagger and hurriedly looked down at where my feet should have been. 'Hurry up, Blue-bum,' Rich whispered. 'Which way, left or right?'

But it was neither. Instead, Blue-bum headed towards the stone stairway, tugging me after him. At its foot I hesitated. This couldn't be right. I felt a none-too-gentle shove, and a familiar voice growled: 'Go on then, Zephyr – or d'you want me to go first?'

This time, the challenge in Rich's voice was clear. I pressed myself as close to the wall as I could and started to climb crabwise, my back to the drop. There'd be a doorway at the top – we just hadn't been able to see it from below. That was what kept me going: the thought of having solid stone on both sides of me and a level floor underfoot . . . and the simple fact that once we were on the stairway there was no place to go but up. Behind me I could hear Jamie scrabbling and snuffling like a baby bulldog, and I found myself mumbling encouragement as I climbed – or was it to myself? '*Keep going . . . one step at a time . . . nearly there now . . . stay close to the wall . . . you're doing great . . .*'

One thing's for sure, I thought grimly: it can't get any worse.

But I was wrong.

I stopped just below the place where the stairs left the wall and jutted into space, staring in disbelief. Where the doorway had to be there was nothing. Worse than nothing: solid wall. We were strung out on a staircase no wider than my desk at school, the equivalent of four storeys up with no place to go. I heard a strangled bleat from behind. And at the same time, impossibly, the softest chatter came from above me to my right – from the stub of steps suspended over the postage stamp of courtyard way below.

Two words collided in my brain. *Blue-bum* and *No*. The chatter came again, urgent, insistent. I opened my mouth, but all that came out was a wordless croak. At last I understood. Very cautiously, I lowered myself to hands and knees. Almost hugging the uneven surface of the stone, I turned my back on the wall and crept out over the drop. With both hands on the last step, I stopped. Peered over the edge, feeling the world tip. Another soft chitter came from up ahead, suspended in mid-air. I groped with one hand, feeling the roughness of stone ahead of me. Somehow the fact that I was still invisible made it easier to believe – easier to trust my weight to the void. I heard a little whimper behind me. 'Remember Rainbow Bridge, Jamie?' I croaked. 'You did that. You can do this too. Close your eyes and pretend it looks as real as it feels – as real as it *is*. And . . . be careful.'

One behind the other we crawled over the abyss, fumbling with invisible hands for steps we couldn't see. I closed my eyes, pretending it was all a dream – a nightmare where if I fell I'd jolt harmlessly awake in my own bed.

At last, after an eternity, I opened my eyes a chink

and there was an opening ahead of me in the wall. It was just in front, damp stone close enough to smell, close enough to touch . . . and then I was scuttling on all fours into the dank mouth of the tunnel, hearing Jamie's whimpers change to sobbing echoes behind . . . staggering to my feet and leading the others away from the nothingness at a stumbling run.

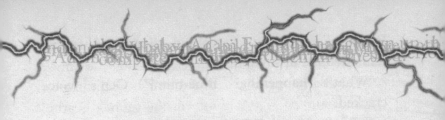

BIRD IN A CAGE

'One thing's for sure,' whispered Rich, 'if any entrance is secret, that one is. Way to go, Blue-bum.'

We were huddled in pitch dark in a tiny room off the main passage. Blue-bum had dragged us in and pulled the door tight shut behind us. For the first time we felt safe, and having hard rock under my bum had never felt so good.

'I vote we stay here a while.' I could tell Jamie was struggling not to cry. 'Maybe till morning . . .'

'What say we have something to eat?' I wasn't hungry, but it was the only sure-fire way I knew to cheer up Jamie.

'I don't . . .' There was a choking catch in Jamie's voice. 'I think I'm going to throw up.'

That's when I felt it too: a weird sinking feeling, as if my stomach was being sucked out of the soles of my feet. Instinctively I threw my hands out, clutching for the walls . . . beside me one of the girls gave a low cry. My body felt as heavy as an elephant, as if gravity had doubled and I was being squashed through the floor.

55

Even in my panic, I realised dimly the feeling reminded me of something . . .

'What's happening? Blue-bum?' Gen's voice cracked.

'What's going on?' Rich, angry – or afraid.

'Blue-bum? Where are you?'

'Answer us!' A cold certainty flooded through me. Blue-bum had gone. He'd led us into a trap – some kind of time-warp, or a gateway to another world – and now he'd gone. The floor beneath me was shuddering, juddering with a faint, somehow metallic vibration. Again, it was weirdly familiar: a feeling that was ordinary and everyday and didn't fit with Karazan . . .

There was a gentle bump, then stillness. Then a sound. Blue-bum hadn't gone. His familiar chatter came from behind me, but now it didn't seem friendly or encouraging. It was low and menacing and some-how triumphant and it turned my blood to ice.

There was the faintest click, a wheeze and a section of the back wall slid open. I stumbled to my feet, shielding my eyes from the sudden dazzle of light. Somewhere at the back of my mind a memory was struggling to surface: a long-ago school trip up the sky tower in the lift . . . Then my eyes snapped into focus, and two facts smashed into my brain like bullets.

We were no longer invisible.

And we'd found King Karazeel – or rather, he had found us.

★

Blue-bum was sidling towards him, grovelling and fawning and bowing low. Karazeel ignored him. His eyes were fixed on us, huddled in the doorway. For a long moment the world stood still. My eyes flicked over the room, looking for options, knowing there'd be none.

Karazeel. The twisted crown of Karazan on his head, his hair smooth and dark, his face unlined. He must be more than seventy, but he had the appearance and bearing of a man in his prime. The face was handsome but the mouth had an unmistakable curve of cruelty, and the pale eyes were shadowed with the dull cast of corruption.

To the left, a vast curve-paned window looked onto the night sky. I didn't need the sprawl of stars to tell me we were way, way high. In front of the window stood a gleaming pedestal made of what I suspected must be pure gold. Beside the window was a dome shrouded in black cloth. I had a momentary flashback to the computer room at Quested Court, to the plasma globe and the test that had started it all . . .

There was a whirring sound, and my eyes jerked to the object that dominated the room, the shrouded shape instantly forgotten. It was an enormous square contraption bristling with knobs and levers, buttons and flashing lights . . . a weird device that hummed and blipped and buzzed and gave off an almost visible tingle of electric power.

Electric . . . The room was bathed in harsh fluorescent light. The smoking torches of Shakesh belonged in another world, another age. Karazan had moved into a new era, in this high tower at least.

'So.' The king's voice was as I remembered it: soft as silk, cold as steel. 'You have delivered them. Well done, faithful servant.' He held out one hand. Sickened, I watched as Blue-bum clambered up his arm and settled on his shoulder, chittering softly in his ear.

There was a choking sob beside me. Kenta. 'Oh, Blue-bum – how *could* you?'

Blue-bum looked at us and smirked, and I saw the dribble of dried blood below his slit monkey mouth. '*You* bit me!' Richard growled. 'I'll throttle you with your tail, you mangy little traitor! We trusted you –'

He was interrupted by a shrill squawk from beneath the black cloth by the window. Suddenly I realised what it reminded me of: a parrot's cage, covered for the night. My mind made the connection without even beginning to make sense of it. Jumbled fragments of thought were flapping uselessly round my brain like birds in a dark room, going nowhere. *Blue-bum – Weevil – Zephyr – me –*

Then another thought, clean as a blade: *This is the man who killed my father.*

And suddenly, on a tide of roaring redness, I knew that what I had to do would be easy. I would do it now, with my bare hands – with my fists, hard as stone. I took two long strides into the room, a slow drumbeat of blood pulsing through me. It was as if I was standing in a long tunnel, and at the end, in a circle of light, was Karazeel. I could see every detail of his face, and for the first time I saw how like my own it was. The dark hair . . . the dusky skin . . . the eyes the colour of mist . . .

A smile twitched the corner of Karazeel's mouth, as if he could read my mind. One hand flicked up. A whirr – a rattle – something huge and heavy dropped from above. Faster than a striking snake a gleaming metal cage settled on the floor, enclosing us in a circle of steel bars.

'I have waited long for this moment,' whispered Karazeel. 'Welcome, children – welcome back to the world of Karazan. I know where you come from, and I have plans for your world. The world beyond the Cliffs of Stone . . . the world to which another child was taken, more than fifty spans ago. I did not know that then – but I know it now.'

The tide of rage had drained away, leaving me trembling and dizzy, the room spinning. I clung to a thin thread of hope. Karazeel didn't know who I was.

'My memory is long. You do not steal from King Karazeel and live, though I have replaced what was taken.' He was talking about Tiger Lily, who we'd magicked away from the dungeons of Shakesh. But how could he have replaced her? There were no cats in Karazan. 'You will be punished for the theft of the Mauler.' He smiled. 'Fate has a pleasing symmetry, as you will see.'

As he spoke he was pacing slowly round our cage, staring in. Jamie and the girls stood in a petrified huddle, not daring to look at him; Rich shot him an occasional glare from under glowering brows.

I'd been turning in a slow circle to keep Karazeel in view and keep an eye on Blue-bum. All pretence had vanished. Staring at his contorted face, I couldn't believe he'd been able to take us all in so completely and for so long. During his circuit of the cage Karazeel had somehow managed to ignore the hunched figure on his shoulder jabbering in his ear; but now Blue-bum grabbed a handful of the king's hair and gave a sharp yank, almost dislodging the twisted crown.

Karazeel's face darkened, and I had a second's wild hope he might lose his temper and throw Blue-bum out of the high window, along with everything he knew. But the frown was replaced by a chilling smile. 'Why yes, my furry friend,' he crooned, 'you have a report to make, do you not? I shall be most interested to hear what you seem so anxious to tell me.'

We watched as Karazeel crossed to his throne and reached down to a low table. A rack of crystal phials rested on its surface, a canister the size of a salt cellar beside them. It was full of a transparent liquid that looked like water. Karazeel picked it up and set Blue-bum down in front of the throne. I stared at the two figures, so focused on what was happening I hardly noticed the shrill screeches coming from the parrot's cage.

Karazeel upended the canister and shook once, twice. A fine spray of droplets landed on Blue-bum's fur. He twitched and jerked as if he'd been burned, his

60

monkey mouth stretching into a mockery of a grin. He gave a last chittering shriek; then his back arched and he fell backwards, his furry head connecting with the flagstones with a crack. His body jack-knifed. Beside me I heard Kenta give a choking sob, and I put out one arm and hugged her close. 'Don't watch,' I muttered . . . but I couldn't take my eyes away.

For a second I thought the liquid must be acid, or some kind of poison; that Karazeel had decided to kill Blue-bum. But as the tiny body twisted and writhed, I realised what was happening. I saw the limbs straightening, elongating . . . the scraggy fur melting away. The face flattening, the nose lengthening, the tail sucking itself back into the body.

A pool of purple rippled out around the huddled shape on the floor like blood; it gave a last convulsive twitch and a rattling cry. There was a long silence. Slowly the prone figure levered itself up onto its elbows, moving as stiffly as an old, old man. His back was to us, and at first all I could see was a cloak and a tangle of hair. In a series of arthritic lurches, the figure struggled to its feet. Turned and hobbled towards us, cackling and cracking its knuckles.

Not Weevil.

Evor.

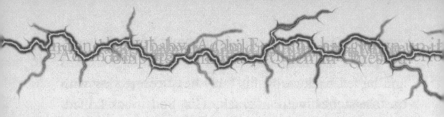

THE MAGIC OF DESTRUCTION

It wasn't possible . . . yet it explained everything. Blue-bum hadn't looked different because he'd been tortured; he'd looked different because he *was* different. He had been Evor all along – ever since we found him half-dead at the edge of Chattering Wood. And he *had* been half-dead . . . hadn't he? It *had* needed the healing potion to bring him back from the brink of death . . . hadn't it? I remembered the dried blood we'd sponged from his matted fur, the cuts and lacerations we'd assumed the potion had healed, but never actually saw . . .

Evor peered up at me from his nest of grizzled hair. 'Well?' he croaked. 'Worked it out yet? A simple matter of having you followed from Arakesh; then a sip of water from Chattering Stream, a little glonk-blood here and there . . . a scatter of kindling to lead you to the bait. A little acting . . . and you children did the rest, in your pathetic eagerness to believe the best of everything.' He leered at Kenta. 'Thank you for the cuddles, little girl. I almost grew to like them.'

He hobbled round to face me again, his eyes

glittering. 'The only one I feared might guess the truth was you . . . *Prince Zephyr*.'

There was a long beat of silence. Karazeel advanced on the cage, his eyes fixed on me so hungrily I felt they were sucking at my soul. 'So . . . that which was prophesied has come to pass. But this is where the legend ends. There will be no triumphant entry into Arakesh for you, nephew. Like the winged horses of Karazan, you will soon be nothing but ash and dust, a forgotten name breathed on the dying wind. But I am one of the mighty, the lords of destiny who shape the future and bend it to their will. Nothing can hinder my rise to greatness.'

In one stride he was beside the massive machine; grabbed a lever and pulled. An electronic humming filled the room. The stars in the vast window began to rotate, faster and still faster, spinning into a vortex of whirling light. Karazeel wheeled to face us, face blazing and demented. 'You see? I have harnessed the power of skyfire. Night and day are at my command. Soon the very galaxies will be in my control; my forces are as legion as the stars.'

He crossed to the golden lectern and raised both hands above it. There was something on its sloping surface . . . something flat with raised buttons that glittered like jewels. A keyboard . . . and the massive box must be a computer, though I was betting most of it was show – the guts would be the microcomputer we'd left behind in Shakesh. With a few modifications thrown in, I thought grimly.

'It's not a window,' whispered Jamie. 'It's a computer screen.'

The whirlpool of stars shattered and fragmented. Jamie was right. It wasn't a window with a view of the stars, it was a screen saver – and now, like a camera, it panned to a sweeping panorama of the mountains below. A dizzying hawk's-eye view of the range, a sleeping dragon blanketed in darkness. The camera panned, tipped and swooped downwards, taking us with it on a roller-coaster ride into the swirling depths of the cauldron.

I'd been wrong: it wasn't bottomless. The Cauldron of Zeel was a seething mass of monstrosity. Here were the hordes of Zeel – computer-generated maybe, but like Karazan itself, transformed into creatures of flesh and blood, with gleaming fangs and burning eyes. We skimmed low over a horde of dog-armadillos, past a legion of slavering shrags . . . and when their forms melted into the wavering grey ranks of the Faceless I closed my eyes and turned my face away. I'd seen enough.

'When the Cauldron is full to overflowing I will give the command. It will be soon, very soon,' crooned Karazeel, stroking the glittering gems encrusting the keyboard.

'Alt Control Delete – the magic of destruction.'

Suddenly Kenta was beside me. I'd always suspected there was more to gentle Kenta than she let on, and now she proved me right. She gripped a bar in each fist and gave a furious shake. The McCracken whiplash was back in her voice and her eyes were snapping fire. 'That's what you think! Call yourself king? You're nothing but a crazy upstart! So you think you're going to take over the world? Well, you're wrong – *we're going to stop you*!'

Karazeel's mouth dropped open. 'I –'

'I haven't finished!' snapped Kenta. 'I knew Blue-bum would never betray us – I never doubted him for a second. Where is he? What have you done with him?'

'Kenta, for goodness' sake shut up!' hissed Rich.

Evor was hobbling forward, with a smile I didn't like. Hobbling to the birdcage in the corner and flicking the cover off with a flourish. There, blinking in the harsh fluorescent light, crouched Blue-bum. His fur was as smooth and silky as ever, his monkey-face unlined and almost chubby-looking compared to the wizened mask of Evor. His paws were wrapped tight around the bars of his cage in a mirror image of Kenta's – the smooth, nimble-fingered monkey-paws I remembered. But it was when I looked into his bright, inquisitive eyes that I knew for sure it was really him.

Evor unlocked the door of the birdcage and grabbed Blue-bum by the scruff of his neck. Sidled over to where we stood staring stupidly out and shook him in our faces. With a fumble and a chink, he unlocked a small door set into the bars, opened it a crack and slammed it shut as Blue-bum sprawled on the stone floor at our feet.

'There is your little friend,' hissed Evor. 'You can all die together.'

'But not tonight.' There was a different note in Karazeel's voice – one that drew our eyes to him like a magnet. The wild frenzy had died away; he had sunk down onto his throne, his skin a sickly greenish-grey. 'The largest part of pleasure lies in anticipation . . . and now, Evor, it is time for my potion.'

'Wait!' What had got into Kenta? She was at the bars again, hugging Blue-bum in her arms. 'If we're going to die anyway, why not give Blue-bum some of that sprinkle stuff and change him back into a boy?'

'Yeah,' snarled Rich. 'Be more fun to watch a boy die than a chatterbot.'

'What a sensitive insight, Richard. But alas, it cannot be done.' As he spoke, Evor selected a phial from the array on the table and held it up, as if checking how much was left. The contents fractured the light like a prism and I caught hints of yellow, red, green and violet. It should have been beautiful, like a rainbow, but the colours were somehow dirty and putrid-looking. The yellow had the sickly cast of pus, the red was the crusty crimson of dried blood, and the green and purple the colour of an old bruise.

'You see,' Evor continued, 'the antidote will only work once. We have turned your little friend into a boy once before – a most talkative and knowledgeable boy, as it happened, once his tongue had been loosened by a drop of Truth Potion. No, your friend Blue-bum will remain a chatterbot for the rest of his life.'

'You're lying! There has to be a way!'

Evor's eyes flickered. 'There is one way he can be restored to his original form, but from what we have come to know of William Weaver, it might as well not exist. And now, my lord King . . .'

'Wait.' The merest croak, but enough to stop the phial before it touched Karazeel's lips. 'First, bring in the Mauler. It can guard them while I sleep . . . and the perfume of their terror will scent my dreams.'

Rich and I exchanged a glance. Last time, in Shakesh, the dreaded Mauler had turned out to be nothing more sinister than Hannah's little Tiger Lily, curled smugly on a velvet cushion. My heart gave a skip of hope. Weird things happened in Karazan. Could it be possible . . .

A faint hum came from the door we'd entered through. The elevator was making its way up from the levels below. It seemed to be struggling. The hum grew louder, and louder still . . . then stopped. The curved silver door slid smoothly to one side to reveal the dark interior. There was a subtle shift in the shadows, as if the darkness itself had moved.

A figure backed out: a youth, tall and broad-shouldered. He was moving very slowly, with exaggerated caution. Thonged sandals were on his feet; leather greaves protected his shins and forearms. He wore a short tunic and a pleated skirt of pliable leather, with a moulded leather breastplate covering his chest. His head was bare, and even from behind I could see the cow's-lick of brown hair sticking jauntily upwards. Kai – our friend, and the Keeper of the Mauler.

In one hand he held a leather whip, the base as thick as my wrist, tapering to a point as thin and supple as a serpent's tail. In the other hand was a trident. He eased backwards in a slow shuffle, his whole attention fixed on whatever was inside the chamber. His body was tensed, leaning slightly forward as if poised for instant flight. The skin on his back between the wide straps that held the breastplate in place was slick with sweat.

I was conscious of a peculiar smell, a fetid stink like algae in a stagnant pool. I darted a glance at Karazeel and Evor. If the Mauler, whatever it was, was so dangerous, then surely . . .

Behind the throne was what I'd thought was an ornamental golden screen, but now I realised it had a more practical purpose. Karazeel and Evor had retreated behind the protective barrier and were watching from safety, eyes fixed avidly on the open door of the elevator. Suddenly I felt sick.

Kai's whip snaked out with a crack like a rifle. There was a shuffle, a guttural, grunting roar – and a dark mass of muscle leapt out of the blackness and smashed into our cage with a force that carried it halfway across the room. Steel shrieked on stone; the air shook.

We cowered at the back of the cage, guts quaking.

The creature was scrabbling for a foothold, trying to heave itself on top of the cage. I saw a pulpy expanse

68

of pinky-grey belly – webbed feet bigger than flippers ending in hooked claws that scraped uselessly against the metal. The thing flopped to the floor and squatted there for a second, then gathered itself into another lurching leap that shoved the cage back into the computer casing with a crunch.

'*No!*' bellowed Kai, brandishing the whip. 'Get down! *NOW!*' His voice cracked. The creature was trying to force its head through the bars. Strings of drool stretched like slimy cling film between the metal and its gaping jaws; mottled lips peeled back from fangs the size of butcher's knives. Bulging eyes the colour of custard stared at us . . . then the mouth opened and it roared: a bellow that blasted our faces with the stink of rancid drains. It turned its head sideways, clamped its teeth on the bars and shook. The massive metal structure creaked and juddered; again, the whip cracked. The creature's head twitched as if it had been stung. It released the cage and waddled slowly round . . . and its eyes locked on Kai.

His whole being was focused on the Mauler, the force of his will bent on it. Three, maybe four paces separated them . . . one bound, and it would be over. Kai raised the trident and took one menacing step towards the crouching beast . . . then another. '*Down.*' A snarl of a word; the growl of a dominant predator.

For a second the muscles of the great haunches seemed to bunch and flex . . . then slowly the great body lowered itself to the floor and squatted, slimy hide glistening, the dangling dewlap pulsating.

'It's a toad,' croaked Richard in disbelief. 'A mutant toad!'

Kai eased forward and clipped a thick chain to the metal shackle circling the creature's front leg. His hand was shaking; it took three tries before the bolt snicked home. Slowly he backed away, the toad dragging itself after him, the chain grating on the floor. Slowly, slowly, without taking his eyes off the Mauler, he groped for a heavy metal retainer in the wall and snapped the other end of the chain home. Then he turned to the king and bowed. His knees were trembling, but his voice was steady.

'I am at your service, my lord King.'

Karazeel's eyes were glazed, his skin like dirty dishwater. 'The Mauler . . . has it eaten?'

'Not these three days, my lord.'

The grey lips twitched. 'It will dine well tomorrow. Good night, children – I wish you pleasant dreams.'

CANDLEWAX

The tower room was still. The flame of a single candle hung suspended in the darkness, a drop of molten gold surrounded by a dusty halo of radiance. The only other light came from the white pinpricks of the stars on the giant computer screen. I'd been gazing at them for what seemed hours, trying to memorise the unfamiliar constellations. Even though I knew it wasn't the real sky, I found it somehow comforting . . . yet at the same time it gave me the unsettling feeling of being inside a giant computer, staring outwards, as if the window was a star-spangled screen between two worlds. On one side of the screen, I was Adam Equinox . . . on the other, Zephyr, Prince of the Wind.

And Q, who'd invented the Karazan computer games . . . here, in the world he'd created, what did that make him? Which was reality – Karazan, or what I still thought of as home? Or was reality a time, not a place . . . wherever I happened to find myself, *now*? But even time was flexible, not fixed; Karazan had taught us that. The only certainty was inside myself;

the only reality was me. And in this moment – *now* – I was Zephyr. I felt it in every beat of my heart.

Some time after sunrise, Zeel and Evor would return. There was no doubt what would happen then. The vast shape against the wall snuffled and stirred as if it could smell my thoughts; a slit of pale light blinked open, then vanished. Between now and then, a plan must be made.

'Told you we shouldn't trust anyone . . .' Rich had muttered bitterly before he fell asleep. 'We should never have told Blue-bloody-bum anything . . .'

It was hard to see how we could be worse off than we already were. And anyhow, I thought with a bleak half-smile, there was nothing left to tell; no one left to trust. Only the motionless huddle of the others, exhausted by a day that seemed to have gone on forever – and would almost certainly be our last.

I was in no hurry for it to end.

My eyes jerked open. The kaleidoscope of stars had shifted. Time had passed; I must have slept. Had I dreamed it? No – the sleeping hum of the computer had deepened into a new note: a swelling buzz. It wasn't the computer. It was the elevator.

The hum snapped abruptly into silence. I sat still as stone, the bars digging into my back, staring past the candle – lower now, guttering in a puddle of wax – at the closed door of the lift. It slid open.

The dark bulk of the toad hunched and hissed. There was an answering growl. The creature sank back into the shadows where wall met floor, the two dim, hooded lamps of its eyes following the moving shape across the room. The door sighed shut.

Kai's face peered through the bars. 'Adam,' he breathed, 'be you awake?' At the sound of his voice my throat tightened. There was something in his face . . . an odd kind of shyness.

'Yes,' I whispered back. 'I'm awake.'

'Give me your hand.'

Puzzled, still half in a dream, I reached my right hand through the bars, expecting him to give me something, or grasp my wrist in the traditional handshake of Karazan. He didn't. He kissed it.

My face flamed in the darkness. I drew a breath to make some light-hearted quip that would brush his gesture aside and turn it into a joke – into something I'd feel comfortable with. The words were halfway to my lips when I saw his face. The rounded cheeks of the boy we'd known had hardened into the strong, flat planes of a man – and they were streaked with tears.

I thought about what those tears meant and something deep in my heart clicked into place. To me . . . well, I was just me, Adam Equinox. I'd blundered through life inside my own skin, messing up and picking up the pieces and somehow soldiering on. But that wasn't who I was to Kai. It wasn't who I'd have the luxury of ever being again . . . even to myself.

Kai had lived for this moment, risked everything for it, for Karazan . . . for me. I took a long, slow breath and tightened my fingers round his hand. 'Kai, look at me.' We locked eyes. I lifted his hand, turned it, and touched the back to my cheek for a second; tried to smile, but my eyes had filled with tears.

In a hurried whisper I told him everything: about Highgate, Q, the diary, me. 'Kai,' I finished, 'we need your help. If we all try together can we lift the cage? Or open it? Is there some way we can get the key?'

He shook his head wordlessly. We'd all watched the tiny silver key Evor had used to open the cage disappear into the folds of his purple cloak.

'Then there's only one thing for it. We'll have to wait until they let us out in the morning. With luck I'll be first. I'll need a weapon . . .'

Again, Kai shook his head. There was something almost apologetic about the way he was looking at me. 'My lord, there be two secrets I have discovered in the service of Karazeel. They are of great import, and I must reveal them to you now, though I cannot see how they will aid you. The first is this. We know there be a magic portal in the Cliffs of Stone: a door that opens but once in four spans, at Sunbalance.' I nodded. We'd spoken of it moments before: it was the portal Zagros told of in Queen Zaronel's diary, the one I'd been smuggled through as a baby, and our escape route last time we'd been in Karazan.

'At first it was a secret known to none but Meirion the Prophet Mage. But Meirion vanished; the years passed, and the legend of the Lost Prince refused to die. It was whispered that the infant had been taken into another world: a world beyond the Morningside.

74

Karazeel sent out his scouts, and for many moons they searched the Cliffs of Stone for any sign of an opening. In vain, for they found nothing.

'But a trusted servant of the King, second only in favour to Evor himself, crept out at dawn on the infant Prince's birthing day and resumed the search. How they happened upon the portal, I know not. Enough that they did. Four years later, this same spy crossed into the other world in search of the Lost Prince.'

My head was spinning. 'Hold on a minute. You're saying that somewhere in the world I come from there's someone from Karazan, looking for me?'

'Aye.' Kai's whisper was so faint I had to press my face against the bars to make out the words. 'I know little more. I cannot even tell you if the creature was male or female, only that it was human – once. The name of the spy was Tallow: a dissembler.'

Even though I had no idea what Kai's words meant, a chill trickled down my spine. 'A dissembler? What's that?'

'It is the name we give to those whose form and spirit have been melted and remoulded to the will of King Karazeel and the service of evil. They say their faces forever bear the scars, taking the form of the molten wax of a candle.'

'Well,' I growled, 'if he's got a face that looks like a melted candle, he wouldn't be hard to spot.'

'Nay, for the art of dissemblers is in disguise. They are adept at cloaking their true being, concealing their identity so skilfully it is impossible for any to guess it.'

'I'm glad you've told me.' But I wasn't. It gave me the creeps to imagine a creature from Karazan searching for me. I gave myself a mental shake. Truth was, there wasn't much point worrying about it, not here in Karazan, with the prospect of being eaten alive by the Mauler and the desperate need to find some way of dealing with Karazeel.

'Kai,' I whispered, 'about the morning. Time's running out. If I could borrow your trident, and find some way of hiding it . . .'

'That be the second thing.' Something told me I was going to like this piece of news even less. 'Evor has brewed potions for many things. Potions to kill . . .' I thought of my father . . . 'and a potion to bestow eternal life.'

'*What?*'

'Aye: a potion of immortality, the potion Karazeel was calling for. It has become a hunger for him, a need greater than food or water or air itself. While it flows in his blood he will not age, and nothing under the twin moons can do him harm.

'So, my Prince, your quest is ended. Nothing and no one in this world can overthrow Karazeel – not even the child of legend grown to man and King.'

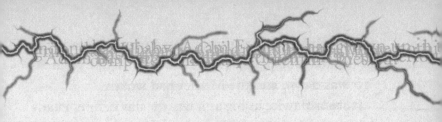

TRUST AND BETRAYAL

My brain felt numb. It had all been for nothing. We might as well give up and head on home.

I stared blankly round the dark room, praying for inspiration. But there was just the computer, humming softly under its breath; Blue-bum's empty cage, its shrouded dome-shape reminding me of Q's plasma globe. The computer screen . . . but now the stars that had been so comforting seemed cold and mocking. *Nothing under the twin moons can do him harm . . .*

Behind the screen I thought I caught a faint flicker of lightning as another storm gathered. Karazeel's demented voice echoed in my mind: *I have harnessed the power of skyfire. Night and day are at my command. Soon the very galaxies will be in my control . . .*

Then Kai's words, flat, defeated: *Nothing and no one in this world can overthrow King Karazeel . . .*

'Kai,' I said slowly. 'What was it you just said?'

I was jolted out of sleep by a bull-like bellow that shook the walls of the tower. I leapt to my feet and the sound came again, a deep-throated roar that made the air tremble.

It was dawn, and the Mauler had woken.

It seemed twice as big as it was the day before. Pearl-coloured light reflected from the computer screen onto its glistening green-black hide. As I gawked at it, still half-asleep, it pumped itself up like a gigantic bellows and roared again, its mouth gaping like a cavern, its eyes fixed on us.

It lunged forward in a clumsy leap, its shackled leg dragging it sideways; righted itself, and leapt again. The ribbon of its tongue flickered, tasting the air; then slowly, crab-wise, it dragged itself as close as it could to our cage and crouched there, panting.

For once even Richard didn't have anything to say. He was huddled with the others at the back of the cage, eyes huge in white faces. I stumbled over to them, horribly conscious of the toad following every movement, terrified of setting it off into another leap. Squeezed between Rich and Jamie, hunkered down between the two girls and put an arm round each of them. 'Listen up, guys,' I whispered. 'Here's the plan . . .'

The elevator door sighed open. First to emerge was Evor, cracking his knuckles and leering. Next came Karazeel, his face smooth and composed. Newly drugged-up with potion, I guessed. His eyes flicked from Rich to Jamie; from Gen to Kenta . . . then to me. He gave a low, ironic bow.

Last came Kai in his Keeper's regalia. He avoided my eyes, crossing to the throne and taking up his position. The Mauler gave a series of coughing burps and shambled round to face him. It was clear it knew its master, and equally clear from the strings of drool dangling from its jaws that it was expecting to be fed.

'Good morning, children. I trust you slept well.' No answer. 'Not afraid, are we? No need, I assure you – the Mauler may not be a tidy feeder, but it is invariably a rapid one. Now, who will be first? You would do well to remember the process will become slower as the edge is taken off his hunger . . .'

'Me.' I'd hoped to sound grimly determined, but the word came out in a pathetic croak. I tried again. 'I will.' My hand crept to my pocket, feeling for my knife – the Swiss army knife Q had given me. The blade was open and ready, cold under my fingers. Behind me, I heard Gen's breath catch in a sob.

'Well, children? Do you not wish to bid farewell to your little friend? I beg your pardon: to his lordship Prince Zephyr, Lost Prince of the Wind, briefly found and soon to be lost once more . . . this time forever.'

'My lord King.' It was Kai, his face expressionless. 'I pray your gracious permission to speak.'

'Later. *After*. Unleash the Mauler. Evor, the key.'

Evor hobbled forward, silver key at the ready.

'But, my lord, *after* will be too late.'

'Do not presume upon my favour, Keeper. Now, Evor –'

'Wait, your majesty! Last night I came to check

upon the Mauler. The boy who calls himself Zephyr was awake. I tricked him into telling me things – things that will bring your lordship powers beyond your wildest dreams.'

Evor paused, the key halfway into the lock; glanced at the King for the signal to continue. Time stopped.

Zeel raised one hand the merest fraction, but enough. He inclined his head towards Kai, his voice menacing and satin-smooth. 'Well?'

Kai was looking anywhere but at me. 'He spoke of a great wizard, a lord of creation named Q, by whose power the world of Karazan was made. He told of a magical globe which resides in the other world – the source of skyfire itself.'

There was a strangled gasp behind me. Turning, I saw Kenta's face, chalk-white and blank with shock. Beside me, Richard growled, 'Adam, you fool! I *told* you not to trust him!' His eyes were blazing with disbelief.

Karazeel took one look at the stunned denial on the others' faces and was on his feet in a flash and over at the cage. A hand like steel twisted into my collar. One jerk, and my face was mashed against the bars, Karazeel's eyes a hair's breadth from my own. 'So,' he hissed, 'the source of skyfire lies in your world? Does the Keeper speak truth?'

'No, he's lying –' I choked.

'*Yes!*' The mad light was back in his eyes. 'You will take me to it! You will deliver the skyfire into my hands and lead me to the creator! I will devour his heart and drink his blood, and his power will be mine. And *you* . . .' a cruel smile twisted his lips, and he pointed at the four children staring aghast, 'you will remain here as hostages. Evor and the Mauler will guard you.'

Jamie bit his lip. 'Don't feel bad, Adam,' he began loyally. 'It wasn't your fault. You . . . you . . .' Then his face crumpled and he burst into hiccuping sobs. Kenta threw her arms round him, glaring daggers at me over his head.

Richard shook his head helplessly, shrugged, and turned away, his face like stone.

'Kai,' hissed Gen, 'you are a slimy *toad*!' She turned away and buried her face in her hands.

None of them saw Kai shift the trident into his sword-hand and flick me an almost invisible wink.

Evor dragged me through the tiny door struggling and cursing, but inside I was jubilant. I couldn't believe how well the plan had worked. I felt bad about fooling the others, but there was no way they could have faked the shock on their faces . . . and that had been the clincher for Karazeel.

Protected by the potion of immortality, nothing under the twin moons of Karazan could do him harm . . . but things would be different in our world, or so I hoped. And that's where he was 'forcing' me to take him. I was banking on him being sandbagged by the transition, the same as I always was – but I was expecting it, and I'd be ready.

I had my pocket knife. It would be one on one.

As for the others – judging by the look on Rich's face he'd be more than a match for Evor. The Mauler was still chained to the wall, and likely to stay that way.

And Kai – I stifled a grin – Kai was on our side, just as he'd always been.

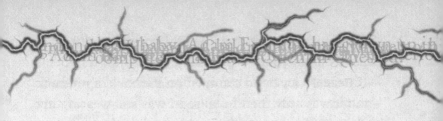

SKYFIRE

Evor dragged me over to the golden pedestal. The grin was gone; my heart was a swelling throb in my throat, almost choking me. What if Hannah was in the computer room? What if Evor's modification to the VRE Interface didn't work and Karazeel got stuck? What if, despite the fact that he was from Karazan like me, he didn't find the transition as tough as I did . . . what if he jumped me at Quested Court and went on the rampage? What if I'd made a stupid mistake?

Too bad. It's done. From here on in, it's all down to you, Zephyr. And you'll only get one shot – so quit worrying and do your best.

The giant screen was a rippled expanse of pink-edged cloud. Early morning. What time would it be at Quested Court? I'd soon find out. I made one last pretence at trying to escape Evor's grip, and felt my boot connect with his bony shin with a satisfying crack. 'Any more trouble from you,' he hissed, 'and I will feed the fat one to the Mauler. You do not seem to understand that the welfare of your friends depends upon your cooperation, *Prince Zephyr*.'

Karazeel's icy hand clamped on the back of my neck – and it was only then I realised I was still wearing my backpack. I'd unpacked it earlier to find the knife and it was practically empty; I must have shrugged it on automatically, as I did at the start of any journey. Some journey, I thought grimly.

I stared down at the keyboard. It was laid out like a normal keyboard but set in solid gold, the keys cushion-cut gems: the letter-keys diamonds as clear as water, the numbers sparkling emeralds, the function keys what I guessed must be sapphires. Four keys stood out from the rest, flawless rubies: Alt. Control. Q. And Delete. I positioned my fingers carefully. Double-checked. I wouldn't want to press Delete by mistake.

Karazeel breathed in my ear: 'Remember, dear nephew: no tricks.' I didn't trust myself to speak. Just closed my eyes and pressed.

I'd done it twice before, but it was worse than I remembered – way worse. Like being in a car wreck in pitch dark without a seatbelt . . . or a human pinball in a real-life game of Galactic Starburst. I rode it out curled like a foetus, breath held, eyes screwed shut.

At last I felt it: the rushing-water rising that meant it was almost over. Gasping for breath in the gluey air, battered and disoriented, I struggled to my feet, staggering and falling against the corner of a table, staring round for Karazeel. Punch-drunk from the transition, my brain registered fragmented images, a slide-show in shades of grey.

Night, pale moonlight slanting through the window. The room deserted, computers silent, the globe under its cover in the corner; the door open; the sleeping house beyond. No Karazeel.

I needed to make the most of every second. Stumbling to the corner I pulled the black cloth off the plasma globe. I could throw it over Karazeel, blind him – then I thought of turning it on, as a distraction. I flicked the switch. Purple-blue tendrils of lightning sprang to life in the glass sphere, twisting and writhing as if they were searching for a way out. For a moment I was mesmerised. I longed to touch it, to feel the cool tingle of the dancing strands under my fingers. The plasma globe was harmless, everyone knew that . . .

To most people, but not to me. And suddenly, like another jigsaw-puzzle piece falling into place, I realised why.

As I hesitated beside the globe there was a change in the air behind me. Not a noise; a presence where before there'd been nothing. I shuffled into the shadow of the doorway as a shape materialised out of the darkness, sprawled over the computer table. There'd be no better chance. He was face-down, groaning, his back a perfect target.

Flick the cloth over his head – and strike.

My hands were shaking, my chest filled with sick hollowness that made it hard to breathe. There was no sign of the red haze now, nothing to mask what I was about to do, only emptiness. I groped in my pocket for the knife, my hand shaking and slick with sweat. Tightened my fingers round it, yanked it out. It caught on something – pain stabbed up my arm and the knife was falling, spinning in slow motion onto the floor and under a table. My hand was on fire. I stared at the welling blackness at the base of my fingers, dripping into the shadows at my feet.

Time turned treacle-slow – but not slow enough.

In a single lithe movement Karazeel was on his feet, spinning to take in the room, me, the open door . . . the globe. He stared; gave a single, shuddering sigh. For an instant the wavering strands of plasma were reflected in his eyes like fluorescent blue veins; then he turned from me and advanced on it, hands outstretched.

This was it – my last chance, my only chance. *I had to do it.* I fell to my knees, scrabbling desperately for the knife. It was nowhere. I had no time. I had to do something – fast. The globe would hold him, but not for long. Then he'd be through the door and after Q.

I couldn't let it happen. I lurched to my feet, grabbed the heavy crystal pitcher of water from the nearest table. *Yes.* It would be enough to knock him cold while I ran for help or found the knife. I took two swift strides forward . . .

What happened next was encased in a fragile soap-bubble of time, stretching thinner and thinner in a moment that seemed to last forever. Karazeel, crouched like a vulture over the dancing electric tendrils of the plasma globe. Me, creeping nearer, jug poised.

A sudden shriek from the dark hallway – a trailing feral screech that froze me where I stood. A skittering rush – then something knocked against my shins and bounced away . . . and something else, swift as thought, smashed into the back of my knees and sent me flying.

Words seeded in my brain – *Bluebell* – *Tiger Lily* – *tag* – and I was falling forward, clutching the jug as its contents curved in a shimmering arc to shatter over Karazeel and the plasma globe.

WHAT THE MOONLIGHT REVEALED

A crack like a thunderbolt – a blinding explosion of blue-white light. I was flying backwards through the crackling air, my head connecting with the back wall with a *thwack*. Dimly I heard a patter like falling rain as the glass from shattered computer screens fell onto the table-tops . . . but my eyes were fixed on Karazeel.

Impossibly, he was dancing.

I stared, my head still ringing. Karazeel was dancing; dancing to the tinkling music of falling glass. A queer, graceful, twisting dance that reminded me of the tendrils of light from the plasma globe . . . and like them he was lit up in a brilliant blaze of fluorescent blue.

I stared, still not beginning to understand, as the electric glow of Karazeel's writhing figure dimmed and faded . . . as the contortions of his dance slowed and bent and crumpled . . . as his body shrank in on itself like an autumn leaf, twitching and jerking till it was the size of a child – of a doll – of a playing-card, shrivelled and black. I stared as the faint breath of a breeze from the open door wafted a grey feather of ash from the floor . . . but before it could drift to the ground again, even that was gone.

I leaned against the wall like a broken puppet while Tiger Lily purred and rubbed herself against me and pretended the pale fur at the tip of her tail wasn't frizzled and scorched. It was the end, wasn't it? I'd done it – or rather Tiger Lily had. Karazeel was dead. Our world was safe. So why did I have such a feeling of dread? Could it be because my mind kept replaying, not what I'd seen, but what I'd heard?

What I'd thought at first was Karazeel singing as he danced; then thought was a high, wavering scream . . . but now echoed in my memory as a sound I'd never heard before and never wanted to hear again: Karazeel's triumphant laughter.

After what seemed a long time I clambered unsteadily to my feet. There was only one thought in my mind: *Find Q*. More than anything else I longed to be held safe in his arms, to hear him tell me I'd done it; it was over.

Something caught my eye: an angular shadow under one of the tables. The knife. Too late now – but then maybe this was how it was meant to happen. I bent to pick it up.

It wasn't the hard metal of the knife that met my fingers. It was something solid and velvety, that tickled my fingertips with the tingle of magic. I drew it out, and it fell open in my hand. The *Book of Days*.

It must have been in my backpack and fallen out when I was thrown across the room. Moonlight fell full on the open page. Words leapt out at me, and in the pale silvery light they seemed tinged with gold, as if they were written not in moonlight, but in liquid fire. They were words I hadn't seen before, in a new hand, strong and compelling: the hand of Meirion the Prophet Mage. *It is not over . . .*

The words of the final entry in Zaronel's diary echoed my own thoughts of seconds before. Numb, disbelieving, I read to the end. A few disjointed sentences, scrawled in haste . . . sentences that changed everything. Meirion was right. It hadn't been over then – and it wasn't over now.

My quest had just begun.

Q – I had to find Q.

I ran.

Past computers with their plastic covers melted onto the casings, their shattered screens gaping shark-mouths rimmed with jagged teeth – past the table where the plasma globe had stood, now just a blackened, shapeless base with a half-melted cord. Through the door, past the grandfather clock in the hallway, up the stairs two at a time. Left at the top past Hannah's room, realising I didn't know which door was Q's. I'd never been to his bedroom; never needed to.

I needed to now. Logic told me it would be the next one – the one beside Hannah's. I skidded to a stop, raised my knuckles and rapped as loud as I dared.

Nothing.

I lifted my hand to try one more time before moving to the next door down where a deep voice reached me through the wood: 'Who is it?'

'Me – Adam.'

A pause . . . then the doorknob turned and the door opened. I blundered in on a wave of relief, already starting to gabble.

But it wasn't Q. It was Shaw, standing with one hand on the doorknob and the other at the neck of his paisley gown. If it hadn't been for the dressing-gown I would have hugged him.

'Shaw,' I gasped, 'thank goodness I've found you! Where's Q? I have to talk to him *now*. Stuff has happened with Karazeel and I've found out –'

'Adam! Yer back! But 'ang on, 'ang on – 'old onter yer 'olly-'ocks.' He lumbered past me and shut the door. 'Don't want ter wake the whole house, do yer? Now, wot's the problem?'

I was tempted to blurt out the whole story, knowing he'd take it all in his stride; it was next to impossible to rattle Shaw. But it was Q I needed . . . and something was niggling at the back of my mind, something I didn't have time to think about right then. I pushed it away; steadied myself. 'Shaw, which is Q's room? I need to speak to him.'

Shaw shook his head slowly. 'Sorry, Adam, Q's 'ad ter go ter Winterton with wee 'annah. Last night she were took bad.' I thought I saw a glimmer of something in his eyes. Could it be tears? I felt my own throat close. Hannah was over her terrible illness – wasn't she?

'Is she . . .'

'Touch an' go, Adam; touch an' go. But Q left you a message. If yer came back unexpected, like. Said ter tell yer . . .' Shaw paused, as if trying to recall exactly what Q's words had been; '. . . ter say that if yer needed 'elp, just come straight ter me.' His eyes glinted in the gloom. 'That . . . and ter give yer 'is love.'

I stared at his face, so solid and reassuring in the candlelight. Candlelight . . . the explosion must have blown the electricity. I shivered. It was cold in the room; no wonder Shaw was clutching the neck of his dressing-gown closed.

To give you his love . . . Tears filled my eyes, and my knees turned to jelly. I sank down on the bed. 'Shaw,' I stammered, 'so much has happened . . . and now, the biggest secret of all . . .'

'Steady now, Adam; just take yer time.'

I was trying desperately to order my thoughts. 'Zephyr, the Lost Prince of Karazan . . . it's me. I know it sounds crazy, but he – *I* – was brought to our world as a baby. Time's different here, it's slower. And Karazeel has been taking a Potion of Immortality, so I tricked him into coming to our world and . . . and . . .'

'And?' There was a new note in Shaw's voice now; I'd hardly have recognised it.

'The plasma globe – the water – he's . . .' I couldn't

say it, but I could tell Shaw understood. His face had gone very still, his eyes were burning into mine with an intensity I'd never seen before. 'But . . . he was laughing – *laughing*. And that can only mean one thing. Something has gone horribly wrong and Karazan is in terrible danger.'

The suffocating dread was back, half panic, half paranoia. 'There's more,' I whispered. 'There's a spy of Karazeel's here in our world, looking for me.'

And here, in the gloom of Quested Court, I knew without a doubt who that spy must be. 'It's Usherwood – it has to be! The plasma globe gave her a shock once too, remember? You told me – that's why you won't go near it. But it doesn't shock just anyone – only people from Karazan. Usherwood's a *dissembler*, and her real name's Tallow.' The pieces of the jigsaw were falling into place so fast I was gabbling to keep up with them. 'She was the one who searched my room – she'd taken invisibility potion so I couldn't see her! That's why she's been watching me all this time! That's why she wanted to adopt me, to find out more about me. She must have suspected –'

Something in Shaw's face flickered in what could almost have been a smile. 'There, there. Don't fret yerself, Adam. Usherwood ain't 'ere now; I am. The door's closed and it's just the two of us. Now, is there anything else yer need ter tell me?'

'Yes.' I hesitated. 'But . . . it's so secret only three people in the entire universe have known it up till now. And it changes everything. I read in Queen

Zaronel's diary that there wasn't one baby born that night. There were two. Prince Zephyr – and Prince Zenith. The Prince of the Wind and the Prince of the Sun – one silver, one gold; one for each of the twin moons of Karazan; one for each strand of the twisted crown.

'Somewhere I have a brother . . . and it will take both of us to save Karazan.'

A SPY IN THE NIGHT

The candle flame flickered, and Shaw's shadow wavered huge and dark on the closed door behind him. His face was as impassive as ever, but I thought I saw a glimmer of approval in his eyes.

'Well, young Adam, yer've certainly put two and two tergether and come pretty close to makin' four. Some of wot yer've just said is news ter me – some, but not all. So you're Zephyr, are yer? Well, well, 'oo'd'ave thought it? Me, mebbe, if I'd only known about the time difference.' He rubbed his face, grimacing slightly as if it was stiff or sore.

'And looking at you now, it isn't so hard to believe. Like I said, young Adam, you've done well. And you're right about Usherwood, she is a spy. But there's one thing you don't know. There are two spies from Karazan here at Quested Court. One sent by King Karazeel . . . and one sent by those they call the Believers. Both on the same mission: to find Prince Zephyr. Think of it as a race, if you like, or a complex game of cat and mouse.'

I stared up at him. He watched me, dark eyes expressionless. He was scratching the base of his neck thoughtfully, almost as if he was waiting for something . . . waiting for me to say something, make some connection . . .

Suddenly the niggle I'd pushed to the edge of my mind leapt back centre-stage, fully formed. What had Shaw said when I knocked on his door? *Who is it?* I'd been so focused on what Shaw was saying I hadn't noticed how he was saying it: not 'oo – *who* . . .

I felt a grin spread over my face. 'It's *you*, isn't it?' I said slowly. '*You're* the Believer. That's how you know all this stuff! You've been looking for me all this time – and I've been right here, under your nose!'

'Almost right, Prince Zephyr. All except for one small detail.' He turned away, scratching the base of his neck. There was a sound like ripping plaster and he turned back to me, the loose skin of his face and head dangling from his hand inside-out, pale and flaccid. Shaw's dark eyes peered out at me from a featureless mass of scar tissue, salmon-pink and grey. *It's not like candle wax*, I thought stupidly; *it's like brains, as if his brains have melted and run down his face* . . .

And now finally, with his mask removed, Tallow was smiling as he advanced towards me.

Instinct took over, powered by adrenaline.

I pushed off from the bed like a rocket, head low and arms pumping, and bolted straight for Shaw – my head rammed him in the gut like a charging bull. I heard his breath *whoof* out as I dodged round his doubled-up body and clutching hands, and fumbled for the doorknob. Grabbed it, twisted, wrenched it open and ran.

Out of the door and down the dark corridor to the end, a long passageway at right angles. Left or right? Didn't matter, as long as I made the turn before Shaw saw. Like a rabbit on the run, I dodged and dived left and right and left again . . .

I hurtled down corridor after dark corridor, swinging round corners, my feet hardly touching the carpet – but I could feel him behind me and closing. I risked a frantic glance backwards; wished I hadn't. He was closer than I'd thought.

Another junction – or was it the same one? Right again, breath coming in ragged gasps – no, this was different. This passage ended in a stairway, heading upwards. I raced up the stairs, two, three at a time, stumbling, crawling, my legs and arms scrabbling for grip, for extra speed. At the top I looked back – he was halfway up, gaining fast.

Left; left again. The passages on this level were narrower; the carpet replaced by worn linoleum that squeaked under my feet. Another left, and ahead of me was a short passage ending in a blank wall, a door leading off to either side. One of them was open just a crack . . .

I made the decision in a split second. He'd never look for me here – only a fool would duck down a dead end. The open door could lead into a room, a hallway, maybe, with another exit; I'd slip through, lose him, sneak on down.

The door opened inwards. I pushed the crack wider and slipped inside, easing it closed behind me and crouching in total darkness, trying not to breathe. I knew instantly there was no room, no hallway, no other door. I was in a broom cupboard. Just like my dream . . . There was the fusty floor-polish smell of dusters and brooms and something was tickling the back of my neck . . . I breathed shallowly and waited, praying I wouldn't sneeze.

How long till he'd be safely past? I heard a sound. Stealthy footsteps, like someone playing hide and seek. The heavy, measured breathing of someone who'd been running, but didn't have to run any more. I heard the door creak slowly open across the passage; snick softly closed again. Soft footfalls, coming closer. The doorknob gave a little jiggle. I realised I was holding it, on the dark inside of the broom cupboard. It was trying to turn against my hand.

I locked my fingers, twisting against him, willing the handle not to turn. My other hand fumbled desperately in my pocket. Looking for something, anything. My hand slid helplessly on the smooth brass surface; the doorknob turned.

I threw my weight on the door, my foot wedged against the back wall for purchase, but I knew it was useless. Shaw was a huge man, heavy and fit. *Thud!* The wood juddered as he flung his weight against the

98

door; a chink of light appeared. I heaved back, but it didn't budge; he'd have his foot against it, holding the gap while he readied himself for another push. And this time I wouldn't be able to hold him.

Then my fingers found something in my pocket, something small and sharp I'd squirreled away in front of another door in another world. Something that held that door open when we wanted it closed. Would it hold this door closed for me now?

I dropped the little wedge-shaped stone onto the floor, hearing the tiny chink of it landing. Felt for it with my foot, kicking it under the doorjamb. Softly I moved away from the door. I had one chance left, and I'd need both hands free. If it was still there. If I could find it in the dark. If there was time.

I ripped my pack off my back and groped inside. Recoiled from the door as a massive weight rammed into it and it leapt inwards – and stuck fast. My fingers raked desperately through the jumble of oddments in the bottom of my bag, sending lightning picture-messages to my brain: *pen, muesli bar, diary, matches* –

Crash! Another shuddering blow; the door shifted a fraction, and held.

And there it was in the corner, smooth and heavy and unspeakably wonderful.

The microcomputer.

I lifted it out, hands shaking, squinting at the keys in the darkness. *Crash!* The door opened another notch. *Now or never.*

Alt – control – Q.

There was an animal roar, a crash like a battering ram that blew the door inwards as if the tiny stone didn't exist. Grey light flooded the darkness.

My fingers clamped down on the keys . . .

THE LOST YEARS

. . . and I was in Karazan.

Something was wrong. It was dusk . . . but it couldn't be. I'd left the Stronghold of Arraz in the early morning. An hour maybe had passed since then, four hours Karazan-time at most. It should be the middle of the day, bright sunshine, birds singing.

But it was almost dark, and there was a terrible stillness in the air. It was as if the sun had gone out.

I took two slow steps forward, staring round me. The standing stone, the magic portal between the worlds, had fallen. It lay smashed in two on the sloping hillside, an angular stub sticking out of the ground like a broken tooth.

A pall hung in the sky; not cloud, more a heaviness of the air. To the northwest, way, way up where the cliffs met the horizon, there was a faint reddish glow. The air smelled burned, not of fire, not the gunpowder smell of thunder, but the coppery, metallic smell of fused electricity. My skin was covered in tiny

101

dots of black that rubbed away when I touched them,
like fallen ash.

> *Words of the past will show the way*
> *To turn the darkest night to day;*
> *When twain is one and one is twain*
> *Wind blows and sun shines forth again;*
> *When man is child and child is man*
> *True King will reign in Karazan.*

The words came into my mind from nowhere. It was
the end of the prophecy, the one part we hadn't been
able to understand. Except Jamie, with his lofty talk
of poetic licence and symbolism. Well, he was wrong.
It meant exactly what it said. But how could he ever
have guessed? How could anyone?

But what had happened? Had I done it? Was it
somehow my fault? That didn't matter. One thing I
knew: it was up to me to put it right. I had no idea
where the others were: I hoped they were safe. There
was no one to help me decide what to do next.

That didn't matter either. I'd read the end of the
diary, and I knew what the poem meant. And I'd done
some figuring out of my own.

I knew what I had to do.

I made my way slowly down the sloping hillside into
the forest. It was darker here, but at least I could pretend the darkness was because of the trees. I followed
the sound of the stream till I was roughly where I

remembered finding the beautiful red flower – the flame vine – the first time I'd come to Karazan. The flower had clamped onto my face; I'd fallen, kicking and struggling . . . Argos had severed the vine and led me downhill.

There was no path; never had been. Hesitantly, following my instincts and uncomfortably aware that every tree trunk looked the same, each patch of tangled undergrowth identical, I wound my way between the trees. At last I reached a place that looked almost familiar: it was where I remembered the clearing being – where I'd looked for the cottage before, with the others, and found nothing. Again, there was nothing. Or was there?

Narrowing my eyes I stared into the shadows, feeling, or imagining, the tingle of magic in the air. The back of my neck prickled as if I was being watched. I braced myself; took a breath. Called out, as loudly as I dared: 'Argos. *Argos!*'

Waited. I heard nothing: not the crack of a twig, not the rustle of a leaf. But a voice spoke behind me, soft in my ear: 'Who are you that calls my name?'

I turned slowly. Last time he'd towered over me; now we were eye to eye. He hadn't changed. The same untidy tangle of grey-brown hair, the same weathered skin and tall, gaunt frame. The same watchful distance in his eyes.

'Look at me, Zagros,' I said quietly. 'Who do you see?'

We looked into each other's eyes for what seemed a

long time. During the walk through the forest my mind had been a jumble of worry – what if I couldn't find the cottage? What if I couldn't find Argos? What if I'd got it wrong, and he wasn't Zagros? What if he was on the other side? And if I did find him, what would I say?

But the words had come into my mind fully formed, and the instant I said them a kind of peace settled over me. This was the way it was meant to be. Now all I could do was wait.

At last he spoke, as much to himself as to me. 'You have your mother's eyes. How could I not know you?'

He led me back the way I'd come. We retraced our steps – almost, but not quite. 'Follow me closely,' Argos had said long ago, and now I understood why. Before, I'd thought he was picking a random route through the trees, but now I realised he was following an invisible path. Left round this tree, right round that, through a narrow gap between two tree trunks like massive gateposts . . . and we stepped out into the clearing – the clearing that had been nothing but an empty glade with a few saplings and a tangle of overgrown brush five minutes earlier.

And there it was: the little grey cottage. The log-pile was higher than before, newly stacked; the flagstone path had been swept, the broom still leaning against the wall. The soft glow of lamplight shone from the window.

I followed Zagros up the path onto the covered

porch. Tucked away in the corner was what I realised must be a spinning wheel, the beginnings of a blanket or cloak folded neatly on the arm of the rocker. I reached out and lifted the soft wool to my cheek. There it was – the faint spicy fragrance that still clung to my own shawl, as familiar to me as my own heart-beat from further back than I could remember.

Zagros paused with one hand on the latch and shot me a questioning glimmer from under his brows. *Ready?*

But suddenly I wasn't. I couldn't do it. This was the moment I had dreamed of all these long, lost years. And now that it was here I couldn't go in.

Zagros reached out and took my shoulders in hands clumsy with gentleness. 'She knew it was you. That lost boy in the woods . . . it was impossible, and yet she knew. Let us not make her wait any longer.'

I followed him inside.

She was there at the fireplace. It wasn't how I'd dreamed all those times. She was old, but the years cloaked her as softly as a mantle. I'd always imagined she would be bigger than me, but she only came up to my shoulder. Her eyes reflected mine like clear water, and in them I could see the same question, the same uncertainty that was filling my heart.

She was the mother and I was the child, and the lost years trembled between us for what seemed an eternity.

And then she held out her arms.

RIDDLES BY FIRELIGHT

'And now,' said Zagros, 'it is time for business.'
I took a second bowl of stew from Zaronel, tearing off another hunk of crusty bread to mop up the gravy. Zaronel – *my mother* – had tended to the cut on my hand with gentle fingers, smearing it with a salve that burned, then soothed; now a little stiffness and a tidy bandage were the only reminder it had ever happened.

I shovelled another spoonful into my mouth and looked over at Zagros with what I hoped was a politely enquiring expression. He and Zaronel were sitting at the table watching me with a kind of pride, as if gobbling down stew was something not many people are capable of. Zagros – Argos and Ronel had been their nicknames for each other when they were playmates in Antarion, he'd told me – looked back at me, his eyes crinkling in what passed for him as a smile as he nodded towards the inner door.

Puzzled, still chewing, I followed his gaze and at the same time a voice – deep, strange and yet familiar

106

– spoke into the silent room. 'Well met once more, Prince Zephyr.'

There in the doorway stood Meirion, Prophet Mage of Karazan.

I almost choked on my stew. Last time I'd seen him had been at the edge of the shroud after our escape from Shakesh; he'd been filthy and half-starved, wearing nothing but a dirty loincloth. We'd rescued him from the dungeon where he'd been imprisoned and tortured; even now I could hardly bear to look at the hollow sockets that had once been eyes. We'd planned to take him back with us to Quested Court, but when we emerged from the shroud, he was gone. I remembered the brief tingling hand-touch that had meant farewell; the shadow of a smile; the words, dismissed as gibberish at the time, dust-dry in darkness: *The five are come, Man-child . . . the time is nigh . . .*

'You knew,' I breathed, staring across at the tall, robed figure. '*Man-child*, like in the prophecy – all the time, you knew. But how . . .'

'The inner eye sees through a veil of darkness. Some things can be seen and yet not spoken of; some seen and yet not changed.' As he spoke, he crossed to stand before the fire. Watching him, it was hard to believe he was blind.

'How did you know it was me, I mean?' Then suddenly the questions were falling over each other. 'Why didn't you tell me? Why did you just disappear like that? Where did you go? How did you find your way here? And how did you get to Shakesh in the first place? There's so much I don't understand . . .'

I heard myself burble to a stop. The flames flickered and steadied, and my thoughts steadied with them. I pushed my plate aside. Everyone was watching me, even Meirion, with his empty eyes – but watching in a different way from before. Watching . . . and waiting.

Hesitantly I rose and crossed to where the mage was standing. I reached for his right hand and raised it, touching it to my lips and then my cheek in a gesture that already felt familiar. When I spoke, uncertainty cracked my voice into a gravelly croak completely unlike my own. 'Well met, my Lord Meirion. Please . . . tell me . . .'

'What is it you wish to know?'

Again, all the unanswered questions pushed up inside me like a gigantic bubble, but this time I swallowed them. Sifted through them; found the ones that really mattered. Spoke my thoughts aloud, slowly, hesitantly. 'Is Zeel dead? On the other side, the plasma globe –' I knew I didn't have to tell him more – 'it's linked to the darkness here in Karazan, isn't it?'

It is not over yet . . .

'My brother, Zenith . . . I need to know where to find him, and what we must do to bring back the light. And Meirion, if you can . . . please help me follow in the footsteps of my father.'

Perhaps it was just a trick of the light, but the creases in the seamed cheeks seemed to deepen. 'For the last: you will make your own footprints upon the soil of Karazan, Prince Zephyr. As to your other questions . . . I will tell you what I can, but this is Karazan, and the way to the truth is crooked and hard to find. I will point the way, but it is your steps that must lead you there. You will stumble upon many things on your path, some of use, some not. Some you have, and some have yet to come. Listen, and look deep into the fire.'

The room seemed suddenly darker. The flames that had burned so brightly moments before had died down to a sullen red glow. Zagros and Zaronel had gone; we were alone. I sat cross-legged beside Meirion, my heart thudding in my chest.

He felt for the worn leather pouch that hung at his belt and drew out a small parchment, folded like a tiny envelope. As he opened it, a dry, musty smell filled the room. On the paper lay two leaves. Staring down at them, I could imagine they might once have been golden; now they were pale skeletons, brittle and faded. As he spoke, he rubbed them gently between his fingers, so that they crumbled into fine grey dust.

'The dark night of the prophecy has come to pass. But there cannot be dawn without nightfall, nor spring without the cold of winter. You ask where you should seek the Prince of the Sun. You, the firstborn, were taken west by Zagros; and into his keeping was given also the Queen, near death from loss and labour. I bade him build a bower in the depths of Shadowwood, its foundation the sloughed skin of the Serpent of Invisibility, and there await my return.

'I carried the second-born to the east, and left him in safe hands. On my return to the shores of Karazan, I was captured by a servant of Zeel: one who went by the name of Tallow. The rest, you can guess.'

It wasn't a guess. They'd tortured him to make him tell where he'd taken the baby. I didn't need to ask if he'd told them. If he had, he'd be dead; if he had, everything would have been over a long, long time ago.

Silence hung in the air.

'Tell me . . .' I cleared my throat; tried again. 'Tell me where you took him.'

A log crumbled on the fire. Meirion's answer, when at last it came, was softer than the falling ash. 'A heart is broken; salt tears turn to stone. A cradle-craft sets sail for Limbo; in those lost lands I left him.'

There was an eerie, almost sing-song quality to his voice that sent a shiver down my spine. 'Is there nothing more you can tell me?' I asked gently. 'Is Limbo a place? How will I know it? Who did you leave him with?'

Slowly, painfully, Meirion shook his head. Before, he'd looked somehow ageless; now he seemed an old, old man, his face carved from stone. As if in slow motion, he reached into the parchment and sprinkled a few of the tiny flakes onto the glowing coals. They snapped and crackled, igniting in sparks bright as stars: red, green and brilliant blue. A sharp smell like burned cinnamon stung my nostrils, and there was a strange, hollow ringing in my head. I watched the sparks drift down, a faint thread of smoke twisting up where each one fell. I wasn't sure whether the next words were Meirion's, or my own thoughts, or came somehow from the fire itself.

Look for grey smoke on a grey horizon.

Meirion cast another pinch of powder into the fire. His voice came again, deep and harsh: 'What has befallen the Prince of Darkness?'

The powder hissed and spat, sucking the flames inwards to a sullen purplish glow.

He has passed into the Realms of the Undead. The birds of the air will point the way; truth and lies will lead you there.

Blue smoke swirled through the room. I stared, my breath catching in my throat, as Meirion reached his hand into the fire and set the parchment itself in the depths of the coals.

The room exploded in a blaze of light. I flinched, squeezing my eyes shut . . . and an after-image floated in the velvet darkness behind my eyelids: two identical circles, drifting in nothingness.

The twin moons of Karazan follow each their own orbit, one near, one far, tracing their own path through the skies; but at Sunbalance they rise together as one, silver and gold, a perfect pair balancing the heavens.

The vision of the full moons faded. I opened my eyes. Meirion was beside me, ash-pale. The fire had burned down to embers. The room was dark and silent.

There was nothing to say. I felt dizzy and sick.

Meirion had given me all he could: I'd been shown everything, yet I understood nothing. And I realised now – too late – that there was something else I should have asked, something that was lying like lead in my heart, though it had nothing to do with my quest or the future of Karazan.

Hannah – what about Hannah?

Meirion stirred and turned towards me. I leaned forward to catch his words, for a wild moment half-believing he might have read my mind and be about to answer my unspoken question . . . but then he spoke, and the hope faded.

'One last thing I will tell you, Prince Zephyr. For you, Child of the Wind, your destiny lies where you least look for it – the beginning will be the end, and every end a new beginning.'

I set out alone as the dark of day was deepening into night.

At my side hung my father's sword. Zagros had taken it from the Summer Palace on the night I was born; now it belonged to me, Zane's firstborn son. It was plain and unadorned: no elaborate engraving, no jewels, no crimson velvet or golden cord. Worn strips of leather bound the hilt; it fitted my hand as if it had been made for me. The fine blade slid from its casing with barely a whisper, its gleaming length chased with the faintest tracery of leaves, flowers and birds. The edges were razor-sharp. As I belted it on, standing tall and square-shouldered to take the unaccustomed weight, I felt for the first time that I was my father's son.

My pack was on my back; in it, neatly folded, was a clean square of bleached calico the size of a small tablecloth, heavily patched and darned. 'It is all Meirion had when he came to us,' Zagros told me. 'He bade me tell you to take it with you and use it well.' I could hardly recognise it as the ragged loincloth Meirion had worn, but as I stowed it away my fingers prickled and I felt a sudden certainty that, like so much in Karazan, it would have a use – one I hoped I'd recognise when the time came. As for the mage himself, I hadn't seen him again, nor expected to: we had said all the farewells we needed by the dying light of the fire.

Above the cloth, wrapped in a napkin, were dried fruit, bread and cheese . . . and in my head rattled a useless jumble of meaningless contradictions and confusing images.

Zagros waved me away from the door of the grey cottage with my mother beside him, as bright and brave as a candle flame.

THE DRAGON WAKES

I turned my back on the shadows of the forest and headed north, keeping to the foot of the cliffs. Soon, as Zagros had told me it would, my route joined the new road forged through the mountains by Zeel's men: a raw scar cutting westwards through the range like a jagged lightning bolt. It was utterly deserted, as we'd hoped it would be. I was going to find my friends. It was like a lantern lighting my way: the thought of them there at the Stronghold of Arraz, waiting for me.

As I walked it seemed a strange false dawn was breaking on the high horizon ahead: the sky was streaked with crimson slashes banded with black. But no morning came, and there was no way of keeping track of time. No setting sun, no stars, no moons – gold or silver – in the dark sky. So I had no way of knowing when it was that I finally reached the summit and looked down on the Stronghold of Arraz . . . or where the Stronghold had once been.

The Cauldron of Zeel had become a lake of fire and the fortress itself had vanished. Even where I stood

114

the searing heat of molten lava scorched my skin, a red glow bathing Dark Face in a hellish other-worldly light.

To the north the twin peaks of the two vast volcanoes stood out against the sky, one spouting a fountain of fireworks into the night; the other gushing a thick, impenetrable pall of black smoke that mushroomed out to blanket the sky. I could just make out a thin line of fire in the far distance: the narrow neck where the depths of the cauldron rose to meet the higher ground of the plains. To its right were the Brimstone Caverns. The molten core of the mountain must have risen and poured from the two caves in a deadly tide that had engulfed the valley below in minutes. The dragon had woken.

It was a long time before my mind made sense of what my eyes were seeing; even longer before my thoughts groped for the first threads of hope, and found none. From when I left the high tower room until the plasma globe exploded – how long? A minute, maybe, two at most. Long enough for the others to . . . to . . . to what?

To nothing. It wasn't long enough.

Everything was gone. The tower, the computer, Evor, the monsters that had crowded the deep, awaiting Zeel's signal. One world at least was safe.

But the other . . . and the others . . .

My mind stuck there.

The others.

There was a pain in my chest that made it hard to breathe, a steel band tightening round my throat. Something touched my cheek – ash? I raised my hand to brush it away. It was a single tear, drying to salt in the swell of heat before it could fall.

A heart is broken; salt tears turn to stone.

I turned and walked down and away, alone.

ECHOES IN THE MIST

I'd been banking on the knowledge that soon I would be with the others; together we'd be able to unravel the riddles that had come from the fire.

Now that wasn't going to happen. And now, when I most needed to think clearly, my mind seemed to have crept away somewhere inside itself like a wounded animal – and instinct told me to let it rest there in the healing darkness. I could barely remember what Meirion had said. Only one sentence stuck in my mind: *I carried the second-born to the east.* That was the only thing I understood.

So I let my feet carry me eastwards towards the sea, following the course of the River Ravven. Somewhere behind the dark pall that covered Karazan the sun rose and set; in another world, safe and far away, I tried to imagine a pale moon and bright stars shining in a clear sky.

Time passed.

It was only when I reached the shores of Lake Stillwater that I finally stumbled to a halt. It took a

moment for me to realise where I was. The last time
I had seen the lake its still surface had reflected the
moonlight like a silver mirror; now, in the gloom, it
was almost impossible to tell where land ended and
water began. A light mist, fine as cobwebs, swirled
over the water, hiding the Citadel from view.

I sank down onto the hard ground to rest, and was
instantly asleep.

The faces of my friends drifted through my dreams.
Gen the way she used to look, a princess in disguise:
knobbly nose, jug ears, straggly hair awry. Jamie,
pink-faced and earnest, puffed-up as a marshmallow
and just as soft inside. Kenta, quiet as a mouse,
fierce as a tiger. Rich, with his swagger and sheepish
grin. Even old Blue-bum – the real one – bright
eyes, monkey-tail, blue behind and all. Words, voices,
snatches of remembered laughter . . .

I'll go first; I'm bigger, and stronger . . .

My feet are hurting, and I'm hungry . . .

It seems so unkind . . . not like you at all . . .

It was a dream, wasn't it? Only a dream . . .

My eyes snapped open. Only a dream . . .

Wait up, guys – wait up!

The mist had thickened: it was dense and smothering, echoes of my dreams still tangled in it. Stupid
with sleep, I struggled to one elbow, peering into the
swirling whiteness. My mind was tricking me like it
had in the Singing Swamp. I groped with clumsy
fingers for my larigot, fumbling with the strap of
my pack, desperate to block the ebb and flow of the

118

voices, now louder, now softer, harder and harder to ignore.

I say we stay where we are till this mist clears . . . Richard's voice, so matter-of-fact and real I could almost reach out and touch him.

We should go on . . . he'll be looking for us . . .

I can hardly see a thing . . .

What if we get lost?

We're already lost!

Already lost . . . already lost . . .

I hardened my heart and closed my ears, put the larigot to my lips and began to play. At once its song filled my head and the lure of the voices retreated. The familiar spell wove round me, soothing and protecting . . .

'Adam? *Adam!*'

Jamie was blundering towards me out of the whiteness, his chubby face one massive beam, with Rich and the girls panting at his heels and Blue-bum lolloping behind. The larigot dropped from my numb fingers and tumbled to the ground. I goggled at them open-mouthed.

'Trust you to sit there playing that darn whistle while we yell ourselves hoarse hunting for you!' growled Rich with a fearsome scowl – and then the frown crumpled and for the first, last and only time, tough-guy Richard burst into tears.

'I still don't believe you're real,' I said for what felt like the zillionth time.

'Oh, we're real all right,' said Rich cheerfully, tossing another log on the fire. 'Though I have to say there were times I didn't think we'd make it. It was all thanks to Kai, of course – I just wish there was some way of letting him know we've found you and you're OK.'

Kai had left the others as soon as he knew they were safe, and headed back to Arakesh to *prepare the way*. 'Though none of us has the faintest inkling what he meant – it was all super-secret Believer stuff, you see,' Jamie confided.

'He wanted us to go with him, but we knew you'd try to get back to Karazan,' said Gen.

'And when you did, the first thing you'd do would be look for us – and the first place you'd look would be the Stronghold of Arraz,' said Kenta.

'If there's anything left of it,' grinned Rich. 'So that's where we were heading when we heard your penny whistle. Back into the frying pan, I suppose you could say. But I bet you're wondering how we got out of Arraz in the first place, and then all the way down here. I guess we've kept you in suspense long enough. So if you're sure you've had enough to eat, settle down and pin back your ears, and I'll tell you the whole story . . .'

OUT OF THE FRYING PAN

*O*ne minute Adam and King Karazeel were silhouetted against the glow of the computer screen; the next they were gone.

Rich stared through the bars of the cage, sick to his stomach. He didn't know which was worse – Kai betraying them, or Adam being idiot enough to trust him.

The plan had been for Adam to volunteer to be the Mauler's first course, but with his Swiss army knife stashed away in his pocket. Once he was clear of the cage he'd make a sudden lunge for Karazeel and get him in a stranglehold, the knife at his throat. Then they'd have the so-called King of Karazan as hostage, and they'd be calling all the shots.

But then Kai had snuck in and somehow tricked Adam into telling him stuff . . . stuff Rich would need a few quiet moments to get his head around. Q as a 'lord of creation' was hard to swallow if you actually knew him, but kind of made sense if you were a power-crazed nutter from Karazan; but Kai had got the wrong end of the stick about the plasma globe. It wasn't the 'source of skyfire', at least as far as Richard knew – so why had Adam said it was?

121

He scratched his head. Something didn't quite add up . . .

'And now,' hissed Evor, 'I am ready for a little entertainment. The Mauler's patience is wearing thin, and there are five of you, after all. Who shall it be?'

The toad was staring fixedly at the cage, ropes of drool swinging from its jaws. Its haunches tensed for another leap; then it shuffled forward slightly and subsided again, panting.

Suddenly Rich's blood froze. The metal retainer embedded in the wall had pulled loose. Before, it had been fastened at all four corners; now, after the Mauler's frenzied leaps, it was held only by a single bolt – and even that was hanging by a thread. Rich was suddenly glad of the sturdy bars separating them from the toad. It would take only one tiny thing to set it off, and this time he wouldn't put money on Kai being able to control it, Keeper or not.

Rich looked uneasily across at Kai – and frowned. Kai had moved behind Evor and was standing very close to him, his trident poised and an expression Rich had never seen before on his face . . . almost as if he was psyching himself up for something. Evor's attention was fixed on the cage, leering from one face to another, rubbing his hands and muttering to himself.

Without warning the world began to shake. It started as a trembling Rich thought came from somewhere inside himself – fear, he supposed, though it wasn't something he'd often felt before. But within seconds it had grown to a shuddering vibration that made Rich grab onto the bars for support, and Jamie give a wail of terror.

It's Adam, *Rich knew instantly.* He's made this happen, somehow. He must have had another plan –

And then the Mauler leapt.

With a roar of rage it flung itself towards the cage, the shackle tearing from the wall as if it was made of paper. The mass of muscle and blubber arced across the room in a single gigantic leap, knocking Evor aside and smashing into the cage halfway up with an impact like a freight train. The cage tipped and swivelled, the front edge of its circular rim lifting clean off the floor. For an endless moment the cage teetered in the balance, the children cowering under it, staring up at the massive structure suspended above them with the toad spread-eagled on its bars. Then the creature's back legs gave another jerking spasm and the cage fell backwards, to crash onto its side on the stone-flagged floor with the Mauler half-crushed behind it.

Evor sprawled on the floor – the toad lying stunned – the air ringing with the vibration of the falling cage – the world jack-hammering . . . and then Kai's frantic shout brought Rich to his senses: 'Quick – run!'

One glance at Kai's face, and Rich knew. 'He's with us – follow him!' he yelled, grabbing the others and dragging them towards the open lift, staggering to keep his feet against the dizzying sway of the tower. 'Get in – quick!'

In seconds they were all in, Kai bringing up the rear. He pressed his palm to a recessed panel set into the wall and the curved double doors slid smoothly shut. Just before they closed Rich caught a glimpse of the Mauler struggling to its feet, slavering as it squeezed its bulk past the cage and across the floor towards Evor.

Then the doors snicked to and the lift started its descent. But it wasn't a smooth, controlled fall; it was a series of hitching, hiccuping drops, jarring first against one wall of the shaft, then against the other as the tower swayed from side to side. Who cares? thought Rich. At least we're out of there. Things can't get any worse.

He was wrong.

There was a CRACK, as if the core of the universe had snapped. A nanosecond later came a sonic BOOM as the massive computer above them exploded. The steel cable snapped like a strand of cotton, the shock wave from the explosion blasting the lift down the shaft like a bullet down the barrel of a gun. Gravity turned head-over-heels: bodies flew upwards, arms and legs flailing, heads colliding with the roof. Time froze in an instant of terror so pure it was almost holy. An image of his pet mice flashed into Rich's brain, part-touch, part-smell – a jigsaw-puzzle tangle of softness and sawdusty silken sweetness. Who will look after them now?

Before the thought had time to form the lift hit the bottom of the shaft. There was no pain: just crippling deceleration, shock, and roaring emptiness. Spread-eagled on the floor, Rich felt a drifting sense of wonder. Dying isn't so bad after all, he thought with mild surprise. What's everyone so worried about?

Then, in hops and jerks, his thoughts began to catch up

with themselves. He was aware of a rushing sound . . . a bulging in his eardrums . . . a darkness blacker than night – deeper surely than death could ever be. Groggily, he lifted his head.

'Water,' croaked Jamie's voice beside him.

The lift hadn't smashed onto bedrock; it had hit water. The realisation surfaced in Rich's mind with a whoosh of relief – and at the same moment the lift itself burst out of the water with an answering WHOOSH *like a breaching whale, bobbed up and down, and then settled on its back, rocking gently to and fro.*

'So there we were,' said Rich with relish, 'floating along on a sub . . . sub . . .'

'Subterranean,' prompted Jamie.

'Yeah, a sub-whatsit cave under the Stronghold of Arraz, with no clue what to do next.'

'But then Kai opened the doors of the lift,' chipped in Kenta, 'and it was like being in a little boat . . .'

'And best of all, we could see! And you'll never guess what we *did* see,' said Gen.

'Glow-worms!' supplied Jamie triumphantly. 'Millions of them, all over the roof and walls of the cave.'

'Like tiny stars. It was like being in a fairy grotto.'

'Though actually I think it was an underground aquifer,' Jamie amended, with an apologetic glance at Gen. 'More of a tunnel than a cave, with a current that drifted us along, on and on . . .'

'And all the time, above us, the rock was rumbling,

and we were expecting that any moment the whole mountain would fall on top of us . . .'

'But it didn't,' said Rich with a grin.

'Is it getting lighter,' Gen asked, 'or is it my imagination?'

It was lighter, Rich realised; and something else was different. The water, which had been so still, was rippled with tiny corrugations that were slapping against the flat front of the lift-boat with a rhythmic lapping sound. And there was another sound, far off in the distance, amplified by the rock walls: a hollow booming.

'Whatever that is,' whispered Jamie uneasily, 'I have a hunch we're not going to like it.'

The boat bobbed on, and the sound grew till it filled the tunnel with a roar that made the air tremble. The little boat was frisking about on the water now, lilting and bouncing cheerfully as it drifted faster . . .

It skipped round a bend and they saw it: the exit from the caves. Horror wound icy fingers round Rich's heart. The underground river had carried them right under the mountain range, but the way out was blocked by a wall of water. It was the same waterfall they'd crossed on Rainbow Bridge, but now they were beneath it. From far above, the roar of the falls had been deafening, the spray a blinding mist that obscured the far bank; from below, it was a thundering devil's cataract Rich knew meant certain death.

It was way too late to turn back. Already the little craft was accelerating towards the swirling eddies at the edge of the cascade. It would fill the boat in less than a second;

126

sink it without a trace. Rich knew what happened to people trapped under falls like this: currents kept you churning round as helplessly as clothes in a washing machine; it could be hours before you resurfaced, if you ever did. And by then . . .

Sorry, Adam, *he thought numbly.* We did our best, but it looks like the River Ravven's won.

Then Kai was screaming in his face, his words drowned by the roar of the water – but Rich could read his lips, his frantic hand signals: 'Down! DOWN!'

Rich spun and threw himself onto the others, dragging them face-down onto the metal floor, screaming along with Kai, whether aloud or in his mind there was no way of telling: DOWN! DOWN!

The doors of the lift snicked closed above them just in time. A giant fist smashed into the tiny craft, and the next eternity was a surging, pummelling horror-ride in pitch darkness.

At long, long last – black and blue with bruises, green with dizzying nausea – they felt the tiny airtight capsule bob to the surface, still spinning and corkscrewing wildly, and hobble and bobble into calmer waters. They lay half-dead, retching and groaning and gasping for breath in the stifling dark. At last, with a wordless croak, Kai fumbled for the panel and the doors slid open.

Rich raised his head drunkenly. The world whirled, then tipped and steadied.

They were cruising sedately along in the centre of the river. Rich peered cautiously over the side. Here and there tiny translucent spiders scrabbled momentarily at the shiny

127

steel sides of the little craft, then swirled helplessly away.

In the distance was a pale ribbon of falling foam, framed on either side by the bush-clad slopes of the gorge. Above it, the sky was washed in a strange red glow.

Rich sucked in a deep, grateful draught of fresh night air . . . then frowned. The air should have been fresh and clean, but it wasn't. It was dark, so it must be night – but it wasn't.

They'd made it out safely, against all the odds. So everything was fine – or would be, once they drifted to the bank and made their way back to Adam. Yes, everything was fine.

Except in his heart he knew it wasn't.

SALT TEARS AND
BROKEN HEARTS

'You're right,' I said bleakly. 'It's anything but fine.'

And slowly, haltingly, I told my story.

They listened in silence. Though I knew we were completely alone, I found myself lowering my voice almost to a whisper, as if the swirling mist might have ears; glancing up, it was easy to imagine faint shapes drifting like grey ghosts in the whiteness.

Once I'd finished, Jamie was first to speak. 'Well, one thing's obvious: our top priority is to find Zenith. *When twain is one and one is twain, wind blows and sun shines forth again . . .* that can only mean one thing: the two of you need to be together again for everything to get back to normal.'

'Yes, for once it's crystal clear,' agreed Gen. 'Maybe you won't even have to do anything else, just find him.'

'*Just*,' said Rich with gloomy emphasis. 'I can't believe Meirion wouldn't simply tell you where he left him. He must know, surely?'

'It was *couldn't*, not wouldn't. He said that in

Karazan the path to the truth is crooked and hard to find, and though he could point the way, I must get there on my own. And then he went into a kind of trance . . . it's hard to explain.' I looked at Rich's scowling face and knew it would be a waste of breath even to try. He saw things simply, in black and white; the shifting sands of my strange conversation with the prophet mage had more to do with images than words.

'Well,' said Jamie, 'even though what he said was cryptic, we have to assume he gave you all the information you need to find Zenith. In which case . . .'

'We need go over exactly what he said, and see where it leads us,' said Gen, sitting up straighter. The familiar sparkle was back in her eyes, and I felt a rush of hope. This was what I'd thought would never happen again. The others were here; we were together. Even Blue-bum. He peeped up at me with his bright button eyes, and gave an encouraging chitter.

'OK then,' I said, frowning with concentration. 'First of all, he said we – I – would find things on the way, some useful, some not. He said we already have some of them –'

'Like Zaronel's diary and the cylinder!' interrupted Jamie. 'Do we have anything else?'

'There's this, I suppose.' Rather doubtfully, I produced the small green mosaic I'd found in the grass in the Summer Palace. 'But it's just a bit of mosaic from the pool.'

'It's beautiful!' said Gen. 'Can I see it?' I handed it

over, and she frowned. 'I wouldn't be so sure, Adam. It has that tingle . . . Suppose it is precious, magical in some way, and someone dropped it . . .'

'It could have lain there for years,' agreed Jamie earnestly, 'just waiting for the right person to come along and pick it up.'

'Or it could just be a bit of stuff from the wall of the pool, like you said,' grinned Rich, tossing it from hand to hand. 'I don't feel any tingle, Gen.' He handed it back. 'Carry on, Adam.'

'He said that he carried the second-born to the east, and left him in safe hands. *A cradle-craft sets sail for Limbo; in those lost lands I left him.*'

'So,' said Jamie, 'Limbo is a place, and you have to get there by boat.'

'Which makes sense when you consider that our map of Karazan shows nothing to the east but sea,' said Kenta.

'Maybe if we get back into our lift-boat and set off eastwards, the map will magically extend to show where we were going – and bingo! There will be Limbo, large as life,' said Rich hopefully.

'Yes – and maybe not,' replied Jamie with a dark look. 'Go on, Adam, what else did he say?'

'He said . . . he said . . .' I was battling to separate the words from the images. What *had* actually been said? Had there been any words at all? '*The birds of the air will point the way . . .*'

'Yes?' prompted Kenta.

'And there was something to do with moons, the

131

twin moons of Karazan rising together and balancing the heavens . . .'

'That's real helpful, I must say,' muttered Rich.

'And *look for grey smoke on a grey horizon*.'

'Well, there's no shortage of grey horizons.'

'Oh, do shut up, Richard,' snapped Gen. 'Adam's finding this hard enough without you chipping in with smart remarks every two seconds. Was there anything else, Adam?'

I hesitated. I had a strong sense that some of what was said was meant only for me, and had nothing to do with our quest. There were two things . . . things that seemed to have imprinted themselves onto my soul so clearly I knew without question I'd never forget them. *You will make your own footprints upon the soil of Karazan* . . . and *For you, Child of the Wind, your destiny lies where you least look for it – the beginning will be the end, and every end a new beginning.* I was silent for a moment, then decided to trust my instinct and let Meirion's words stay in my heart where it felt they belonged, for the time being at least.

There was something else bothering me. 'What you said before, Gen: about just finding Zenith being enough. I have a feeling there's more. Meirion said Zeel had passed into the Realms of the Undead . . . *truth and lies will lead you there*, he said. And that can only mean one thing. Once we've found Zenith we're going to have to find our way to the Realms of the Undead and do . . . something.'

There was an uncomfortable silence. Looking

132

round at the circle of solemn faces, I knew I wasn't the only one who hoped it wouldn't come to that.

'Well, never mind that,' said Rich at last. 'Going back to this whole Limbo mission, Adam: are you sure you've told us everything? Do we just go along to Kaladar, that port on the map, and hop on the next ship?'

'I doubt it,' said Gen regretfully. 'That isn't the way things work in Karazan. Crooked paths, remember?'

And then, out of nowhere, Meirion's other, forgotten words came back into my mind, the words I'd spoken on the mountainside above Arraz. *A heart is broken; salt tears turn to stone . . .*

'What did you say, Adam?' Kenta was staring at me.

I blushed. 'Nothing,' I muttered. 'It's just . . . that's what Meirion said at the very beginning, when I asked where he'd taken Zenith. But it wasn't about him; it was about me.' I gulped; looked down and mumbled, 'When I thought you guys had . . . when I thought I'd never see you again . . .' I saw in their faces that they understood. 'Meirion knew. He could see it all.'

'Maybe,' said Kenta slowly. 'Maybe, and maybe not.'

'Adam,' said Gen urgently, 'give me that mosaic again!' She held it up for us all to see, her eyes glowing. 'Look at its shape!'

'What about it?' grumbled Rich.

'It's a teardrop. Salt *tears*.'

'But it's not stone, it's glass.'

'Don't be so literal, Richard!' Gen popped the mosaic into her mouth. We goggled at her. 'I'm right!' she said, rather indistinctly.

'Don't swallow it, Gen, whatever you do!' cautioned Jamie. 'Especially if it really is important!'

Gen spat it daintily out into the palm of her hand. 'It tastes of salt!' she said triumphantly. 'Which means . . .'

'What?' asked Rich. 'What does it mean?'

There was a silence. Gen stared down at the mosaic. 'It must mean *something*.'

Kenta had been rummaging through her pack. Now she pulled out the map and unrolled it. 'I could be wrong, but *salt* . . .' Her face lit up. 'Yes!' She pointed.

We all peered at the map. There was Lake Stillwater, with the dark bulge of Shadowwood to the south; lower still was a place called Crescent Cove. But that wasn't what Kenta was pointing to.

'Salt Rocks,' read Richard blankly. 'What about them?'

'Don't you see? *Salt tears turn to stone*. Come on, everyone: if salt water turns to stone, what do you have?'

'Salt rocks,' said Rich slowly, but now he was grinning. 'Give that here a minute, Kenta.' He lifted the parchment up so it was almost touching his nose and squinted at it; then lowered it again, staring round at us. 'And guess what, guys? There's a little bay here, just below the writing . . . and it's the exact shape of a heart.'

A CALL OF NATURE

We thought the heart-shaped bay would be simple to find – after all, there it was on the map, clear as day. But we were wrong. The coastline beyond Lake Stillwater was wild and rugged – sheer cliffs plunging to meet jagged rocks that would have smashed any boat to matchsticks in moments. A steep climb from the river valley took us out of the mist; we followed the grass-covered cliff-top south, staying well away from the edge and trying not to look at the ominous swell of the waves far below. I'd expected the exposed headland to be scoured by a strong sea-wind, for there to be gulls wheeling and crying above the cliffs; but there was only still air and silence.

In spite of the lack of wind, or perhaps because of it, a deep chill was seeping into my bones; I pulled my cloak closer round me and plodded on. It was as if we were walking in a dead world – or a dying one.

'Jamie,' I said quietly, as we tramped along side by side, 'what do you think would happen if it stayed like this forever?'

Jamie gave me a sideways look it was impossible to read. 'I dunno,' he muttered. 'Don't think about it, Adam; it won't happen.'

We walked on for a minute or so in silence. Then: 'Tell me.'

He shook his head; then slowed and stopped, turning to face me. 'It's true,' he said defensively. 'I *don't* know. No one could, for sure. But . . .'

'But?'

'Well, in Science Club at school . . .' his voice wobbled. I knew what he must be thinking: how very far away those safe, sunny afternoons at Science Club seemed now. 'In Science Club,' he went on resolutely, 'we did an investigation into what made the dinosaurs extinct. There's a theory that it was a massive asteroid that smashed into the earth. I was thinking about it before: it would have had an effect almost exactly like this. Dust, smoke, ash, whatever, blocking out the sun. The first thing that would happen is the temperature would drop, like at night. You can feel it happening now. But there'd be no morning, so it would keep on dropping. And if the temperature gets too low . . .' He shrugged and gave me an apologetic glance.

'Just as important would be the effect on the food chain. It starts with sunlight. Plants need that to grow – it's called photosynthesis. It wouldn't be long before the food chain began to break down, and then . . .'

We stared at each other. He didn't need to say anything more.

'But don't worry,' he said flatly. 'Like I said, it isn't going to happen.'

There were no people about: none. Normally I'd have been thankful, but now I'd have given anything to see a lone fisherman down on the rocks, or a traveller in the distance. I imagined people huddled by their fires against the creeping cold, shutters closed tight to keep out the unnatural darkness, doors barred against the unknown. I imagined them whispering to one another, full of dread; putting on false smiles and cheerful voices for the children.

I imagined Kai hurrying along the deserted road to Arakesh bearing the news that the lost prince was found – and the grim truth that his return had brought destruction to them all.

At last we came to Crescent Cove. I'd pictured a bustling little fishing village, with people and boats and the cheerful smells of fish and cooking fires. But we nearly walked right past it: a desolate huddle of half a dozen shacks on a narrow beach of grey pebbles way below us, at the foot of a steep path. A twist of smoke wound up from one chimney, and the sour tang of ash hung on the air.

Past Crescent Cove the landscape changed abruptly. Grass gave way to scrub and then dense coastal forest. The ground fell away slightly, the cliff face easing from vertical to a slope we could just about have slithered down. What had been a ruler-straight cliff edge changed to a series of inlets almost completely concealed by smothering vegetation. While before we'd been striding along open moors, now we were shoving our way through thick foliage in near-darkness, in danger of missing our footing and sliding down the slope. Worst of all, the undergrowth obscured the coastline: what was clear on the map was completely hidden now that we were actually there.

It wasn't long before Rich stumbled to a standstill. 'This is no good,' he grumbled. 'We could go right past the bay without ever knowing. It's down there somewhere, but where?'

'We need to look out for fresh water,' said Kenta. 'We've only got enough for tonight, and tomorrow morning if we're lucky.'

'We could climb down to sea level and pick our way along the beach . . .' said Gen without much enthusiasm.

'If there is a beach,' said Jamie. '*Salt rocks*, remember, Gen? I'm betting it's called that for a reason.'

'What if only a couple of us go down?' suggested Kenta. 'That way there'll be someone at the top to help them up again.'

'Well, don't look at me,' said Jamie firmly. 'James Mortimer Fitzpatrick's staying up here. I'm not built for climbing.'

I looked at him standing there, four-square and determined – and suddenly felt myself begin to grin. 'True enough, Jamie, you're not,' I said, feeling more cheerful than I had for hours. 'But we all know someone who is.' I shrugged off my backpack and plonked it down none too gently on the ground. 'Wakey-wakey, Blue-bum old pal,' I told him. 'Now's the time for you to use up some of that energy you've been saving and make yourself useful!'

It grew steadily darker, and we searched on. Night was falling, and soon I could barely see the dim forms of the others pushing through the trees, keeping pace with Blue-bum, swinging through the forest far below. And still the excited chitter we were waiting for didn't come.

At last, reluctantly, I suggested we call a halt. 'There's no point carrying on in the dark. Let's give Blue-bum a shout and have some dinner and an early night.'

It wasn't long before the others were curled up in their sleeping bags fast asleep. I snuggled down in mine, glad of its comforting warmth, closed my eyes . . . and for the first time allowed myself the luxury of thinking about everything I'd discovered over the past few days. My thoughts kept coming back to one fact, almost more incredible, more amazing to me than anything else.

I had a brother.

For as long as I could remember I'd dreamed of one day finding my parents, or at least discovering who they were. But it had never, ever, even in my most extravagant daydreams, occurred to me that I might have a brother or sister. And not just a brother: a twin. And now I did. Zenith.

All this time, while I'd been battling through the lonely years at Highgate, he'd been growing up too, living his own life, just like I'd been living mine. I lay smiling, thinking of our parallel lives, each completely unaware of the other's existence. While I'd been at school, he'd have been at – what? Trentice, I supposed, like Hob and Kai. Making friends; having fights; getting in trouble. Eating, sleeping, laughing, crying. Wherever he was, he'd have grown up part of a family not his own. Did he know, like me, that somewhere he had a mother and father he'd never met? Did he know, deep in his bones, that there was somewhere else he belonged; a destiny he had to fill?

Now – soon – we'd meet.

Zenith. Would he look like me? Would he be bad at spelling too? Would we laugh at the same jokes, like the same food? Who'd be taller, him or me? I was older, even if just by a few minutes. I grinned up at the ceiling of leaves. I wouldn't let him forget it.

Zenith. One thing I knew for certain. When I found him, I'd know him instantly. Just like Zaronel had known me.

The truth shocked me awake in the middle of the night with the suddenness of a gunshot. *Our parallel lives*. Me in 'our world'; Zenith in the world of Karazan.

Thirteen years for me – more than fifty for him. My twin brother wouldn't be a kid like me any longer. We were searching for an adult four times my age.

Our quest had come full circle. We'd been looking for the Prince of the Wind, an adult man grown into a king, but it had been me. Now we were looking for the Prince of the Sun – an adult, not a child.

I lay awake for a long time in the darkness, aching for the brother I'd thought I was going to have; the friend and companion I'd lost.

I was woken by cold seeping through the down of my sleeping bag and into the marrow of my bones. We ate a hurried breakfast huddled round a sullen fire that hardly gave out any warmth. There was a chill about the morning that even the normally cheerful chatter of the campsite couldn't dispel, and no one seemed keen to linger.

Almost before we finished eating Blue-bum shimmied up the nearest tree and swung away downhill to continue the search. While I strapped on my sword and stamped out the fire, the others started drifting in the direction we'd been heading the previous day – all except Jamie. I looked round for him, frowning, eager to get going.

There he was, a pale splodge blundering in the wrong direction. 'Other way, Jamie,' I called, trying not to sound impatient.

An anxious moon-face peered at me through the undergrowth. 'Hang on a sec, Adam. I'm not ready. I have to . . . you know . . .' He waved a fluttering streamer of toilet paper, and crashed off through the bushes.

I gave an inward sigh and settled down to wait for him, my hands tucked into my armpits for warmth – and suddenly I realised which way he'd been going in his quest for privacy. 'Hey, Jamie,' I called, 'don't go too far, OK? Remember the –'

But before I could say the word I heard it – a slither and a warbling wail that could only be one thing: James Mortimer Fitzpatrick falling over the edge of the cliff.

A CRADLE-CRAFT

I said the worst word I knew – then I was smashing through the bushes after him. I reached the place he'd gone over in moments: a tempting screen of leaves just dense enough to conceal the crumbling precipice; a tell-tale skid-mark, a half-uprooted shrub, and a single, pathetic square of toilet paper impaled on a twig.

I knelt, parted the leaves and peered cautiously downwards. 'Jamie?' I called. 'Are you OK?' It was a steep slope rather than a sheer drop, I saw with relief, and there seemed plenty to grab onto on the way down; but if he'd fallen onto rocks, or twisted his leg under him as he fell – well, with Jamie's weight . . .

There was a muttered 'Trust Jamie . . .' behind me. Rich.

'I'm going after him.' I swung my legs over the edge ready to start half-climbing, half-sliding down – and then Jamie's voice drifted up from way below, slightly shaky, but unmistakably triumphant. 'I'm OK – well, almost. But guess what? I've found the heart-shaped

144

bay, and something else as well. Something you'll never believe in a million years! Come and see!'

Very carefully, and way more slowly than Jamie, we made our descent, Blue-bum in the lead. And there at the bottom was Jamie, muddy, scratched and beaming, busting to show us his discovery.

There was no doubt we were in the right place. The bush-covered cliff face reared behind us; gazing up, I could see that the bay would be completely hidden from above. If Jamie hadn't literally stumbled on it, we'd have walked right past.

The rocky sides of the tiny cove extended out to sea like protective shoulders, and between them nature had carved two identical crescent-shaped inlets, side by side, the exact shape of a heart. Curving beaches of fine white sand sloped down to the sea; between them, where the two halves of the heart joined, was a pointed outcrop of flat rock, bisected by a deep cleft extending down to the water.

'*A heart is broken . . .*' murmured Gen.

'Yup, we've found it all right – way to go, Jamie!' said Rich with satisfaction. 'Though you were lucky not to hurt yourself. What on earth were you doing so close to the edge?'

At Rich's first words Jamie had swelled with pride; now he deflated like a popped balloon, turning pink. 'I *was* lucky,' he admitted, ignoring Rich's question. 'I landed on those bushes . . .' He pointed. Sure enough, the cliff met the ground in a cascade of lush green undergrowth. It would be like falling on a

145

mattress, springy and resilient. 'Fell right through them – and look what I found.'

He parted the branches and we peered into the leafy gloom. It was so well hidden that at first I couldn't even see it; but then I made out the blunt end of what looked like a pole lying on the ground, and beside it a curved rise of tight-sealed planks.

'It's a boat!' squawked Gen.

'It's more than that!' corrected Jamie. 'It's a *cradle-craft* – I'm betting the exact same one Meirion set sail in with Zenith all those years ago!'

It didn't take us long to haul the little boat out of the thicket and over to the water. Then, with the bow pointing out to sea and the blunt stern safely on the sand, we stood back to admire our find.

It was solid-looking and seaworthy, plenty big enough for the five of us, plus one little chatterbot. But it wasn't a sea-going galleon, that was for sure. 'Cradle-craft' was about right: a simple dinghy with three bench seats and a tiny cupboard built into the pointed front.

'Is it a rowboat, d'you think?' asked Gen, giving it a doubtful prod with one foot.

'I hope not,' said Kenta. 'I don't fancy rowing all the way to Limbo, wherever that is.'

'Well, it's not a motorboat, that's for sure,' said Rich. 'And you can relax, Kenta: it isn't a rowboat. There are no what-d'you-call-thems?'

'Rowlocks.'

146

'Yeah, them; and no oars either.' His face clouded.

We all stared glumly at the boat. The question was all too obvious, and none of us had an answer.

'Hang on, though,' I said suddenly. 'I thought I saw . . .' Back to the bushes I went, and burrowed inside. Yes! There was the pole I'd caught sight of earlier. A couple of tugs and it was lying on the sand: a smooth length of timber with two cross-pieces.

'So,' said Jamie, 'it's a sailing boat, and this is its mast.'

'Give me a hand, guys.' Rich was struggling to hoist it upright. 'It'll slot in that hollow cylinder sticking up from the floor. I wondered what it was for.'

'If there was ever a sail, it'd have rotted away years ago,' said Gen. 'But look at these cross-pieces. They're hinged, to make a long kind of clamp . . .'

'And there's a spring-loaded metal clasp at each end to hold them tight,' grinned Rich. 'So it doesn't have to be the actual sail, anything would do. To take a random example: our trusty tarpaulin!' As he spoke, he was throwing stuff out of his bag; last of all out came the bright blue plastic tarp. Rich shook it out with a crackle and held it up.

'It looks about the right size,' said Kenta. 'Come on, Gen: help me with this side!'

Together we stretched the tarp out flat; Blue-bum scampered up the mast and clamped the top: it fitted perfectly and in no time the sail was rigged.

The little boat looked jaunty and ready for anything. Rich dumped in the gear and rubbed his hands.

147

'In you hop, let's give it a trial run!'

Jamie and the girls clambered in, and Blue-bum settled himself on the little triangular seat in the bow, hanging on tight. 'You can be our figurehead,' said Kenta. 'That seat could have been made for you!'

Rich and I heaved and with a rasp and a wobble the boat was floating. Rich flopped down on the sand and yanked off his boots and socks, then waded into the water after it. He didn't have to go far: it was still wallowing within easy reach of the beach. Rich scrambled in and the boat tilted dangerously, to squeals of alarm from Kenta and Gen. He settled himself at the back with one hand on the tiller, every inch the captain, and they all sat there waiting for something to happen.

It didn't.

It was Jamie who finally spoke, in an aggrieved tone. 'But . . . it isn't going anywhere, Richard.'

'Well,' said Rich a touch defensively, 'it won't till there's a wind.'

'But,' said Gen, '*When twain is one and one is twain Wind blows and sun shines forth again*. Remember? If we wait for the wind, we'll wait forever.'

'Or at least till Adam and Zenith are together,' amended Jamie.

'But that isn't going to happen till we get to Limbo,' Rich pointed out.

'And we won't get to Limbo or anywhere else until the wind starts to blow,' said Kenta.

There was a silence.

And that's when I remembered.

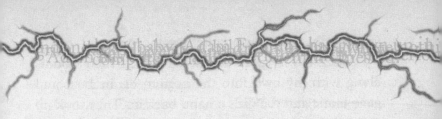

INTO THE DEEP

'Well, even if it *is* a sail I don't see how it can possibly help,' grumbled Rich as we manhandled the boat back onto the beach. 'I know you think old Meirion is the best thing since sliced bread, Adam, but fifty years' solitary confinement in a pitch-dark dungeon with water dripping on your forehead would be enough to send anyone off their rocker.'

Jamie was examining the cloth I'd extracted from the depths of my pack. 'It's definitely magical,' he announced; 'it has that tingle. But who says it's a sail? It could be a magic tablecloth that covers itself with food when you spread it out . . .'

'In your dreams, Jamie,' retorted Richard. 'And now, if you've finished drooling over it, how about giving us a hand?'

It wasn't long before the blue sail had been replaced by a far more flimsy white one. But even if it was the sail Meirion had originally used, it would be as useless as the tarp had been with no wind to fill it.

'But we may as well try doing it Adam's way,' said

Gen kindly, with a sympathetic glance at me.

Feeling like a spoilt toddler, I tossed Rich's boots along with my own into the bottom of the boat and gave Jamie and the girls a hand back in. They took up their places, but the excited anticipation of the first launching was noticeably absent. Jamie was muttering about lunch, and Kenta and Gen were busy hatching a plan to send Blue-bum to the top of the cliff to fill the water bottles. As for Rich, he was standing high and dry on the sand, arms akimbo, an *I told you so* look on his face.

I gave the boat a rather half-hearted shove – and it shot forward as if the sandy beach was a greased slipway. Blue-bum, who'd been perched on his special seat, flew backwards to land in a tangled heap with the boots and smelly socks. I staggered after the boat into the icy water, grabbing for the back with one hand, the other windmilling wildly to keep my balance. My fingers snagged the wooden edge and gripped it tightly – and the next thing I knew I was being dragged through the water at a flailing run.

Without thinking, without time to wonder what was happening or why, I threw myself forward in a headlong lunge and heaved myself over the back of the boat, landing on top of Blue-bum in a jumble of knees and elbows. Rolling over, I gawked up at the others' shocked faces and past them at the sail, in stunned disbelief.

The flimsy white cloth that had drooped so forlornly when the boat was aground was fat-bellied and straining with non-existent wind that was propelling us out to sea at an alarming rate. Scrambling to my hands and knees, I stared back at the beach. Already, a widening expanse of water separated us from land. Rich was a rapidly dwindling silhouette performing an agitated war-dance on the sand, waving his arms and yelling, 'Come back, you guys! *Come back!*'

'The tiller!' gasped Jamie, pointing.

I knew less than nothing about boats, but I grabbed the wooden lever with both hands and pushed; then yanked it towards me. It didn't budge. I threw my weight on it, at the same time searching frantically for something that might be holding it in place. There was nothing. I heaved again with all my strength but it might as well have been set in concrete.

'It's jammed. Quick, Blue-bum, climb up and undo the clamps! We have to get the sail down!'

Already Gen and Kenta were fumbling with the clips that secured the bottom edge; Jamie seemed completely immobilised, his face a picture of woe. As for me – uppermost in my mind were jubilation and relief. *Yes!* Meirion had come through! The sail was magical and once we'd collected Rich it would take us straight to Limbo in double-quick time!

Then Gen spoke, and something in her voice wiped the smile clean off my face. 'The clamps won't undo. The sail's stuck! Adam, *do something* – quick!'

There was only one thing I could do. I cupped my hands round my mouth and yelled. '*Richard! We can't turn back! Swim for it – before it's too late!*'

For a moment he stood frozen and I thought he hadn't heard me. I sucked in a giant breath and raised my hands to try again, choking down the panic pushing up inside me. But then, as if a starting pistol had fired, Rich sprinted down the beach and flung himself into the water in a shallow racing dive.

The sea around us was silvery and still, only the smooth swell of the boat's wake disturbing it. But behind Richard it churned white and foamy, as if he was being driven by an outboard motor. His arms scythed through the water, his head flicking first one way, then the other as he breathed. 'Wow,' breathed Jamie enviously, 'he sure can swim!' I remembered what Rich had told us on the banks of the River Ravven: he was freestyle champ at school. Watching him now it was easy to believe.

'He's gaining,' Gen whispered. 'He has to be!'

And he was. The gap between his thrashing figure and the boat was shrinking. Blue-bum skipped about, jibbering with excitement; Gen raised clenched fists in the air and jiggled up and down like a cheerleader shrieking, 'Go, Richard! *GO!*'

Kenta was kneeling, leaning out over the water with outstretched hands as if she could somehow drag him towards us by sheer force of will . . . but then she raised a tear-streaked face to us: a face sick with despair. 'He's slowing,' she said flatly.

Richard was exhausted. His rhythm had gone; the motion that had been so fluid and effortless had become choppy and uncoordinated. The beach was a thin pale line in the distance, the cliffs dark smudges on either side. If he didn't make it to the boat, he wasn't going to have the strength to get back.

He was close enough now for us to hear the ragged gasping of his breaths over his splashing strokes – only the width of a tennis court away – and still the little boat sailed on. Jamie thumped to his knees, scrabbling frantically in his pack. 'The rope!' he panted. He thrust a coil of red nylon into my hands. 'You do it!'

I'd only get one chance. Richard's arms were all over the place, his head bobbing up with every stroke; we could see desperation in his face. I wound the free end of the rope round my hand and threw.

The thin nylon curled up and out, unravelling, snaking through the air and over the shimmering water like a serpent. Up, out and down. It wasn't going to be long enough, I realised with a gut-wrenching jolt of despair; it wasn't going to reach.

Richard gave one last sweeping lunge forward, reaching with one hand like an Olympic swimmer stretching for the finish line – and the rope snapped tight, almost jerking me out of the boat.

I threw myself backwards, feeling the others grab whatever bits of me they could reach; heard my voice shouting hoarsely over and over again: 'Hang on! *Hang on tight!*'

Then Rich flopped half into the boat on a freezing wave of sea water and we were dragging him over the

back and in, gasping and spluttering and shivering
with cold and cussing a blue streak with what little
breath he had left.

WATER EVERYWHERE

'The good thing is,' said Rich with a crooked grin, 'we'll get to Limbo in no time flat at this rate.'

'I hope so,' said Gen in an odd little voice.

'And now,' fussed Kenta, 'you need some food, Richard. I only wish we could make some hot cocoa to warm you up . . .'

Rich was huddled in the bottom of the boat. He'd exchanged his sodden clothes for my spare polypropylene underwear – red and white pirate-striped long johns and a long-sleeved vest, stashed away by Hannah's Nanny in a side pocket of my pack and promptly forgotten. Now, swathed in my cloak for the sake of modesty, he looked cosy and snug and remarkably cheerful. He accepted a handful of scroggin from Jamie and began wolfing it down hungrily.

'Want some, Gen?' Jamie asked, proffering the packet. Gen shook her head. She was staring towards the invisible horizon, her face pale and pinched-looking. Jamie reached out shyly and touched her hand. 'Everything's OK now, Gen. Try not to worry.'

Gen didn't even look at him; just stared out over the dark water as if he hadn't spoken.

'Maybe she's seasick,' suggested Richard through a mouthful of scroggin. 'Though this sea's as calm as a duck-pond. Have some water, Gen, that's supposed to help.'

Slowly, Gen turned her head to look at him, and the instant I saw her eyes I realised something was badly wrong. 'No thanks, Richard. We'd better save the water for when we really need it. Because we never did fill those bottles – and there's only about a thimbleful left.'

It was mid-morning the following day when we weakened and shared out what was left of the water. Gen had been wrong: there was more than a thimbleful. When we pooled the dribbles left in the bottom of everyone's canteens, there was about half a cup. In spite of Jamie's token objection to 'sharing spit' we passed the tin mug round in a solemn ritual, each taking a tiny sip from a different place before passing it on. It went round exactly three times before Rich upended it over his open mouth and let the last crystal drop tremble and fall.

Time crawled by, and the little boat surged steadily on towards the unchanging horizon. Now and again someone would crawl over to Kenta's pack and pull out the map; unroll it, stare at it for a minute or two, then replace it without speaking. It hadn't changed since we left the shores of Karazan, and we knew in our hearts it wasn't going to.

Lunchtime came and went. 'We should eat,' muttered Jamie. 'Food with a high moisture content, I remember reading that somewhere.' But all our food was dehydrated. *Just Add Water!* was printed on the front of every single pack.

Jamie offered round the scroggin again; I took a pinch so as not to hurt his feelings, but it tasted like sawdust. All I wanted was a barley sugar, and they were long gone. The chocolate was thick and tacky, turning what little spit I had to glue, the sultanas dry as bullets in my mouth – and there didn't seem to be any of Hannah's *imagination* left at all.

And still the sea stretched on forever.

I spent the afternoon staring out at the water, dreaming of drinks. Coke, ice cold with a slice of lemon the way we'd had it at Quested Court, the bubbles fizzing under my nose. Milk, gulped straight from the fridge at Highgate when Matron wasn't looking, leaving a creamy moustache on my lip. But by the time night fell all I could think of was water. Cool, clear, fresh, pure, life-giving water.

As we were settling down to sleep Jamie produced five grimy-looking pieces of chewing gum, which the others fell on with eager croaks. I snapped mine in half and gave one of the grubby morsels to Blue-bum, who sniffed it dubiously before tucking it behind one ear. Saving it for later . . . with a ghost of a smile,

I slipped my piece into my pocket too. It would be good to have something to look forward to.

I slept fitfully, sprawled with the others on the hard planks that made up the bottom of the boat. Tormenting dreams circulated in my brain. I was at Highgate, asleep in bed; woke with a raging thirst and padded through to the boys' cloakroom for a drink. But there was Matron, tight-lipped, guarding the door . . .

I was in a forest in Karazan, following the tinkling music of a stream through the trees. But when at last I reached it and bent to drink, the reflection of a faceless, hooded head stared back at me . . .

When at last I woke it was almost a relief. I lay listening to the others' breathing, rocked by the now-familiar motion of the little boat on the water. My mouth was as dry as paper. I closed it, working my tongue and cheeks to try and generate some moisture. My tongue felt like leather; my throat like an old, dried-out drain. My breath stank.

For the first time, I wondered what would happen if we didn't reach land soon. For the first time, I seriously considered asking the others to use their microcomputers to go back to Quested Court, and leave me to face whatever lay ahead alone.

Morning came.

My eyes grated open and there was Rich, bum in the air, bent over the side of the boat. He glanced back and saw me watching and something in his eyes sent a bolt of alarm through me. 'Richard,' I whispered, 'what are you doing?'

'Nothing.' He turned, trying to hide something behind his back. It was the battered little saucepan we'd used to make all those countless rehydrated meals.

'Rich,' I croaked, 'you haven't – have you?'

A slow blush crawled up his face, but he met my eyes defiantly. 'No. But I'm going to.'

'You can't!' Gen was awake now, staring at Rich as if he was mad. 'You go crazy if you drink sea water!'

'It's an old wives' tale.' It was hard to make out Rich's words; they were slurred, as if his tongue was too big for his mouth. 'What's crazy is dying of thirst in the middle of all this water. Water's water – so what if it's salty?'

'No.' Jamie struggled up on one elbow. His face seemed to have shrunk overnight, and his eyes looked dull. 'The more sea water you drink, the more dehydrated you get. It's to do with osmosis. There's more salt in sea water than in your blood, and your body has to get rid of it . . .' he swallowed, making a horrid clicking sound. 'You excrete the extra salt in your urine, but that uses more water than was in the sea water in the first place. You don't go crazy, you dry up. It kills you, sure as poison.'

Very slowly, with a mixture of shame and bravado, Richard drew the saucepan out from behind his back. It was almost full; the water sloshed gently to and fro. He stared from one face to the next, his face expressionless.

'Richard, wait. Here –' I was fumbling in my pocket for the gum I'd saved last night. 'Have this – it'll help, just for now, while we decide what to do . . .' My fingers felt numb and awkward, but at last they found the smooth fragment and pulled it out. 'Jamie, girls: we have to talk. There's something I want you to do for me. But first, Rich,' I summoned a rusty grin from somewhere, and held out my free hand for the saucepan: 'swap.'

Rich hugged the saucepan closer. His face was clenched in a stubborn scowl . . . but his eyes dropped automatically to the piece of gum in the palm of my hand. Puzzlement replaced the frown but he didn't pass over the pan. 'Why would I want that?' he croaked.

I looked down. It wasn't the gum. It was the teardrop-shaped mosaic from the gardens of the Summer Palace, deep sea-green inlaid with shimmering gold glitter. 'This is seriously weird . . .' I muttered, staring at it.

'What?' Jamie shuffled closer, peering into my hand. 'What's weird?'

They were all watching me, even Rich. Oh well, I thought, at least it's distracting him from the sea water. 'It's changed. Before, it was green. And now . . .'

I held it up for them to see. The colour had completely disappeared. It was no-coloured, crystal-coloured . . . a perfect teardrop the colour of water.

160

The others looked at me blankly. An idea was rising slowly through my mind. A memory. Hope.

Playing on the computer long ago with my friend Cameron, we built up a collection of useless-seeming stuff, just like Meirion had talked about – an inventory, Cam called it. And sometimes the appearance of things changed, just slightly, when the time came that they could be used. I stared at the teardrop, willing it to be true. Then I slipped it into my mouth, and sucked. Gen had said it tasted of salt. Now it tasted of nothing.

'Richard,' I said quietly, 'pass me the saucepan . . . please.'

He hesitated. Then slowly, reluctantly, he passed it over.

I lifted it to my lips.

'*Adam – no!*'

I took the tiniest sip. It tasted brackish, salty – like the poison it would be if we drank it. I dropped the teardrop into the pan with a tiny *plop*. It sank straight to the bottom; I couldn't see it, but I knew it was there. Raised the pan to my lips . . . took another tiny sip. It was fresh water. Cool, clear, pure, life-giving water. I held the saucepan out to Richard. 'Drink.'

That night I slept without stirring, without dreaming. And when I woke there was an edge to the darkness – a broad bar of dusty-looking gold hanging under the greyness.

We were sailing towards it.

FOUR WINDS

With every hour the light grew brighter, the strip of clear sky wider and closer. Soon, below it, we could make out the unmistakable smudge of land – and the following morning we sailed our little craft into a harbour busy with boats and bright with sunlight.

No one had been surprised when, in sight of land, the tiller started working again; now Rich steered us deftly between the vessels lying at anchor while the rest of us stared round, eyes squinched to slits against the dazzle reflecting off the water.

After days at sea, in near-darkness and almost total silence, my senses were reeling. Colour was everywhere – sails every shade of the rainbow; sailors scurrying about on deck and townsfolk thronging the quay, their clothing a kaleidoscope of every hue imaginable. Small square buildings in the cool pastel shades of ice cream crowded the hillside – pale green, baby pinks and blues, and white so bright it made me squint.

All around us was a cheerful hubbub of sound.

The splashing of oars, the flutter of flags, the crackle of canvas in the breeze; the squawk and squabble of seagulls; voices calling and joking from boat to boat; the brassy fanfare of some kind of band on the wharf.

But most of all – the smells! A stinking stream of sewage emptying from the bilge of a beat-up fishing boat; the clean tinge of paint and the tacky tang of tar; the silvery scent of fish, fresh and not-so-fresh; a greasy whiff of roast meat that made my mouth water; the powdery dryness of dust . . . and beneath it all the loamy richness of fresh-turned earth.

Everywhere white teeth flashed in tanned faces as men and women bustled about their business, nimble-footed children shrieking and giggling round their feet. It was as different from Karazan as day from night. But it was how Karazan had once been, I was sure – and how it could be again.

'Look!' squealed Gen, pointing. 'Over there, Richard! There are moorings where you can tie boats up, and a market on the waterfront.'

Rich parked the boat with a bone-shattering bump beside a barge loaded with barrels, and Jamie used one of his famous scout knots to secure it to the rusty ring set into the dock. Taking down the sail was easy this time; I folded it carefully and stashed it in my pack, then shouldered it and hurried after the others up the slippery steps to the pier.

In Arakesh we'd felt horribly conspicuous, as if we were being constantly watched, but here no one paid us the slightest attention. Even if they had, in our salt-stained clothes, tousled and grimy and no doubt stinking to high heaven, we blended in with the crowd.

'I think I'm going to like it here in Limbo,' grinned Rich as we were swept along between the stalls. Protected from the sun by striped awnings and manned by cheery-looking vendors, they were laden with everything from bolts of cloth to wooden carvings, from intricately tooled chalices to musical instruments. There was even a stall selling weapons – daggers and richly embossed shields; armour and wicked-looking double-edged battleaxes.

We passed what I guessed must be an apothecary: a musty-smelling cubicle tucked away in a corner, every surface covered in weird-looking bottles and jars of potions and powders, dried leaves of every size and shape you could imagine hanging from the rafters. A russet-haired boy was at the counter, having a heated argument with the storekeeper.

But it was the food stalls that drew us like magnets. Trestle tables groaning with jars of honey and pickles and preserves; bakers' stalls with crusty loaves; a cheesemonger in a striped apron with a lethal-looking cleaver and cheeses the size of wagon-wheels, and brightly coloured pyramids of glossy, juicy-looking fruit.

'Look over there,' said Rich. In the shade of a tree at the edge of the village green a whole sucking pig was sizzling on a spit. A woman wandered past, a little boy tugging at her hand. Smiling, she bent to listen to him, then passed a coin to the vendor. He carved off a couple of slices of meat, sandwiched them between two slabs of bread and passed them to the boy.

I looked at Rich, Rich looked at Jamie – and Jamie just kept staring at that sucking pig. Then we were hustling towards the stall, me fumbling in my pocket for the coins we'd been given in Drakendale, the girls tagging along behind.

'Excuse me,' I said to the stallholder, 'do you accept Karazan money here?'

'And why wouldn't I?' he replied, holding out a hand the size of a ham. 'This be a trading post, don't it? Any coinage be good to the merchants of Four Winds.'

'Four Winds?' Jamie echoed, aghast. 'But . . . isn't this Limbo?'

'Limbo?' the man gave Jamie an odd look that made me wish he'd kept his mouth shut. 'Nay, lad, this is not Limbo. And you should thank the twin moons 'tis not – for you'd find nothing there but dust and emptiness.'

'And people, of course,' chipped in Gen craftily, giving him her best smile.

'People? Nay, lovely lassie, there be no people in Limbo.' He was assembling our doorstoppers as he spoke; now he pressed the last one into my hand.

'Yes there are!' objected Jamie. 'There must be, otherwise where would Mei–' Rich gave him a kick and he broke off abruptly, turning pink.

The man frowned. 'Well, doubtless you know best, young smartboots,' he said, selecting a small six-sided gold coin from the assortment I was holding out.

Jamie was onto him quick as a flash. 'Surely they can't be that much? A couple of silver ones, maybe . . .'

'I will take silver if you prefer, but you will be the losers. Do you not know that silver and gold be of equal value in Four Winds and the lands beyond? Now take your food and your questions elsewhere.'

Rich gave Jamie a warning glare and took over, speaking as politely as possible through a mouthful of bread. 'Could you tell us where Limbo is?'

'Best ask Master Know-all,' grumbled the man, but then he saw Gen's woebegone face and relented. 'Truth to tell, I know not. If you're after tales of Limbo, them's the folk you should be asking.' He nodded towards the far side of the green.

'Who?' asked Gen. 'The villagers?'

'Nay, the travelling circus,' he said with a dismissive jerk of his head. 'What there is of it. But you'd best be hurrying, for they were packing to leave, last I heard, and a good thing too. Barbaric, that's what I call it but that's Borderfolk for you . . .' He turned away to serve another customer.

'A travelling circus!' whispered Jamie, eyes sparkling. 'I love circuses. They're not barbaric as long as they don't have animals. I did a Circus Arts course once –'

'*What there is of it* . . .' interrupted Kenta thoughtfully. 'What an odd thing to say. I wonder what he meant?'

166

Rich stuffed the last of his doorstopper into his mouth. 'Let's find out.'

The travelling circus wasn't hard to find. Like Jamie, I'd been hoping for a striped marquee and a string of brightly painted wagons; but it turned out to be a cluster of dilapidated caravans with *Troupe Talisman* painted on the sides and a rickety trailer parked up under a tree, with several mangy-looking glonks tethered nearby.

As we drew closer we slowed and huddled together, shuffling our feet and whispering. 'What now?' muttered Rich. 'Do we just find the guy in charge and ask for directions to Limbo?'

'I suppose so,' said Kenta. 'Though I don't see many people about.'

But as she spoke a figure strode towards the caravan, scowling fearsomely, hair blazing in the bright sunshine. The boy from the apothecary. Though he was just a kid our age wearing ordinary clothes – breeches, loose shirt and leather jerkin – I knew instantly he must be from the circus. It was partly the way he moved, with the fluid ease of an athlete or an acrobat, and partly the placard he was dragging in the dust behind him. Being upside-down made it hard to read, but behind me Gen whispered the words aloud: 'Join Troupe Talisman today! See the world and discover your hidden talents in the Brotherhood of the Arena. Hiring now! All training provided. Enquire on village green.'

'Quick,' hissed Rich, 'grab him!'

Too late. The boy disappeared round the side of the caravan, and there was a crash that could only be the placard being thrown to the ground.

'Well?' growled a deep adult voice. 'What fortune, Lyulf?'

'Ill fortune!' snarled the boy. 'I tell you, Borg, we waste our time. The people of Four Winds have their faces set against the circus arts. We would do best to pack our goods and go.'

'And then what? It will be a moon at best before our injured are fit to perform. I say we stay and see what the next boat brings. There be strange tales on the lips of townsfolk and travellers alike – something is afoot in Karazan: change blows in the wind, for good or ill I know not. You know as well as I that we garner the flotsam and jetsam of fate, the desperate who have no refuge. If there is darkness and destruction across the water, the debris will drift on the tide and we should be here to harvest it.'

'What's he on about?' muttered Rich.

'Dunno,' whispered Jamie, 'but I say we butt in and find out what we need to know before they pack up and go.'

'I left Blade at the harbour,' continued the boy. 'They say the wind has dropped in Karazan, but there is word of a galley before sunset.'

Cautiously we edged round the caravan. A short distance away a huddle of dark figures was hunched over a sullen fire. One head lifted momentarily; it was swarthy and unshaven, the eyes sunken and dull. I glimpsed a splinted leg stuck out at an awkward angle, a head swathed in filthy bandages, rough crutches flung where they lay.

Then my whole attention was on the bearded, dark-faced man glaring down at the boy. The moment we appeared he switched his gaze to us and it wasn't friendly. He had a rugged, almost savage face, and his black beard did nothing to hide a livid scar that ran from eye to chin, pulling the corner of his mouth down in a permanent snarl. 'What do *you* want?'

We exchanged awkward glances; then Blue-bum, perched on my shoulder, gave my earlobe a tug. 'We were just wondering . . . someone said you might know the way to Limbo.'

'Limbo!' Instantly the boy's full attention was on me and I felt myself flush. It was like being in the full beam of a searchlight. Shorter than Rich and me, but somehow older-looking: strongly built and muscular, with a strangely adult-looking face and something smouldering in his eyes I'd never seen before: a fierce, almost animal fire.

'What business have you in Limbo?' growled the man.

'Their business is not yours, Borg.'

I glanced at the big man to see how he'd take a telling-off from someone so much younger but he ignored it and carried on staring at us through narrowed eyes.

'We are looking for . . . someone . . . there,' I said evasively.

'But the stallholder said no one lives there,' chipped in Jamie. 'It isn't true, is it?'

'Limbo lies on the far side of the Borderlands,' said the boy. There was a slight hesitancy about his speech, a carefulness as if he'd once had a stammer, or was having to mentally translate what he was saying from another language. There was the trace of an accent, though none I'd ever heard before.

'But *do* people live there?' persisted Jamie.

'Aye – and nay.' The boy switched his gaze to Jamie, then back to me, as if weighing up whether to tell us more. 'Limbo is not a city. It is a barren wasteland peopled by creatures of the wild, a buffer between the Borderlands and . . . that which lies beyond. They say a band of nomads lives there: the Lost Tribe of Limbo, men call them.' He shrugged. 'But I have never seen them.'

Rich gave me a painful dig in the ribs which said louder than words *Yes! We've hit the jackpot!* Though I tried not to flinch I saw from the boy's eyes that it hadn't gone unnoticed – not much did, I suspected.

'So you've been there?' Gen was saying eagerly. 'To Limbo?'

'We travel there, but only to the borders – never beyond.'

'So,' said Rich, all business, 'what direction do we go? Is it far?'

Man and boy exchanged a glance. The man's

mouth twisted, and for a moment I thought the boy might be about to smile. 'You cannot journey to the wildlands,' he said flatly.

'Why not?' demanded Rich. '*You* do.'

The glance again. Without answering, the boy shrugged again and made as if to turn away.

'Why can't we?'

'The nature of the circus arts allows us to travel in safety where none other dare,' growled the man, continuing in an undertone, as if to himself, 'though our arts bring their own perils from the lands beyond.' He scowled at us. 'We have work to do. Farewell.'

But Jamie hustled forward, pink-faced and earnest. '*We* need to get to Limbo, to find . . . to find our friend. And you're looking for circus performers. Well, how about us? We'll join your circus; you take us to Limbo.

'What d'you say?'

TROUPE TALISMAN

'Jamie, are you crazy?' hissed Richard.

'We may seem a little on the young side,' Jamie told the boy, ignoring Rich, 'but you're young too. You provide training, it says so on your billboard. And I'm already trained. I went to Circus Arts School one holidays –'

'Your parents – where are they?' Borg demanded.

'Well, it's a long story . . .' began Gen.

'Dead – all dead!' Jamie interrupted loudly. He arranged his face into a mournful expression and gave a small, pathetic snuffle. 'I guess . . . I guess you could say we're victims of fate, desperate and helpless, with nowhere to call home.'

'Indeed.' The man's crooked mouth twisted into what I guessed was supposed to be a kindly smile, but it didn't reach his eyes. The boy was frowning at us, obviously unconvinced.

'And what did they teach you at this *circus arts school*?' he asked. 'You seem an unlikely –'

'It matters not, Lyulf,' interrupted Borg smoothly. 'As the boy says, full training is provided.'

'But the girls –'

'What of them?' growled the man. 'The public likes nothing better than to watch young maidens in the arena, and if they do not last as long, what of it? And the chatterbot will be useful to collect the takings, if it can be trained.' Blue-bum gave an indignant chitter. 'Let us waste no more time. Fetch parchment and quill – I wish to be well away by nightfall.'

The boy disappeared into the largest caravan and emerged holding a piece of dog-eared parchment and a ratty-looking feather. He passed them to Borg, who sat on the top step, rested the paper on his knee and began to write, with many frowns and pauses.

The five of us took advantage of the chance for a lightning council of war. 'What d'you reckon?' hissed Rich. 'Do we give it a go?'

'I don't think we have much choice,' I whispered. 'Do keep still and shut up, Blue-bum!' He was jigging about on my shoulder, chattering in my ear and tugging my hair, still nose-out-of-joint about Borg's comment, I was betting. Trying to ignore him, I went on: 'We don't know the way to Limbo, and even if we did, it sounds as if it would be dangerous to travel there alone.'

'I say we do it!' said Gen. 'Remember Kai and his *tapestries of fate*? Things happen for a reason – and anyhow, it sounds like fun.'

'I suppose I could use my gymnastics,' said Kenta doubtfully; 'though I don't much like Borg. Can we trust him? And there seem to be an awful lot of injuries . . .'

At that moment the boy sidled up to us. With a wary eye on Borg, he spoke, in a voice almost too low to hear. 'You must be desperate indeed. Are you certain you wish to join us? Once the contract is signed and we have left Four Winds, there can be no going back.'

'Well, we do have just one question,' whispered Kenta. 'Why –'

'Right: who will be first?' Borg was striding towards us, holding out the parchment and quill. Jamie snatched it eagerly, scanned it and signed his name with a flourish. Then he handed it to me with a whispered, 'Here you go, Adam: our ticket to Limbo!'

Less than two minutes later we were all signed-up members of Troupe Talisman.

To our delight we were given a caravan to ourselves, though it was the smallest and shabbiest, and also allocated a doleful-looking flea-bitten glonk the colour of an old carpet, with one ear longer than the other. We immediately christened him Gloom, and set to work trying to figure out how to harness him to the shafts of the caravan.

A cheerful voice interrupted us. 'That be back-to-front. His tail goes through that loop, not his nose.'

I stumbled round, blushing, my arms full of tangled leather. A slim figure in a tight-fitting black bodysuit and cloak was watching us. At first, seeing the sharp angles of the face and the short-cropped dark hair, I thought it was a boy, a year or two older than us. But then she spoke again, stepping forward and taking the harness from me with a sidelong smile, and I realised my mistake. 'My name is Blade. Who be you?'

'We're the new circus performers,' said Jamie proudly. 'I'm Jamie.' By the time he'd introduced us the harness was fitted and Blade's nimble fingers were doing up the last buckle. 'So I guess that makes seven of us – if you don't count Borg and the other men.'

'Eight,' she said briefly, nodding towards Borg's caravan.

'You found someone?' Lyulf was busy with the trailer, which contained the circus equipment. Jamie'd been itching to get a peek, but Borg had ordered him gruffly away. 'It'll be stuff like the Big Top – that's the tent – juggling batons, stilts, a unicycle, maybe even a flying trapeze . . .' Jamie had told us.

'Then you had better fortune than I did, Blade,' Lyulf went on. 'I came back empty-handed, nothing but abuse from the townsfolk, and to hear that apothecary, you would think fire-tongue was silver dust.'

'And so it is, in our business,' said Blade. 'We dare not leave without it, Lyulf.'

'There will be some growing wild along the way, though it is early in the season. Closer to Limbo, perhaps . . .'

'Fire-tongue!' breathed Jamie reverently in my ear.

'That'll have something to do with fire-eating, the most dangerous act there is!'

But my attention was focused on the exchange between Lyulf and Blade. I figured the more we could find out about the circus set-up and our new companions, the better.

'I don't know how much use he'll be,' Blade was saying. 'I asked if he had any experience, and he said he did. But . . . well, you know how they are.'

'What's his name?' asked Gen curiously, staring across at Borg's caravan. A tall, strongly-built figure was deep in conversation with him – or rather, Borg was firing questions at him while the man stood impassive as a rock.

'I don't know,' said Blade. 'He was standing near the docks. The galley from Karazan had just come in, and at first I thought he was waiting for someone. But everyone was already off and still he stood there. So I asked if he was from Karazan.'

'And what did he say?' prompted Jamie.

Blade shrugged. 'Nothing.'

'Nothing?' echoed Lyulf.

'He's . . . well . . . different,' said Blade. 'But when I said we were looking for performers, leaving for the Borderlands tonight, he seemed keen enough to join us. And you know Borg,' she finished, with a meaning glance at us. 'He's hardly fussy.'

'In what way is he different?' asked Kenta.

'He doesn't talk, for one thing. Could be he can't. They cut people's tongues out in Karazan for

176

speaking out against the king. And for another . . .'

She didn't finish – didn't need to. At that moment the tall man turned away from Borg and stared towards us. At least, I assumed that was what he was doing: it was hard to tell. His face was completely hidden by something I thought at first was a kind of helmet . . . but then I saw it was a shapeless mask, a leather hood over his head with two slits for eyes.

Lyulf grunted, almost as if he was approving, or even amused. 'Well, it seems we have one at least with a ready-made stage name. He can be the Masked Man. And if he doesn't talk, so much the better – he won't argue.'

But Blade was watching him with a small frown. 'I hope I did right,' she muttered. 'He'll keep to the company of the men, or so I hope. And I'd counsel you all to stay well away from them. They're hardened, professional performers: a rough lot, made the more surly and ill-humoured by injury and idleness.

'And now, we're ready to leave.'

We took up our place at the rear of the straggling cavalcade, and by nightfall, as Borg had promised, we'd left Four Winds far behind.

CIRCUS ARTS

Much to our relief, what Blade said was true. From the start there seemed to be an unspoken division between the men, who smelled of dirty dressings and unwashed flesh, spoke in growls and grunts and behaved as if we didn't exist, and our cheerful campfire. Borg kept to the men's group, ignoring us as much as possible, barking the occasional order and generally treating us with dismissive contempt, which seemed at odds with his initial eagerness to sign us up. And the Masked Man seemed happy to keep to himself.

'So tell us about your circus course, Jamie,' said Rich after our first breakfast, a silent meal of lumpy porridge made by Lyulf and choked down by all of us to be polite.

We were parked up among some trees beside a river, the caravans and trailer grouped in a rough circle with the campfires in the middle. Borg had growled something about a 'training session' and stumped off, presumably to fetch the equipment, leaving the five of us – you could hardly count Blue-bum – to do the clearing-up.

'Yes,' said Gen, 'show us some tricks, Jamie!'

'Well,' said Jamie, looking rather bashful, 'all I can do is juggle a bit with three balls . . . sort of, and not for very long. I'm out of practice.' He hesitated, then took a deep breath and went on: 'The course was part of a youth programme my parents sent me on. It was supposed to help with *personal and social development, confidence, cooperation and creativity*. I think Mum and Dad hoped I'd make some friends.

'But actually it turned out to be a dumping-ground for problem kids over the holidays. You'd be surprised how many things kids like that can find to do with juggling scarves and fire torches.' He swallowed. 'It wasn't much fun for me. Though I guess it was for them.'

I didn't know what to say. He was staring miserably at the ground, mouth set in a determined line, chin trembling. Then suddenly Gen was giving him a hug that made him blush bright scarlet. 'Never mind, Jamie. You've got *real* friends now. And you've joined an *actual* circus, not some silly course. Hopefully Blade will be the one to teach us; she's really nice.'

'It's an odd name, isn't it?' said Kenta. 'I wonder –'

She broke off as Borg appeared, staggering under the weight of a battered wooden crate the size and shape of a coffin. The equipment had arrived. Hastily we stowed the dishes away and kicked out the fire,

179

then gathered round to look. Juggling batons, stilts, a unicycle, Jamie had said . . . I couldn't wait to try it.

Borg opened the little leather bag that hung on a thong round his neck and withdrew a tiny key. We held our breath as he opened the padlocks and slowly lifted the lid.

I blinked. Had he brought the wrong box? Where were the devil sticks and the clown outfits? I looked at the others, and saw my own bafflement reflected on their faces.

The box was full of weapons. Swords, long and short, made of metal and of wood; tridents like the one Kai had used; nets, staffs, daggers and spears; weird things like spiked knuckle-dusters; clumsy-looking gloves made of steel and leather and woven chain-mail, and what looked like padded frisbees.

The Masked Man strode up, arms piled high with huge shields the size of cartwheels; they must have weighed a ton, but he carried them as easily as if they were a pile of pancakes. He dropped them on the ground with a ringing crash, dust puffing out all round. Was it some kind of joke? I stared at the stuff, not even beginning to understand. On my shoulder Blue-bum was still and silent; his little hand twisted firmly into my hair for balance. For once it felt oddly comforting.

For what seemed a long time no one spoke. Then Gen piped up, in a strangled bleat: 'What . . .' Her voice trailed away.

Why ask the question, with the answer right there in

front of us? We'd joined a circus all right – but not quite the kind of circus we'd thought.

Borg stalked off to fetch his 'sword-master' and while we waited we discussed the contents of the box in agitated whispers.

'Maybe they're juggling swords,' said Jamie. 'In some circuses –'

'Yeah, right, or they're planning to teach us sword-swallowing for starters, before we graduate to fire-eating,' growled Rich. 'Face it, Jamie, we've been conned.'

'But I don't understand,' said Kenta. 'Are they bandits, or what?'

'Not bandits; gladiators.' Lyulf was standing a few paces away, arms folded. He had an unnerving knack of appearing silently out of nowhere, moving quietly as a cat.

Gladiators! It was the one thing in the world I knew something about, from my ill-fated Gladiator Project. A memory of hours hunched over the computer at Highgate flashed through my mind, vivid images of clashing steel and blood-soaked sand mingling with the orphanage smells of overcooked cabbage and disinfectant. Without meaning to, I found myself glancing up at Blue-bum, remembering how, as Weevil, he'd stolen my project and passed it off as his own . . . his bright button eyes met mine full-on for a second, then squeezed tight shut.

I'd always thought being a gladiator would be way

cool – the olden-day equivalent of an Olympic gold medallist . . . my heart did a flip-flop of mixed nerves and excitement and I felt the beginnings of a grin tug at the corners of my mouth.

But Gen spun to face Lyulf, eyes blazing. 'Why didn't you tell us? You said it was a circus – and so did Borg! And anyhow, gladiators don't . . .'

Lyulf watched expressionlessly as she wound gradually down, realising the pointlessness of what she was saying. They might not exist in our world, but she could hardly say so – and here they all too obviously did.

'I suppose it's just a question of definition,' said Jamie, always a stickler for accuracy. 'Come to think of it, in Ancient Rome the gladiator tournaments were called *circuses* – it's where the term originated. They taught us that in . . .' Then Jamie too gulped and was silent.

'Now it all makes sense,' said Kenta. 'The men – the *hardened professionals* – haven't hurt themselves falling off the high wire.'

'No wonder Blade told us to stay away from them,' whispered Gen.

'They are brigands, criminals, cut-throats,' said Lyulf grimly. 'Blade counselled you well.'

'But what happened to them? If they're as tough as you say . . .'

Lyulf shrugged. 'We cannot always choose who – or what – we fight. Those who remain were the most skilled – and the most fortunate, believe me.'

'Well, Lyulf,' I said evenly, 'maybe you'd better tell us a bit more about your kind of circus. We might as well know what sort of outfit we've joined.'

Lyulf gave a small snort that could have been amusement, but still he didn't smile. 'The circus is an ancient tradition of the Borderlands,' he said, 'and other lands further afield. Borg is the ringmaster. He owns the circus. He employs trained fighters – gladiators – to take part in contests between other troupes, or champions who volunteer for combat. Sometimes there is a tournament in one of the bigger towns –'

'And that's where the real money is to be made,' chipped in Blade cheerfully. 'Don't look so down in the mouth. Whatever you thought a circus was, it couldn't be better than this. Excitement, danger, success – even fame, for some.' She nodded towards Lyulf. 'Pitting your skill against all comers – whether man or beast, warrior or phantom – and never knowing what the next day will bring. Nothing adds as much spice to life as not knowing when it is to end!'

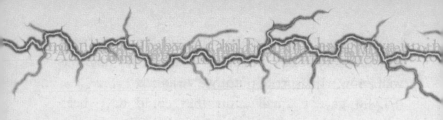

FIRST STEPS

A few minutes later we were standing in a ragged line, each with one of the wooden swords. Jamie held his as if it was red-hot, eyeing it distrustfully. 'I don't know if this is really my kind of thing . . .' he began, casting Blade a doubtful glance.

'Well, don't look at me,' she said. 'Any problems should be addressed to the sword-master.'

'But aren't *you* the sword-master?'

She gave a snort of laughter. 'Me? I'm only a humble gladiator. Lyulf's the sword-master.'

'But he's just a kid!' Rich objected. 'I'd rather be trained by someone with a bit more experience – no offence, Lyulf.'

Blade had been walking away, but now she turned, her eyes flashing. 'And no offence to *you*, Richard, when I tell you to speak only of what you know. Of lesser years Lyulf may be, but he has the skills of a swordsman five times his age and more, coupled with the speed and stamina of youth. He is expert at assessing fighters – and at training them. If ignorance

184

leaps from your mouth when you open it, I'd counsel you to keep it shut.' She turned on her heel and stalked off. Rich, who'd turned bright red, stared at the ground.

Without comment, Lyulf tossed the last wooden sword to the Masked Man, who caught it easily by the hilt. 'Very well,' he said, 'let us see what lies beneath that mask, my friend.'

The two of them circled warily, looking for an opening. The Masked Man was twice the size of Lyulf, and I was glad the swords weren't real. I had a hunch the mysterious stranger might turn out to be better at swordsmanship than any of us expected – and I was right.

He took a slow half-shuffle forward with one foot and suddenly the air was cracking with the clash of wood on wood. In and out the two figures wove, left and right, one fluid movement blending in with the next as if they were partners in some kind of intricate dance, their swords no more than a blur. Then there was a snap and a grunt and something was cartwheeling through the air towards me; I ducked instinctively as one of the swords spun over our heads and clattered to the ground behind us.

Jamie gave a snuffle of dismay, and beside me Richard whistled softly between his teeth. The two combatants faced each other, neither of them even breathing hard. Lyulf still held his sword, but the Masked Man's hand was empty.

'Good enough.' Lyulf's face was expressionless, but

it was clear he was pleased. 'We have one competent fighter at least. Who's next?' We shuffled our feet and tried to avoid his eye. 'No volunteers? Come then – you. Up here with me.' To no one's surprise he pointed at Richard, who shambled sheepishly into the makeshift arena. The hang-dog look on his face showed he knew what he was in for – it was the perfect chance for Lyulf to get his own back and teach him a lesson he wouldn't forget.

But Rich wasn't going down without a fight. He gripped his sword in both hands like a baseball bat, raised it to chest height and narrowed his eyes. I closed mine, hoping that at least Lyulf would make it quick and painless.

Nothing happened.

I opened them a crack . . . and there was Lyulf, his sword beside him on the ground, painstakingly re-arranging Richard's hand on his sword-hilt.

It seemed one look had told Lyulf all he needed to know – or confirmed what I realised he'd suspected all along: we all knew less than nothing. The Masked Man settled himself on a log and watched with undisguised interest as Lyulf coached us through the basics – grip, stance and footwork – using Rich to demonstrate. I soon forgot we were being taught by someone our own age – there was no hint of showing off or arrogance, just patient matter-of-factness tinged with dry touches of humour that soon put us all at ease. 'The footwork is as simple and direct as walking,' he explained. 'Step forward and back, left and right, pivot on one leg to circle your opponent – and remember, balance and timing are everything. Your footwork keeps you at a safe distance, then brings you into the attack. Now, get into pairs and try it . . .'

It seemed we'd only been practising a few minutes when Lyulf glanced at the sun and said it was time to stop. Even Jamie objected. 'Already? But we've only just begun!'

'You have done enough for the first day. As it is, your sword arm will be stiff tomorrow. You have all made a good beginning. The way of the body is the foundation of our craft; the way of the sword will follow. As for the third part of the art of the circus . . . the way of the mind will come to you in time, without you realising it. And now it is time for the midday meal.'

The morning couldn't have passed so quickly – yet it had. Reluctantly we replaced the swords in the box and joined Blade at our campfire, where a cauldron of stew was simmering.

'This is well earned,' she said, ladling out hearty helpings. 'The first lesson's something to celebrate – and you're all doing well.' We grinned at one another. The phrase we'd read on the placard flashed into my mind – *the brotherhood of the arena*. Suddenly it made sense.

'You'll need to be thinking of stage names,' Blade told us between mouthfuls. 'A name that says something about you is best – that is true to your inner core. A name is far more than just a word in our business.'

'Is that what Blade is?' asked Kenta. 'Your stage name?'

Blade shrugged. 'I can't remember being called anything else. I was born to this.'

'What about you, Lyulf?' asked Jamie. 'Is Lyulf your stage name?'

Blade snorted. 'I should think not! You have the honour of being taught by none other than the great Wolf Flame – the finest gladiator the Borderlands have ever known.'

Lyulf frowned and carried on eating.

'Wolf Flame!' echoed Rich enviously. 'How cool is that! How did you choose it?'

For a moment I thought Lyulf wasn't going to answer. But then he finished chewing, swallowed, and said briefly, 'It is the meaning of the name Lyulf in the old tongue – or Lyulf is its meaning, whichever you prefer.'

'What *old tongue*?' asked Gen. 'Have you always been a gladiator, like Blade?'

Again, he chewed unhurriedly and swallowed; but this time he took another mouthful without answering. Blade laughed. 'Persuading Lyulf to talk about himself is like getting rainwater from desert sand,' she said. 'In all the time I've known him, he's told me no more than that.'

'How long have you known each other?' asked Kenta curiously.

188

'Too long,' grunted Lyulf.

'Long enough,' she amended with a smile. 'Lyulf was sword-master of the troupe I joined before this one. I'd been in the arena all my life and thought I knew it all.' She pulled a wry face, glancing over at Lyulf with a look I couldn't interpret. He didn't return it. 'I soon learned differently. I couldn't believe my good fortune when I realised who he was. I'd heard, of course, of the legendary Wolf Flame who springs up wherever he is least expected, never staying in one place longer than –'

She broke off. Lyulf had pushed his bowl aside and risen to his feet, and was walking away.

'Oh, by the twin moons . . .' Blade muttered. 'Lyulf, come back and finish your meal!' But he was gone. She shrugged, her expression a mixture of impatience and remorse. 'My tongue runs away with my words – I know he hates to be spoken of.

'Now: we were discussing stage names.'

'I've already chosen mine,' said Gen. Everyone stared at her. 'I thought . . . Crystal.'

Blade nodded. 'That is like you,' she said. 'Outwardly fragile, with an inner strength; beautiful, and clear and transparent as water.'

By the end of lunch all the names had been decided except mine. Rich was calling himself Tornado, and Kenta decided on Shadow – 'Not the scary sort,' she'd explained shyly; 'the dappled, shifting shadows leaves make in sunshine.'

Jamie had opted for Blunderbuss. 'It may sound

189

comical,' he'd told us when we'd laughed, 'but it's not. A Blunderbuss was an old-fashioned gun, and a lot more lethal than it sounds – just like I'll be once I'm all trained up. So there!'

But – as usual – I couldn't come up with a single idea. The others drifted away, Blue-bum lolloping behind them; I leaned against a tree and took out my larigot to help me think. I'd played it in the stillness of the previous evening; more and more I was finding refuge and strength in its music. It seemed to bridge the gap between past and future, in my imagination at least: to draw my father, my mother and my lost brother closer, into a magical circle of silver . . .

A shadow fell over me and I broke off, startled. It was the Masked Man. As always, his face was obscured by his leather hood, but I could feel the intensity of his gaze behind the narrow slits. 'Whistler,' he said. His voice was muffled and indistinct, but the single word was unmistakable.

I nearly dropped my larigot. 'What? Who . . .'

'Sometimes we choose our own name, and sometimes it is chosen for us. And sometimes the name chooses itself . . . *Whistler*.' He watched me a moment more, then turned and walked away.

I stared after him, then down at my larigot. It felt cool, smooth, familiar between my fingers . . . part of me, like it always had.

Yes, that was it. Whistler.

Sometimes the name chooses itself. But it hadn't. He had chosen it for me . . . whoever he was.

THE BROTHERHOOD OF
THE ARENA

I lost track of time in the days that followed.

Between travelling, eating and sleeping, we did almost nothing but train. Our only free time was in the evenings, when Borg joined the circle of men passing a wineskin round their campfire and the Masked Man disappeared who knew where. The rest of us relaxed by the fire; I'd play my larigot, or Gen would make up a story; we'd talk, sing songs or play blow-sticks.

Lyulf had whittled us each our own pipe from a bamboo-like plant with a hollow centre; Blade would rig the target – rather gruesomely a human body, arms raised and legs spread, the heart and other vital organs marked in red and scoring highest – on a convenient tree, and it would be game on. We'd take turns to aim and fire with lethal-looking feathered darts that smacked into the target with a grisly *thwack*. At first Blade and Lyulf beat us easily, but we soon became more expert, till even Jamie – who was worst – was clamouring to play as soon as the dinner things were cleared away.

As for Blue-bum . . . at first he watched, looking lonely and left out. And then one night Lyulf handed him his own little mini-pipe. 'The fellowship of the arena includes us all,' he said solemnly, a twinkle in his eye, 'even you, Blue-bum.' Who'd have guessed what a tiger would be unleashed? Blue-bum spent every spare moment practising, and was soon better than us all. He showed a fierce and not always sporting spirit, once snapping his blow-stick in half and going off to sulk at the top of a tree when Blade beat him by a whisker – a reminder that the old Weevil was still in there somewhere, I told myself with a smile.

During the day we lived and breathed training. At first Lyulf kept us together to learn the basics: cuts, thrusts, attack and counter-attack, grappling, disarming, and, 'most important of all', as Jamie said – avoidance.

'I'm hopeless!' Jamie wailed miserably on the third day, after he'd tripped over his own sword and fallen flat on his face at Lyulf's feet.

'Not so,' replied Lyulf, while the rest of us looked hurriedly away to hide our smiles. 'In a circus troupe there are many different roles. It is time you all began to specialise.'

From then on, training switched to one-on-one. For Kenta and Gen, out came tall tridents that reminded me with a shudder of the Mauler, and nets weighted at the edges with iron balls. 'You girls are swift and agile,' Lyulf told them. 'We will work on developing those abilities, together with your stamina.'

To Rich's initial disgust, most of his training took place with no weapon. 'You will never make a swordsman, Tornado,' Lyulf told him bluntly; 'you do not have the subtlety. Your strength lies in your physical power. I will teach you a few simple strategies for disarming your opponent; once the weapons are out of the way you will come into your own.' Despite himself, Richard soon began to relish the hand-to-hand combat techniques Lyulf schooled him in: the throws, rolls, kicks, punches, locks, and close-quarter knife-work.

'And for you, Blunderbuss,' said Lyulf gravely, 'something rather different is called for – and for that, Blade must be your teacher.' Off they went together day after day to practise whatever it was in private. They'd return hours later, Jamie grubby, dishevelled and looking very pleased with himself; Blade uncharacteristically mysterious, a brighter-than-usual sparkle in her eyes. It was clear the two of them had some kind of secret, and Gen for one didn't seem to like it, though she didn't say so.

It was only me who didn't seem to have any special role. I longed to ask what my strength was, what my speciality was going to be . . . but I couldn't find the courage. It wasn't that I was worried Lyulf would growl at me: we'd all come to know him well enough to trust him completely, despite – or maybe because of – his characteristic grimness. I was afraid he'd have to admit I didn't have one – that in each of the others he could see talent of some kind, while with me he was floundering in the dark.

For days I plugged on with the wooden sword I'd started with, but it felt as clumsy and unresponsive as a log of wood in my hand; Lyulf, watching me, scowled and shook his head.

He put the sword aside and switched me to a wider-bladed broadsword, with one of the padded leather 'frisbees' – a miniature shield or 'buckler' – strapped to my left forearm; but still he didn't seem satisfied. The buckler was exchanged for a long-bladed wooden dagger, the heavy sword for a lighter version with a longer blade. I sparred two-handed with Blade, getting the feel of the new weapons while Lyulf stood and watched, arms folded, face like thunder. 'What's the matter with me?' I muttered miserably to Blade during a brief break. 'What am I doing wrong?'

'Nothing,' she replied with a grin. 'Don't let it bother you. It's Lyulf. He's never happy till he's found the perfect combination of man – or woman – and weapon. Bear with him and be patient.'

For the next few nights Lyulf didn't join us round the campfire. His absence left an emptiness: though he never said much, his presence was a force that generated heat and energy, like the fire itself . . . unlike the Masked Man, who prowled in and out of the circle almost unnoticed, now here, now gone, always so silent I wondered if I'd imagined those few muffled words.

Then after breakfast one day Lyulf arrived for my training session carrying a long object wrapped in his cloak, in his eyes a mysterious gleam. 'Well, Whistler, let us see how you fare with this,' he said, allowing the cloak to fall away. I stared, speechless. Resting on his palms was a perfect replica of my father's sword made of wood. Length and breadth of blade, balance and proportion were identical; even the hilt had been faithfully copied, right down to the leather binding round the grip. But how? When?

Casting my mind back, I realised when it must have been. Blade had asked to see my sword soon after we joined the troupe; I'd unsheathed it and passed it over, and she'd admired it for a minute or so before returning it. I hadn't even realised Lyulf was there. In those few moments he must have memorised every detail, even down to the tracery of leaves on the flat of the blade. For the first time I had an inkling of the extent of Lyulf's mastery. A weapon of any kind, once glimpsed, memorised instantly in minute detail . . . and now reproduced – for me.

Blood rushed to my face; I didn't know what to say. I glanced up, hoping he wouldn't notice my tears. Our eyes met in an instant of connection so powerful it jolted through me like an electric shock. I blinked, confused and shaken . . . and the moment was past.

'No need,' Lyulf was saying gruffly, as if in answer to a 'thank you' I didn't even know I'd spoken.

★

From the first moment it was as if the wooden sword was alive in my hand. Now at last I saw a smile in Lyulf's eyes as he lowered the point of his own practice sword and stepped back, wiping his face on his sleeve. Blade, 'happening' to pass at that moment, threw me an impudent grin and a wink. I couldn't help grinning back, light-headed with relief and a savage kind of joy. I hadn't realised till then how important it seemed to be for me to be good at this . . . and to see the approval in Lyulf's eyes.

That afternoon he called the Masked Man over. 'It is time you sparred with a partner other than myself and Blade,' he told me. I put my new sword on guard with a sinking heart. I'd seen how good the hooded stranger was . . . but I'd rather have died than let Lyulf know how I felt.

The two blades touched, lightly as feathers . . . and I felt the weirdest sensation. It was as if the wooden blade of my sword was a live conduit, an antenna telegraphing information to my brain. I felt a frown gather behind the leather mask, and my own brain answered with a grin of triumph: so – *he'd felt it too. And he didn't like it.*

Slowly, we began to circle. The blades touched, parted, touched again – and each time they touched, the connection was there. Like a cat's whisker in the dark, semaphoring the other blade's intention the instant it was formulated. Now the Masked Man's sword wasn't a blur; I could follow its movements, almost as if they were in slow motion, tracking them, anticipating them, countering them with my own instinctive parries and thrusts.

Strangest of all, for the first time the wooden sword gave me a sense of *knowing* my adversary – not *who* he was, but *what* he was – his inner core, as Blade would say. With Lyulf, it was crackling energy, fierce as a wolf, bright as a flame. But with the Masked Man the touching blades transmitted a darker force, muted and strangely compelling . . . and with it came an unsettling sense of recognition, almost as if, were the mask removed, the face beneath might be as familiar as my own.

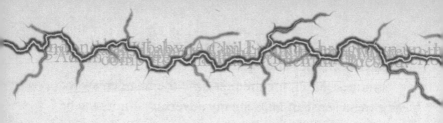

A GREY HORIZON

That night, for the first time, Lyulf said we should take turns at keeping watch while the others slept. 'We are deep in the wildlands,' he told us, 'and still two days' journey from the first town. We would be foolish to rely on the safety of numbers alone, with so many wounded.'

Blade agreed. 'If you leave your caravan at night, do not venture far from the fire – and if you hear anything unusual, wake one of us at once.'

The two of them carried on shovelling down their bowls of gruel as if they'd been discussing the weather forecast, but Jamie turned greenish-grey and pushed his bowl away unfinished. 'What sort of anything?' he croaked.

'Yeah,' said Rich cheerfully, 'what exactly are these famous *dangers of the wildlands*? I thought Borg said the circus arts would protect us!'

Blade and Lyulf exchanged a glance. 'Tell them,' said Lyulf. 'It is better that they know.'

'We are near the border of Limbo.' My heart gave a little skip, but Blade set down her spoon and looked

198

round at us gravely. 'And beyond . . .' she lowered her voice to a whisper, 'lie the Realms of the Undead.'

'The Realms of the Undead . . .' I echoed, remembering the words that had come from the fire. 'So they do exist.' I didn't want to ask, but I knew I must. 'Do you know anything more about them?'

'Only what I have heard – and even that I do not fully believe, for none who have been there return. Limbo lies at the edge of the world; the shadowlands we speak of, further still. Men say they are bordered by a vast forest, and that through the forest run two paths. One path leads to the Realms of the Undead; the other, to your journey's end – wherever that may be. Legend has it that the paths are guarded by two birds which speak with the voices of men.'

'And they tell you which path is which, I'll bet . . .' said Jamie.

'Yes – and no. One bird tells nothing but truth; the other, nothing but lies.'

'So it's all a bit of a lottery,' chipped in Rich cheerfully. 'Sounds like a load of rubbish.'

I said nothing. I was remembering . . . *The birds of the air will point the way; truth and lies will lead you there* . . . My heart felt like a stone rolling slowly downhill. We were close to Limbo – very close. In Limbo, we would find Zenith. Together we would take whatever final steps we needed . . . to wherever they led us.

'Aye, Tornado, possibly none of it is true,' Blade continued sombrely. 'But this I do know. Many of those who roam the wildlands are taken – I know not for what purpose. And though the circus arts protect us, they also put us most at risk. But be of good cheer: we have journeyed this route many times and come to no harm.'

'These *Undead* . . .' quavered Gen. 'Who are they?'

'They are creatures of darkness, the evil and the damned, those who lie restless in unnamed graves.' Blade's voice was low. 'Their bodies retain a semblance of human form; it is their souls that putrefy. They go by different names in different lands, but many know them as the Faceless.'

'Lock and bolt your door,' said Lyulf grimly. 'We will sleep with weapons by our sides tonight. Blade, you and I will take the darkest watches. And remember – if you hear anything, wake us instantly.'

I don't know what it was that woke me.

After my watch I'd roused Blade and fallen instantly into a bottomless sleep that should have lasted till morning; now suddenly I was wide awake, skin prickling, ears straining for the faintest sound. In the bunk below me I could hear Jamie's gentle snoring; across the narrow caravan one of the girls whimpered and was still again.

It was Blade waking Lyulf for his watch, I told myself; the sooner I went back to sleep, the sooner morning would come. Gradually my heartbeat slowed; I squirmed deeper into my sleeping bag and turned to face the door, closing my eyes and breathing deeply.

My thoughts blurred gradually into dreams . . . and then the sound came again, jerking me awake. There was something outside the caravan.

I wriggled out of my sleeping bag and lowered myself soundlessly to the floor, padded bare-chested to the window and drew back the flimsy curtain. Night hung outside like black velvet . . . and through the stillness came the softest murmur of a voice.

I decided to fetch Lyulf; felt for my sword in the darkness, slid it from its sheath and held it ready by my side, my other hand steady but cold as ice as I unlocked the door and drew the bolt. I slipped through the door and drew it closed. Feeling the way with my bare feet over the rough ground, I edged round the side of the caravan towards the glow of the fire – and froze.

Two figures were silhouetted against the soft wash of firelight. Lyulf and Blade. It was their voices I'd heard. They were speaking in whispers, but with an intensity that carried their words further than they intended – across to me, standing stock-still in the shadow of the caravan.

'What are you running from? Just tell me that – trust me that far at least, for friendship's sake!'

Lyulf's growl: 'I trust nothing and no one.'

'Can you truly say you care nothing for me? Look me in the eyes and tell me.'

'Lower your voice – you will wake the others.'

Blade dropped her voice, and I caught only snatches of her next words: '. . . when last we spoke of this . . . held to the hope . . . followed you here, and now –'

'Yes – and you should not have done! The evil I battle is mine alone to face or flee, my curse mine alone to carry!'

Blade reached out to him, arms slender and fragile in the firelight. Her next words were a whisper too soft to hear. I watched helplessly, paralysed by the knowledge that I'd stumbled on something so private, yet terrified to move a muscle in case I gave my presence away.

A mumble from Lyulf – a word or two, broken, indistinct – then Blade's voice, pleading and desperate: '. . . *whatever the enchantment* . . .'

'*No!*' The single word cut through the night like a sword, so full of anguish that for a second I thought Lyulf really had been wounded, somehow, by some hidden enemy lurking in the darkness. He spun and staggered away from the fire towards the dark circle of caravans, moving at a stumbling run as if he'd been cut to the bone.

My heart was in my throat. I was a second away from stepping from my hiding place to help him . . . and then I saw his face. He passed less than an arm's-length away and never saw me; slipped into his caravan and snicked the door shut. I waited for a sound, for a light to flicker on, for something . . . but there was only silence.

By the fire Blade stood like a statue, arms by her sides, head bowed.

I crept back into my caravan, slid into bed and lay, my mind spinning, waiting for dawn.

Morning came, and with it the first hint of autumn. Till now the days had been long and golden, what clouds there were gathering swiftly into sudden thunderstorms that left the world scoured to a shimmering brightness. But today we shivered awake and huddled in our cloaks by the fire, the wood sullen and slow to burn in the damp air.

Blade was at pains to seem her usual self, chatting away in a bright, false voice, though never to Lyulf. He was quieter than ever, keeping his eyes low and his mouth shut. With the Masked Man as silent as always and Borg and the others speaking in grunts if at all, breakfast was a dreary affair. I was glad when my porridge was finished and I had an excuse to wander down to the river and rinse my bowl.

My mind was full of what I'd heard the night before. I couldn't make sense of any of it – not just the words themselves, but the rip-tide of emotion that surged beneath them. Should I tell the others? No – every instinct told me what I'd stumbled on was private, not mine to tell. But could it be important in some way – have some bearing on our quest? I couldn't see how.

I stood gazing out over the water to the riverbank beyond, shaking the last drops from my bowl and drawing the cool, damp air deep into my lungs . . . and that's when I saw it. Way distant, almost invisible

203

against the dull sky: the faintest twist, like a ghost of tattered lace faded faint as a dream.

Grey smoke on a grey horizon.

My mind snapped shut on every thought but one. I turned and headed back to the others, my blood singing.

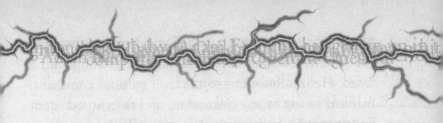

HUNTING THE HUNTERS

With the excuse of washing up I hustled Rich, Jamie and the girls to the riverside to see the smoke. They were quick to agree on what it was, but that's where agreement ended and a heated argument began.

The girls wanted to sneak off into Limbo without a word to anyone. But Rich was all for confrontation: 'I say we tell Borg we're going, and let him try to stop us!'

'I don't think we should burn our bridges,' Jamie objected. 'Let's talk to Blade and Lyulf, and see what they say.'

'And tell them what? Once you start talking, you never know what might slip out,' retorted Rich.

'I guess you're right,' Jamie admitted. 'They're bound to ask . . .'

'They won't ask anything.' I was certain of it. 'Not Lyulf. He already knows we're looking for someone in Limbo, and he hasn't asked a single question. It's not his way. Let's show him the smoke, tell him we need to investigate, and see what he says.'

★

205

Now, side by side, Rich, Lyulf and I stood staring at the smoke. I'd been right – so far Lyulf hadn't said a word. He'd followed us to the river without comment, listened to my brief explanation, and then stood silent and focused, staring at the horizon with narrowed eyes and head raised as if he was sniffing the air.

When at last he spoke it was almost as if to himself, and not with questions at all.

'So, the tales of the Lost Tribe are true . . . yet this is the first sign I have seen of them. They must not often stray as close to the Borderlands. It is smoke from a wood fire – karas, by the scent of it. The change in weather has taken them by surprise – dry, the wood burns clean, but dampness makes it smoke.' He was quiet for a moment, thinking. 'A hunting party rather than a permanent camp, I'll wager. And if it is, they'll strike camp within the hour and move northwards away from the border, travelling fast and far.' Our eyes met. His were a clear greenish-gold, flecked with chips of brightness like sunlight. They held a smile. 'You will have to move swiftly, Whistler. Blunderbuss would slow you, and the girls too . . . take Tornado, keep the sun on your right and meet us a day's journey to the east by nightfall.'

Rich didn't even try to wipe the grin off his face. 'But won't Borg –' he began half-heartedly.

'I will deal with Borg. Go now – and good speed.'

Rich raced off to tell the others the plan, and I hurried to the caravan and threw a few things into a pack. Cloaks, a crumpled bag of dried fruit, a handful of spicy smoked meat, water bottles filled to the brim – and my larigot. Down the steps in one bound – and I just about smacked straight into the Masked Man. 'Sorry,' I mumbled, ducking round him – but he reached out and grabbed my arm.

'If you travel to Limbo, you should not go alone,' he growled.

I gaped at him. I'd almost forgotten the few words he'd spoken before; like the others, I'd become so used to his silent, brooding presence that now I scarcely noticed it. I cast my mind back to the riverbank – had he been lurking nearby?

I pulled my arm free. 'I'm not going alone. Richard – Tornado – is coming with me. I'm surprised you didn't hear that too, if you were listening. And any-how –' it sounded rude, but then he shouldn't have been eavesdropping – 'what's it to you?'

'Something and nothing – the *brotherhood of the arena*, perhaps,' he replied with ironic emphasis. 'I offer you the protection of my sword and the arm that wields it. The choice is yours.'

So he wanted to come along! Why? What made him such an expert on Limbo – and why was it only ever me he chose to talk to? I opened my mouth to ask any one of the dozen questions that had bobbed to the surface of my mind, but I knew I'd never get a straight answer. Instead, I gave him a grin. 'Thanks, but Tornado and I'll be just fine.'

With what I hoped was a comradely wink and a nod, I dodged round him and pelted off to where Rich was hopping from foot to foot on the riverbank, desperate to be away.

We ran and walked and ran again, keeping the sun on our right as Lyulf had told us. The misty cloud soon burned off and the fuzzy smudge became a ball of fire beating down on the bare earth and burning our cheeks. After the first half hour or so I realised with a sickening jolt that with all the talk of swords I'd forgotten my own; another half an hour, soaked with sweat and puffing like a steam train, and I was thankful not to have it.

On and on we jogged across the shimmering desert. 'Nothing but dust and emptiness' was how the sandwich-seller had described Limbo, and it was true. It was hard to believe anyone could live here – impossible to imagine what kind of existence they'd have if they did.

Not just anyone – my twin. This arid, inhospitable landscape was home to him. For the first time I felt something twist deep inside me. What kind of man would grow from this harsh soil? I pushed the thought aside and ran on.

When we couldn't go another step we'd stumble to a halt, doubled up and groaning; swap the pack over, have a swallow of water, catch our breath and then push on. I didn't dare think what would happen if we were heading in the wrong direction; just hung grimly to the belief that Lyulf was never wrong – about that kind of thing, anyhow.

We ran for the most part in silence, exchanging no more than the odd glance of encouragement or grunted word. Exhausted as I was, I knew I could run all day. Because soon – today – I'd meet him. That thought was a bottomless fuel tank of energy I knew would last as long as it took to find him . . . and every stride was bringing us closer. Zenith – my brother.

I was grateful to Richard for not talking. What I was feeling was way beyond words.

When at last we reached the campsite we almost ran right past. But I'd become so used to the sameness of the drab landscape – grey-brown undulating earth pocked with scrub and boulders – that my eyes snagged instantly on the fragment of blackened firewood half-buried in a drift of sand.

We stumbled to a halt and together we unearthed it: a scatter of charcoal and ash, still warm to the touch. Now even I could pick up its scent: a sweet, woody fragrance with a hint of burned cloves.

Apart from that there was nothing – no sign that anyone had been there. In the back of my mind I'd imagined we'd track them once we got closer: follow a trail of footprints and bent blades of grass till we found them. But there was no grass, and not a grain of sand out of place that I could see.

North, Lyulf had said. Fast and far.

We ran on.

At midday we panted to a stop and flopped down into

a sliver of shade under a rock. The sun beat down like a mallet. 'My water's pretty much finished.' Rich gave his bottle a shake and didn't look at me. 'I'm sorry, Adam, I'm not sure we should go on. We may never catch them, and we promised –'

And suddenly they were there.

There was no sound, no movement, nothing: just a presence where before there had been emptiness. Men – five of them – grouped round us, holding evil-looking spears with fire-hardened tips.

Rich and I were on our feet in an instant, shoulder to shoulder, hearts pounding.

Their skin was brown as leather, their heads shaven and tattooed. White paint streaked the skin from cheekbone to jaw; their flat black eyes watched us, unwavering. Their bodies were naked except for a skin breechcloth and a couple of strings of cream-coloured beads circling wrists and ankles; their feet were bare. Something about them – the flatness of muscle, the stillness of eye – made me think of animals rather than people. Animals, wild and free.

Rich had turned several shades paler; now he slid his eyes sideways to meet mine. But for me, shock and fear were tinged with a fierce excitement. These were *his* people – they would take us to him. If they seemed savage, it was because they had to be, to survive. But once they realised we came in friendship . . . I was suddenly even gladder I hadn't brought my sword. I stared from one face to the next, searching for something – a glimmer of warmth, a glint of humanity . . .

One was younger, a year older than me perhaps, his tattoos a brighter blue than the others', his body still holding echoes of the contours of boyhood. But his eyes were as hard and cold as the rest. One was an old man, shrunken and skinny, white powder caked in the deep wrinkles of his cheeks. The other three were warriors, hunters in their prime. One seemed taller, stood straighter ... I turned to him, holding out my hands palm-upward. My mouth felt very dry. 'We come in peace,' I said quietly.

Without taking his eyes from me he jabbered something – a string of harsh, meaningless syllables. Somehow I could tell his words weren't directed at us; the old man replied: swift, sharp words like stones.

The tall man's eyes bored into mine. '*Quicksheeottle?*' he demanded. '*Shannagalore?*'

I stared at him stupidly, my brain in a tailspin. Why hadn't we thought of this? What now? What if none of them spoke English – what if Zenith didn't? What would we do then? You didn't have to be a genius to figure out what he was asking. *Who are you? What are you doing here?* But how could we answer them in words they'd understand?

'*Hasta!*' snarled the man beside him. '*Nga!*'

'We ... I ...' A trickle of sweat ran into my eye. I brushed it away – and instantly the youth leapt forward, teeth bared, the point of his spear digging into my neck. It felt sharper than it looked. Now he was close enough to smell: a gamy pungency that caught in my throat.

211

I raised both hands and took a slow, careful step back, out of range. 'Settle down,' I told him, keeping my voice low and even. His eyes flickered, and I saw something in them I recognised: the glitter of bravado I'd seen a million times in the playground – and only ever in the eyes of boys in a group who knew they had the upper hand. I traded look for hard look. 'And keep your stick and your BO to yourself, OK?' His gaze wavered; sullenly he lowered the spear and took a single, shuffling step back.

'Don't insult them!' hissed Rich.

It's OK – they don't understand . . . But as the words formed in my mind I knew it wasn't true. They might not be able to understand the words, but they could understand the sense behind them – just as I'd understood the tall guy without knowing a single syllable of his language.

I turned to face the old man, and took a deep breath. 'We . . .' I said, gesturing to Rich and then to me, 'come . . .' – I made my fingers into a little man, walking – 'from the river.' I pointed south, and made a rippling motion with my arm. 'I . . . look . . .' – pointed to my eye – 'for brother . . .' I held up one finger, then two, hoping that wouldn't be the one thing that meant the same in their language as in ours. 'Baby . . . ' I made a cradle of my arms and rocked it; 'long, long ago.' I swept my arm up and over from one horizon to the other, again, and again.

And then I waited.

THE LOST TRIBE OF LIMBO

I don't know how much of what I tried to say they understood, but somehow, in the course of those few clumsy words, all the tension drained away. They still held their spears towards us and the points looked as sharp as ever, but the threat was gone.

Though the youth glared and scuffed his feet and darted me sulky glances, I knew we'd won through. The old man's eyes weren't flat and opaque any more; now they had light and depth.

He rumbled some question or comment to the tall man, who gabbled a reply . . . and next thing we knew the whole lot of them were having a lively discussion, fingers rather than spears jabbing away at us to drive home whatever point they were making. One word was repeated so often even I could pick it out: *Temba*.

I wondered if perhaps it was my brother's name.

The tall guy barked an order, and his two mates prowled off behind a nearby rock and retrieved a deer carcass strung on a pole, slinging it between them. A finger stabbed once at Rich and once at me, and a lean brown arm beckoned in a gesture that was universal.

Then the hunting party loped off across the sand with Rich and me jogging along behind.

It was evening before we reached the main encampment: a huddle of rough tents made of animal hide; the glow of campfires; the clear note of voices calling through the twilight air.

On the long tramp our escorts had all but ignored us – I'd had the feeling that while we were welcome to tag along, they wouldn't so much as slow their pace if we fell behind. But now hard hands gripped our arms and we were hustled through the campsite, startled eyes and silence following our progress, children peeking at us from the flaps of doorways.

We reached a tent bigger than the rest, a woman in a beaded skirt stirring something over a fire outside. She gawked at us as if we'd come from outer space; then, at a gruff word from our escorts, scurried into the tent. I could hear an urgent exchange of voices, some kind of garbled explanation . . . then the door flap lifted and a man emerged, straightened to his full height and surveyed us haughtily without the smallest hint of surprise.

He was the leader – of that there was no doubt. His face could have been carved from hardwood; his eyes were sharp as an eagle's, their intensity proclaiming his status more clearly than a crown. His presence seemed somehow larger than he was, a coiled energy radiating from his gleaming-dark skin like heat.

I bent my head, sensing Rich beside me doing the same. When I lifted it he was still staring at me. Then he inclined his head once, deeply, gravely, as if returning the bow of an equal. I felt a moment's confusion: who – or what – did he think I was? What had the hunters told him? Then, looking deep into those eyes, I knew: this man didn't need to be told. In the same way I'd known him for what he was, he had looked beneath the tattered clothes and grime and tangled hair and seen . . . what?

He said his name: 'Jabula.'

This time I didn't bother with hand signs. Slowly, thinking carefully before each word, I told him why we'd come – though I sensed he might already know. 'I am Zephyr.' It was the first time I'd spoken it aloud; saying it made it true. 'I come from Karazan.' A light flickered deep in his eyes. 'Meirion sent me.' He nodded at the name.

'I have come for Zenith.' There was something unsettling in his face now . . . something too deep and complex for me to read.

He spoke haltingly, as if reciting something he'd been taught long ago, each unfamiliar word falling awkwardly from his lips. 'Show me the sign.'

There was only one thing it could be. I drew my ring out from under my shirt and held it up for him to see, gleaming in the firelight. He nodded once. 'Come.'

★

He led me away from the hearth into the darkness beyond, my footsteps keeping time with the beat of my heart in the stillness. We came to a path bordered by flickering torches and followed it, soft-footed; and as we walked I realised the sound I was hearing wasn't my heart, but the rhythmic beat of a single drum in the darkness.

Then out of the night came another sound: a high, wavering ululation; women's voices tangling and parting, twining and unfurling in a lament that wound up towards the stars like a prayer. Part of my spirit twisted upwards with their song – and in that moment, deep in my soul, I knew what I was going to find.

We came to a simple hut made of woven branches. A ring of torches surrounded it; beyond them, invisible in the night, wove the circle of song. There was no door, only a low archway leading into darkness.

Jabula touched me lightly on the shoulder and left me. I stood for a moment alone under the ceiling of stars, the silver moon rising, the golden one already low in the night sky. I bent and entered.

An earthen floor beneath my hands, swept clean; a smouldering wigwam of twigs sending a whisper of fragrance into the still air. And on the far side, a shape huddled motionless on a low bed. On hands and knees I crept closer. It was dark . . . too dark to see anything but a tangle of whiteness, the faint outline of a cheek. There was a tang of something in the air, a sourness the incense couldn't hide, like ashes from a dying fire. Then the figure stirred and turned towards me. I saw skin faded grey, pleats and wrinkles folded in on themselves by time, a pale halo of crinkled hair, eyes quick and bright in sunken sockets.

'So, at last you come. Almost too late.' It was a woman's voice, with the querulous crack of extreme old age, but an edge that told me the mind was sharp and clear.

'Who are you?'

'I am Temba. Mother of the Chief.'

'You speak English . . .'

'I speak the tongue of the Lost People, and the tongue of the Borderlands and beyond – though I have not spoken it these fifty years, and will not speak it again.'

'You knew I'd come.'

'I prayed you would not.'

Everything was still. I whispered the words. 'Why? Where is he?'

'Dead.' The single word fell like a stone into the silence.

I couldn't speak; barely felt the skinny claw creep from the folds of fur and find my hand.

'The mage brought him here: a speck of a thing hardly a day old. My own son was suckling – Jabula, chief-child – but I had milk enough for two.

'*Keep him for me*, Meirion said. *Keep him safe and guard him well, and treat him as your own.* And we did.'

'What . . .' I swallowed. 'What –' My voice cracked.

'What became of him? Two sons, one born, one

217

given, but a few days separating them. Jabula pulled struggling and screaming into the world, kicking, walking, running before the first nine moons were past: a quick mind and strong body to match it; his father's son. I loved him for his strength . . . love him still.

'But the babe Meirion brought . . . I loved him more. He was not my birth-child, but I loved him for his weakness, his frailty, though I knew it doomed him. Slow, so slow to everything . . . yet so perfect. There have been other infants like him, in the annals of the tribe, where growth does not keep pace with the journey of the days.'

'You're saying there was something . . . wrong with him?'

'At half a year the elders were muttering among themselves. I kept him hidden as best I could, pretended nothing was amiss . . . but always there was his breast-brother beside him, a dancing flame to his still shadow. The mind –' she was talking to herself now, her words far away and full of pain – 'the mind was whole! I knew it with a mother's heart – saw the spirit shine from his eyes, bright as fire. But at a year, he was not able even to crawl upon his hands and knees, just lay and smiled at me. *Treat him as your own*, Meirion said . . . and we did.'

I stared at her, unable to look away from those dark eyes gazing back into the past.

'It is the way of our people. A hut was woven for him and ringed with fire; the songs of our ancestors offered him up to the stars. And at daybreak we left him.'

'You left him? A little baby, helpless and alone?'

'He was doomed! Ours is a harsh life, the land of Limbo bitter and unforgiving. The frail, the crippled, the ill, the old – all come to it in time. Oh, I begged, do not think I let him go easily . . . but none can argue with the ancient ways of the Tribe and the laws of the desert land.

'*Treat him as your own*, Meirion said – and we did . . . we did.'

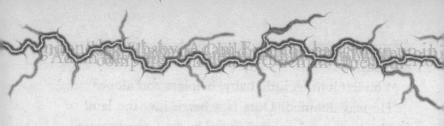

A GIFT FROM BLADE

L ater – how much later I don't know – I found myself alone in the darkness, my larigot in my hand. The golden moon was setting over the far horizon.

I put my larigot to my lips and played: a farewell to the brother I had never known and the mother who loved him, my song mingling with the lament of the women and the wailing cry of gathering wolves. I played until the silver moon shone high and cold alone in the sky, fading with the dawn.

At first light we went our separate ways, a single hut marking the place the camp had been, the Lost Tribe of Limbo a straggle of dark figures melting into grey distance.

None looked back.

'Where have you *been*?' Jamie's voice was an indignant squawk. 'Borg's been ropeable! It's after dinnertime on the *second day*, and you promised Lyulf –' He broke off and stared at me, eyes wide. 'What . . . where's . . .'

'Later, Jamie. Adam needs to sit down and have something hot to drink.' I started to shake my head, but Rich took my arm and drew me to the campfire. 'You do and you will, whether you want to or not.'

I sat; took the cup of hot broth Kenta pressed into my hands. Sipped it and gazed into the fire, dimly aware of Rich taking the others aside and whispering to them.

Borg stumped up and stood glaring down at me, arms akimbo. He looked far from pleased, but a smouldering excitement beneath his scowl told me he had something different on his mind. 'So you're back. High time too – we have our first tournament tomorrow. Gather round, all of you!' The others clustered round, Blue-bum clambering onto my lap and chittering up into my face with an anxious monkey frown. The Masked Man took up his place on the far side of the fire, Blade beside him; Lyulf settled on a log with his usual cat-like grace.

'Tomorrow we enter our first town,' growled Borg. 'None of our seasoned gladiators are sufficiently recovered to fight – which means it's down to you, for better or worse. Tomorrow, your lives as gladiators begin in earnest. If you perform well, riches and even fame await. If you do not . . .' he paused, then drew a flat hand across his throat and made a gurgling sound. 'As first-time performers, there are a number of things you need to know. Firstly, our entrance into town . . .'

I tried to concentrate on what Borg was saying, but

my brain was numb and the words – important as I knew they were – bounced off unheard.

But the hot broth was warming me, thawing something I'd thought frozen forever deep inside. The loss of Zenith changed everything . . . and yet it changed nothing. My quest was still the same. My mind groped blindly for the familiar words:

> When twain is one and one is twain
> Wind blows and sun shines forth again;
> When man is child and child is man
> True King will reign in Karazan.

Jamie had said they could only mean one thing, and at the time that meaning had seemed as clear as day. *The two of you need to be together again for everything to get back to normal.* But now Jamie's interpretation seemed childish, almost naïve in its simplicity . . . because now I saw there was another meaning.

First there had been one baby, then two . . . and now there was only one again.

And the child I'd been only a day ago had transformed overnight into a man – a man in whose hands alone rested the future of Karazan.

'You have all learned well.' Lyulf's voice brought me back to the present. Borg's briefing was over; he and the Masked Man were gone, the fire burned down to glowing embers. 'Put your trust in your skill and you will have nothing to fear.'

Blade stood, reaching into the leather pouch that hung at her waist. She seemed different: lit up inside with a radiance that shone from her dark eyes like candles. She moved round the circle, giving something to Kenta, then Gen. 'Here.' Her words were deliberately offhand, but we knew her well enough to tell that this was important. 'These are for you.'

My turn came. She pressed something small and soft into my palm and closed my fingers round it, holding my hand for a moment in her firm, cool grip. Her eyes met mine in a smile. 'Courage and strength, Whistler,' she said softly, and moved on.

I opened my hand. There in my palm was a soft leather drawstring bag on a thong.

'Our talismans . . .' Kenta murmured. Borg, Blade and Lyulf all wore them: it was no secret that Borg kept the keys to the weapons chests in his, a symbol of his authority he flaunted at every opportunity. We'd never seen Blade without hers, or Lyulf without his scuffed suede one, as much part of him as his rough red hair – but we had no idea what was in them.

'Your talismans,' agreed Blade cheerfully. 'I have crafted them for you – the only time I ever willingly wield a needle rather than a sword.' She was suddenly serious. 'Choose what you keep in them with care.'

'What kind of thing should it be?' Jamie wondered, opening his up and peering hopefully inside.

'Your luck,' said Lyulf grimly, 'whatever that may be.'

*

223

I offered to take first watch, stoked up the fire and sat quietly watching the flames. Any luck I had was inside me, but I knew what I'd keep in my leather pouch. My ring; a whisker from a little cat in a far-away world; a grey striped feather that could mean something . . . or nothing.

A voice spoke quietly beside me. Lyulf. I hadn't heard him come – but who ever did? 'You did not find what you sought?'

'No. And yet . . . perhaps I did.'

'We do not always search for that which we are meant to find.'

We watched the fire together in silence. Then we spoke, at the same moment, almost the same words:

'I'm going to have to leave –'

'I will soon be moving on –'

We each broke off, gesturing to the other to go on; but it was me who continued, finding the words as I went along. 'I need to leave. There's something I have to do.'

'Will you take your companions with you?'

'I don't know. I'd like to – if they can come. But I have a feeling . . .'

'. . . that some paths are made to walk alone.'

I glanced at him. He was no stranger to those paths, I knew . . . and suddenly I wished I could talk to him, tell him about Zenith, my quest, everything.

A shadow shifted beyond the firelight. 'Our friend walks late,' Lyulf murmured. 'The shades of the wildlands hold no fears for him, it seems.' His tone changed. 'And what of the morrow, Whistler? Your friends take courage from you, you know – even Tornado.'

Two days before I'd have been a jumble of nerves, agog with queasy excitement at the prospect of putting my new-found skills into practice. But now I hardly cared; it was what lay beyond that was filling my mind. 'I don't know,' I admitted. 'One more day can't make much difference. I'll stay and fight with the others, I suppose. How about you? Will you fight too?'

'No. My fighting days are over.'

'But . . .'

'I am a teacher now, remember?' There was a smile in his voice. 'And if you learn nothing else from me, Whistler, learn this: every strength has a weakness, and even the creatures of darkest nightmare may be vanquished by the light.'

BLUNDERBUSS

Morning came – the morning of the gladiator tournament.

Blade and Lyulf gobbled down their bowls of burned porridge with gusto, but no one else seemed hungry. Even Blue-bum, whose only role consisted of collecting the takings, sniffed at his little dish and pushed it away. 'At least we've got a cast-iron excuse not to finish it today,' muttered Jamie, looking green.

'I feel the same as before an exam when I know I haven't done nearly enough work to scrape through,' agreed Rich queasily – and from the girls' faces I could see they felt the same.

We cleared the breakfast things away, Lyulf scraping bowl after bowl of uneaten porridge into the glonk manger without comment, to be hoovered up by Gloom, who'd eat anything.

As we were packing to leave Richard sidled up to me, his amulet in his hand. 'Adam, I was wondering . . . you know what Lyulf said last night, about luck?

Well, I don't really have any – not the sort you can put in a bag, anyhow. I was awake half the night worrying about it. That . . . and other things.' He flushed. 'Then I remembered: the magic mosaic that turns salt water fresh. That was lucky for me. And I wondered . . .'

'Of course you can have it.' I fished it out of my pocket and handed it over. 'I gave it to you before, remember . . . you just didn't take it.'

With a grateful grin Rich slipped it into his pouch and headed off to pack his stuff, his confident swagger back in place.

Borg had been banging about impatiently, swearing and snarling and getting in everyone's way. 'Right – gather round!' he barked when we were finally ready. All we were taking was the trailer – the caravans would stay where they were in the shelter of the trees, guarded by the men. 'Remember, we don't know who you'll be pitted against. We'll begin with a demonstration bout to warm up the crowd; then, if we're the only troupe, we'll invite challenges from the public. In that case the combat will not be to the death – unless the challenger wins, of course.' He gave a wolfish smile. 'If there is another circus in town, the ringmaster and I will set up bouts between evenly matched contestants, based on our assessment of your abilities.'

'Lyulf's assessment, he means,' whispered Blade. 'Don't worry – Lyulf won't let you fight anyone you're not ready for.'

'And at worst, you will fight each other.'

227

'*What?*' Rich was on his feet, aghast. 'Fight each other? We *won't*!'

The crooked corner of Borg's mouth twisted. 'It states in your contract that you will,' he snarled. 'And remember – a carnival atmosphere will draw good crowds and loosen purse-strings. I want to see smiles and laughter, not long faces. Anyone would think you were headed for a funeral! The Whistler has his instrument, and for the rest of you . . .' He flung open the lid of a wooden chest on the tailgate of the trailer. A jumble of percussion instruments filled it.

Blade stepped forward and took up a tambourine; Lyulf the wooden xylophone. 'Bags I the drum!' said Rich, 'I can bang that as well as anyone.' Kenta chose castanets and Gen a triangle, and Jamie the brass cymbals. Even Blue-bum scrambled up and peered inside, but all that was left was a battered-looking pair of old gourds. He picked one up and shook it, giving a chitter of approval at the unexpectedly loud rattling sound.

So – on the surface at least – it was a festive parade that made its discordant way towards the town. Borg stamped along at the front, twisted smile fixed in place, looking more like a crazed axe-murderer than ever; at the rear, in charge of the trailer with its grim-looking cargo of coffin-shaped caskets, strode the Masked Man, his expression hidden as always, his thoughts impossible to guess.

By the time we reached the centre of the town we'd

attracted every man, woman and child in the village the way a magnet draws iron filings: they crowded round, pretty girls casting us demure glances from under their lashes, men muttering and pointing and fingering their purses, little children staring at us and giggling at Blue-bum, then shrieking and rushing away to hide behind their mothers, who stood on the fringes of the crowd tut-tutting and craning their necks for a better view.

The village green was our first real reminder that we were deep in the Borderlands, where gladiatorial sports ruled. Instead of the usual smooth expanse of grass and few scattered trees, a deep bowl-shaped depression had been excavated in its centre, its flat bottom thickly strewn with sawdust. The prime spots on the sloping sides were already taken, mostly by boys about our age jostling for position, yelling comments, whacking each other with wooden swords and generally larking about like anyone given a day off school to watch a circus.

On one side of the arena a steep-sided cutting gave access to a kind of backstage area for the gladiators, divided into two – one for each opposing team, I assumed. Makeshift sackcloth screens gave some privacy, though at any time half a dozen grubby faces could be seen peering through, hissing urgent questions: 'Mister, mister, who be you?' 'What be your name, then?' 'Can I see your sword?' and – most often – 'What be your tally?', one it took me a moment to work out.

Borg and Lyulf erected a brightly painted billboard on top of the embankment, and in moments it was surrounded by a pushing, shoving mass of people. 'What does it say?' Gen quavered. 'What are they so keen to see?'

'The names of the contestants,' answered Blade over her shoulder, busy arranging our weapons for inspection by the officials. 'They hope to see ones that are known to them.'

'Lyulf – I mean Wolf Flame – is his name there?' asked Jamie in a loud whisper.

'Hush, Blunderbuss! Nay, nor has it been since he laid down his sword. The one time a ringmaster made the error of advertising Wolf Flame's presence he was gone by sundown, never to return. And he never fights now, of course, not since –' At that moment Lyulf appeared from nowhere with his customary suddenness, and Blade fell silent.

Well, I thought, if it's big names they're wanting they'll be disappointed . . . but I was wrong.

Soon there was a jostling crowd at the makeshift doorway, clapping and chanting, hooting and whistling. 'What do they want?' asked Kenta nervously. 'Why are they shouting?'

But as the chant settled into a steady rhythm, there could be no mistaking it: 'Blade! Blade! BLADE! *BLADE!*'

Blade blushed furiously and bent her head closer to the bright array of steel. But Lyulf put his hand on her shoulder. 'It is your moment of glory,' he said quietly;

'and well earned. Go to them – I will take care of the swords.'

Borg was striding up and down the top tier of the grandstand, bellowing fearsomely. 'Roll up! Roll up, friends and townsfolk! This is your chance to see the skills of the most famed gladiator troupe in the Borderlands: *TROUPE TALISMAN*! Dig deep into your pockets, my friends, for the more you give, the harder my warriors will fight – and the more blood you will see flow! Where be the champions among you? Who has the courage to face the might of the Masked Man – the skill of the Whistler and Crystal? Who among you dares face the incomparable BLADE?'

'He's winding them up,' hissed Rich above the roar of the crowd. 'So far we're the only troupe – and if the villagers don't come to the party . . .' He was interrupted by a great clash that made the air tremble. Borg was holding up a massive circular shield; again and again he struck it with the hilt of his sword, a series of deep booms ringing out and silencing the crowd. I could see Blue-bum skipping over the crowd at head-height, hopping from shoulder to shoulder; he clambered down onto the stage dragging a leather helmet full of chinking silver coins, grinning and chittering as more coins pattered down all round him.

'Ladies and gentlemen, we are ready to begin! I am proud to announce our first bout, a demonstration of skill between the celebrated Blade . . .' the air shook with cheers and wolf-whistles as Blade strolled

nonchalantly out, raising her hand in casual acknowledgement of the uproar; 'and the sensational, the
spectacular . . . *Blunderbuss*!'

Jamie strutted onto the stage, pink-faced and
bowing to left and right. I blinked. There was a perky
confidence about him that didn't add up – even for a
demonstration bout, the Jamie we knew would have
been cowering under the trailer paralysed with terror,
not parading about as if he owned the show.

We stood staring as Jamie and Blade took up their
positions in the arena, turned to face the crowd and
bowed low. 'She won't hurt him . . .' Gen's voice was
the merest tremble '. . . will she?'

'Watch.' Lyulf's face was as expressionless, but
something in the set of his mouth made me wonder.
He knew something we didn't.

They turned to face each other, Blade slim and
upright in her customary black, poised for action, long
blade in her right hand, dagger in the left. She was
wearing a cloak, I noticed, which she'd never done
in practice.

As for Jamie . . . suddenly one of the few toys
there'd been at the orphanage popped into my mind.
Battered and faded, the paint long gone: a chubby
little wobble-man with a lead weight in his base that
made him bounce back up whenever you pushed him
over. One day someone threw him across the room
and the weight shifted, and from that moment on the
wobble-man never stood upright again. I pushed the
thought away.

Jamie had a short sword in one hand and a lightweight shield in the other. Now the cocky, confident expression had been replaced by one of almost comical terror. He held up the shield and peeked at Blade over the top. There were some boos and catcalls from the crowd. She advanced stealthily, leading with her right foot, narrow-eyed; Jamie backed away. Their swords touched – left-right-left – and then Blade brought the flat of her sword down on Jamie's head with what looked like enough force to shatter his skull. Behind me I heard the girls gasp. Jamie keeled over like a skittle – and then he was somersaulting backwards like a roly-poly piece of tumbleweed, Blade – caught wrong-footed – chasing after him. Next instant, impossibly, he was on his feet again, bouncing up as if he had springs in his legs; he leapfrogged over the crouching Blade and spun to face her. Now Blade was moving more cautiously, circling him warily, keeping her distance. The crowd was utterly silent.

Then Jamie darted in, seeming to catch Blade by surprise – and he was gone. I blinked. Blade was staring round in disbelief; slowly, weapons at the ready, she circled, scanning the arena. Suddenly among the crowd there was a murmur; then a ripple of delighted laughter. An extra pair of booted feet was protruding from beneath Blade's cloak, circling in exact time with hers. A grin pasted itself over my face – and I understood.

'It's a clown show!' whispered Gen. 'A carefully choreographed clown show – *that's* what they've been practising all this time!' Jamie had ducked out from his hiding place, and Blade had turned and seen him. The chase was on; it was clear whose side the crowd was on – and it wasn't Blade's.

One outrageous move followed the next, Jamie bouncing out of trouble time after time with a beleaguered Blade in hot and hopeless pursuit. Gradually, impossibly, it was Jamie who was getting the upper hand. Blade was engulfed in her own cloak, groping blindly for her adversary . . . A wicked death-lunge from her dagger skewered nothing more fatal than an apple Jamie happened to have in his pocket . . . Jamie's shield, sword inserted in a special slit, was sent spinning in pursuit of Blade round the arena, Jamie puffing behind . . . and then too soon it was over, a beaming Blade presenting Jamie, pink-faced and victorious, to the howling crowd.

Coins rained into the arena and the cry rang out again and again, a rolling tidal wave of sound: 'BLUNderBUSS! BLUNderBUSS!' The noise was deafening.

I guess that's why we didn't hear the rumble of wheels as the wagons rolled down the cobbled street behind us. It was only when the chant broke up and trailed away to silence that we followed the gaze of the crowd and saw the still figure silhouetted against the sky.

Another circus had come to town.

THE CIRCUS OF BEASTS

'So – you applaud this mockery of the noble circus arts.' Scorn flooded the arena like ice water. Jamie's grin froze on his face and he dropped his upraised arms to his sides as if he'd been slapped. I glanced at Blade: there was an absolute stillness about her that sent a stab of fear through me. Instinctively I looked across at Lyulf; his face was set in stone. *They knew this man – whoever he was.*

'Are you men – or children?' The voice was a whip-lash. Faces that had been open and laughing moments before were covered in confusion, eyes downcast as if they were ashamed. 'Are you proud Borderlanders, thirsty for blood, or milk-sucking merchants of the Coastlands?'

The mood of the crowd was changing – had already changed. And Blade knew it. She was edging Jamie towards the exit, hoping no one would notice their departure.

'So be it.' The stranger shrugged. 'If foolery and horseplay amuse you, this is no place for me. I will move on . . . and take the Circus of Beasts with me.'

A ripple ran through the crowd. A voice rang out, followed by another, and another: 'Stay! STAY! The Circus of Beasts! *THE CIRCUS OF BEASTS!*'

The man raised his arms in a gesture that mirrored Jamie's moments before, and the crowd stilled. 'Those who wish me to stay, say *Aye*.'

'AYE!'

He put a hand to his ear. 'Did you speak? I thought I heard the wind whispering in the treetops ... Those who wish to see the Circus of Beasts, say *Aye!*'

'*AYE!*' The barrage of sound was followed by a vacuum of silence, every eye on the stranger.

There was a hand on my arm ... Lyulf. 'We're leaving. Help pack up – quick.' Something in his voice told me there was no time for questions. Already Rich and Jamie were piling the weapons back into the chest, Kenta and Gen hustling Gloom into his harness, fastening the buckles with fingers clumsy with haste. Only Borg was still staring into the arena, Blade beside him, tense as a bowstring. But the Masked Man ... where was he?

Lyulf grabbed Blade's arm and spun her round. 'Come. We're going – now.'

'But I –'

'*Now!*'

I picked up an armful of musical instruments and headed for the wagon ... and the man's voice went on, cutting across the silent arena. 'But wait – let us not forget we have another gladiator troupe in town.

The most famed gladiator troupe in the Borderlands, I believe: Troupe Talisman. Who here would wish to see a battle to the death between beast and human, between the invincible Candalupus and mortal man? Who here would wish to see entrails spilled – carnage and destruction – bloody defeat – glorious victory? Who here –' His voice was drowned in a deluge of sound.

'Adam, come *on*!' Gen's eyes were wide and scared in her white face.

'Who *is* he?'

'Thrax.' Lyulf's single word fell like the blow of an axe. 'We must leave while we can.'

But it was already too late. 'But will any among the famed gladiators of Troupe Talisman be man – *or woman* – enough to accept the challenge?'

I saw Blade step forward, as if in slow motion. Her voice rang out over the crowd, slicing the air like a sword. 'I will.'

'No!' I couldn't bring myself to look at Lyulf, but Blade turned to face him, her eyes burning with a terrible, fierce joy.

'*Yes!*'

Already the crowd was chanting: 'Blade! *Blade!* BLADE! *BLADE!*'

She stepped into the arena, lithe as a panther, proud as a lioness . . . and even from where I stood there was no mistaking the flash of triumph in the stranger's eyes.

★

We had no idea what kind of creature it was that Blade would fight.

Feeling sick, Richard and I parted the sacking and peered through, but all we could see were massive shrouded cages with steel-shod wheels drawn by great beasts like shaggy oxen. They spilled out into the street behind and out of sight. And the sounds . . . the sounds coming from them made the hair at the back of my neck stand on end. Growls and grunts and guttural roars; the creaking of wood strained almost to breaking point by the weight it bore; the crunch of steel on crumbling cobblestones – and the stench of festering wounds and raw excrement.

We huddled together in the entranceway. My mouth felt dry; my heart had gone lopsided. 'What's a Canda . . . Canda . . .' Richard was whispering.

'Candalupus,' said Jamie automatically . . . and then a quiet voice spoke just behind us: Lyulf.

'Circuses such as these are peopled by age-old creatures of myth and legend, and by newer forms that have mutated. And now there are yet more terrible beasts: monsters of the imagination, spawned I know not where, and the Candalupus is among them. They say it is half an armoured creature like a bear, half wild wolf-dog . . .'

'Karazeel's monster!' Jamie's eyes were like saucers. 'Remember, on the computer.'

I remembered. But nothing could have prepared me for the reality. The creature we'd seen at Quested Court had been small enough to fit on a computer screen, then – shrunk down and cloned – as tiny as a marble. There'd been no way of telling what size it would be in real life . . . but I guess I'd thought it might be my height at most.

There was a hoarse shout behind us and a spine-chilling rattle of chains. '*Make way! Give way if you value your lives!*' A roar rent the air; the ground shook. I threw my arms out, pressing the others back against the earthen wall. We froze there, staring.

The creature lumbering towards us would have dwarfed a rhinoceros. It moved four-footed with an awkward, rolling gait, and as it passed it turned its head, stared me straight in the eyes and snarled. The head was shaggy and wolf-like, overlapping scales interspersed with moulting fur that hung in shreds. Black lips peeled back from yellow fangs the size of sabres. The eyes that met my own were blood-red and burning, radiating savagery, hatred, hunger – yet I recognised in them a twisted, almost human intelligence. Here was a creature in which the worst of man and beast had been merged.

A tick-infested mane of coarse hair gave way to overlapping plates that covered the rest of its body and legs. The scales were tarnished gold and rigid-looking, narrowing from the depth of a hand near their base to finger-thickness at the scalloped edge. I had no idea what they could be made of – something like tortoiseshell or horn, perhaps. But as the creature shambled past it made a squealing, grinding sound that set my teeth on edge: a sound like a thousand knives being sharpened. The scales were metal. Armour, thick and impenetrable.

The weight of it made the ground shake. I quailed to think of the strength it must take to move that giant body, the strength that would soon be pitted against the slender form of Blade.

'Lyulf,' I croaked as the monster vanished into the arena; 'Lyulf – we mustn't let her. Can't you –'

We were standing shoulder to shoulder. He didn't turn his head. 'Have you ever tried to stop Blade doing something she wants to do?' His voice was flat, expressionless.

'No, but . . . she can't *want* –'

'It is more than a want. This is in her blood: what she lives for. I am not her master – no man is. Blade will do as she pleases. All we can do is watch – and pray.'

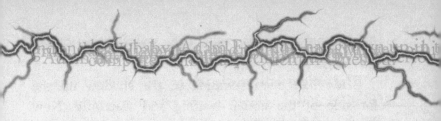

FIRST BLOOD

We stood on the high bank above the cutting and watched.

The Candalupus shuffled to a halt in the centre of the arena; behind it, at a safe distance, followed a man cradling something in his arms, swathed in a cloth that even from this distance reeked of rancid oil. Something heavy, by the look of it . . .

He circled the beast warily, pulled the cloth away and proffered what it had hidden. It was a weapon, the length of a long-sword but broad and heavy, made of dark, dull metal. Vicious-looking curved serrations ran down both edges of the blade like a double-edged saw. I stared, sickened, as the creature reached for a weapon it couldn't possibly need: its groping talon was armed with claws that could have disembowelled a man with a single sweep. The creature rose awkwardly to its full height, fumbling two-handed with the weapon for a firmer grip. I felt a glimmer of hope. Lethal as those clawed talons might be, they weren't made for holding a sword.

'And he is slow and clumsy, and will be quick to

tire,' Lyulf murmured beside me. *Every strength has a weakness . . .*

Blade had been standing in the shadow on the far side of the arena, waiting and watching. Now she strode forward, a spring in her step, head held high. She drew her sword with a ringing hiss of steel; silver flashed in the sunlight. With her free hand she unbuckled her sword-belt and tossed it aside, drew her dagger and moved towards the monster, her body falling naturally into a crouching guard, weapons crossed.

The Candalupus roared and rocked from side to side, scraping its great clawed feet through the sawdust. Slowly it advanced. Just as slowly Blade backed away, never taking her eyes from the apparition that towered before her, circling to draw it after her and avoid being trapped against the side of the arena.

Suddenly, too fast for the eye to follow, a bright blade flashed out and there was the ringing clash of steel on metal; then Blade was leaping out of range again, both sword and dagger in her left hand, opening and closing the right as if to regain the feeling. She'd struck out, trying to penetrate that armour . . .

And now the monster was after her, lurching forward with great, grunting strides. His weapon swung like a scythe, one of his steps equalling four of hers. Blade back-pedalled swiftly, drawing him after her, her right arm hanging limp. Suddenly she tripped and fell backwards, just as Jamie had done . . . and with a roar the great beast was over her, sword raised for the death-blow.

Faster than light Blade's limp hand sprang to life and grasped her sword; thrust up from underneath, between the overlapping plates of armour on the monstrous thigh. As easily as a knife into butter the slender sword slid home, deep into the bowels of the beast.

A roar of rage and pain shook the stadium. A stumbling step back, and the mighty hacksaw smashed down in a cloud of dust and purple blood. I wanted to close my eyes but could only stare transfixed as the Candalupus staggered in a drunken circle, snarling and gnashing its teeth, rooting for its prey.

Then I saw her, on the far side of the arena. No sooner had she struck the blow than she must have rolled and sprung away; the saw-toothed sword had fallen on empty ground. The blood was the monster's. Now, groaning and slavering, it was hobbling across the arena after her. Blade's sword-hilt protruded from its inner leg, angled sharply upward, slick with sticky blood.

Closer and closer it came, and still Blade stood her ground. The only weapon she had now was her dagger, and to use it she'd have to be close . . . too close.

Up came a hand; the wrist flicked, as if tossing sand into the creature's eyes. The great head twitched back; he blinked, raised one arm to his face and gave a roar of agony. Blade stood poised, out of reach, watching empty-handed.

It seemed to take a long, long time for him to fall. It was as if the realisation that he was dead – beaten by a creature a tenth his size – took longer than the steel blade of the knife to penetrate his slow brain. But finally he swayed, took one unsteady step back . . . and fell. He hit the ground with an impact that shook the stadium like an earthquake. He lay still, his purple blood soaking into the sawdust.

Silence stretched on. At last the first voice came, reed-thin, uncertain: 'Blade! Blade!' Others joined it: 'BLADE! BLADE!' Then the arena was pounding with the chant, like the beating of a gigantic heart: *'BLADE! BLADE! BLADE!'*

Wearily, with dragging feet, she made her way towards us. If there was joy in victory, you couldn't see it. Her vanquished opponent lay face to the sky, one outstretched hand still clinging to the sword. She walked past him as if he wasn't there.

And then it happened. With the speed of a snake, the monster rolled and struck. The barbed edge of his sword bit deep into Blade's back, any sound it might have made swallowed by the chanting of the crowd.

For me, it was as if suddenly the whole arena was silent. All I saw was Blade falling, graceful as a swan, seeming to float down to rest on the soft sawdust as if it were a cloud.

FIRE-TONGUE

We took her back to our campsite, pale and still as death. Lyulf carried her like a baby into her small caravan. Though the Masked Man made a gesture as if to help, he would let no one else touch her. The five of us stood in a silent cluster outside, waiting, Kenta hugging Blue-bum close for comfort.

After what seemed a long time the door opened slowly. Lyulf stood there; he must have drawn the curtains, because the room beyond was dark and still. There was something lost about him – the first sign I'd seen of the child that lay beneath his hard exterior. He raised both hands in a small gesture of helplessness.

It was Richard who spoke. 'Is she . . .'

Lyulf shook his head. 'Her clothes . . . I can't . . .' His voice cracked.

It was Kenta who understood. Stepped forward, and gently took his arm. 'Of course you can't. Gen and I will do it. Go with Adam and Richard, light a

245

fire and boil some water; we'll call you as soon as we can.'

At last Gen came to fetch us, her face grim; she met my eyes and gave her head a tiny shake. Together we squeezed into the single room of the caravan and stared down at Blade, our eyes adjusting to the gloom. She was lying on her front, head turned towards us, eyes closed. The girls had undressed her; a light woollen blanket covered her from the waist down. The right-hand side of her slender back was coffee-cream and perfect, smooth muscle a silken covering over a tracery of ribs. But the left side . . .

Kenta was speaking, her voice steady and matter-of-fact. 'I've checked as best I can that nothing's been left in the wound, but the impact seems to have driven fibres from her clothes . . .' she swallowed, and carried determinedly on. 'It won't stop bleeding. We need to apply pressure, but her ribs are broken, and I'm scared they might puncture . . . And the sword has left stuff inside, like grease; it has a strange smell. Once the water's cooled we'll swab it, but we need antiseptic, antibiotics . . . she probably ought to have a tetanus shot . . .' Her voice trailed away.

None of us looked at each other. What Blade really needed was a sip of healing potion . . . but there wasn't any.

At last Lyulf spoke, in a mutter almost to himself. 'Fire-tongue . . . how can it be that we have still not come upon it? Yet it grows this far south . . .'

He turned to us. 'Do you know it? It also goes by the name of wound-wart; it slows bleeding and banishes the ill humours that cause a wound to fester.'

'We don't know it,' said Jamie staunchly, 'but we'll find some, if you tell us where to look. You can stay and take care of Blade.'

The terrible flatness had left Lyulf's eyes. He lifted one hand and rested it for a moment on Blade's tangled hair. 'Look for a straggly low-growing bush – you will think it a weed. It bears long seedpods that turn from green to red as the season advances . . .'

'It sounds like capsicum – cayenne pepper!' said Rich. 'My Grannie grows it in her veggie patch and puts it in everything. It burns like the blazes.'

'Fire-tongue! That'll be it!' yipped Gen. 'Let's not waste any more time – and don't worry, Lyulf, we'll be back in a flash!'

But we weren't. The afternoon wore on into evening, and still we searched. Once Rich found a plant he thought might be right, but all it had were a few green nubs that might or might not grow into seed pods – given a month or so. All of us would have given up hours before if it hadn't been for the thought of the look in Lyulf's eyes when we returned empty-handed.

It was almost dark when we heard a sudden excited chitter from Blue-bum, followed by a cheeping call he'd never made before. I ran towards the sound, hearing the others hurrying through the undergrowth,

247

and there he was skipping round, a whole plant uprooted in his hand. He clambered up my arm, scattering dirt from the loose roots, and shoved it triumphantly in my face.

Lyulf was right, it did look like a weed – except it was covered in crinkly tongue-shaped pods, ranging in colour from green to deep, glossy scarlet. 'That's it for sure!' I crowed.

'Yes – clever boy, Blue-bum!' Jamie said.

'But naughty boy for pulling it up by the roots,' scolded Rich with a grin. 'My Grannie'd have something to say to you if she was here.'

Blue-bum chittered crossly and made a digging motion with one hand, patting with the other. Kenta gave Rich an exasperated look. 'Will you never learn to trust poor Blue-bum, Richard? We're going to take it back and plant it in a pot, so it'll always be there if it's needed – aren't we, Blue-bum?'

We turned back towards the camp, darkness thickening around us. Now that the first excitement of our success had faded we were all uncomfortably aware of where we were, and Lyulf's warnings about the dangers of the wildlands seemed very real.

Kenta was especially quiet, her face closed as she hurried beside me at the front of the group. Of all of us she was the only one with any medical knowledge, and I didn't dare ask how bad she thought Blade's injuries might be.

We'd wandered further than I thought in our search, but at last I saw a copse of trees that looked familiar, and the heavy feeling in my chest lightened. We were nearly there.

Suddenly Blue-bum made a low vibrating sound almost like a growl. Something about it froze Kenta and me in our tracks. 'What is it, Blue-bum? What have you seen?' Kenta whispered.

Every sense on edge, I stared round in the darkness, my ears straining for whatever sound Blue-bum might have heard, whatever movement he might have seen in the shadows. And then I smelled it, the merest whiff on the still air: a cloying, maggoty smell of corruption and decay.

'It's them – the Faceless!' Gen breathed. 'Quick – run for the camp!'

We ran. It was just ahead in the next group of trees: the brightness of the fire, the safety of the others. Rich was in the lead; I forced myself to slow, staying behind the others as rearguard. I could almost feel the icy breath on the back of my neck . . . I ran on, my pack bumping on my back, cursing myself for setting out without a weapon, not daring to look round.

Rich, Gen, Jamie, then Kenta and Blue-bum disappeared into the trees. I crashed after them, not caring how much noise I made. They'd be there now, in the clearing with the others, safe from whatever was coming after us . . .

I reached the clearing. Stopped, staring. The others were there, faces blank with shock.

Where the camp had been, the caravans, the men,

the glonks, the blazing fire . . . now there was nothing. We needn't have run. Nothing was coming after us.

It had already been – and gone.

LYULF'S LUCK

There was nothing left. Just trampled grass, a scatter of ashes, a scrap of fabric I recognised from Blade's black cloak . . . and on the ground where her caravan had been, a dark splash of blood.

Those that roam the wildlands are taken . . . though the circus arts protect us, they put us most at risk. The five of us away, Blade injured and Lyulf at her bedside . . . Borg, the Masked Man and the wounded fighters had been no match for them. They were gone, all of them, right down to Gloom and the glonks – gone to the Realms of the Undead and whatever fate awaited them.

'Well,' said Gen, 'thank goodness we have our rucksacks with us.'

'Yeah – and the good thing is, there's nothing to pack,' said Richard.

'But there's no point setting off in the dark,' Kenta said.

'You're right,' Jamie agreed. 'I vote we make a fire, get some rest and go after them at first light.'

'And at least we've got matches and some food. Jamie's right – we should get all the rest we can,' said Gen.

I stared round at the faces of my four friends – at Blue-bum's face, monkey-mouth set in a determined line. *Some paths are made to walk alone*, Lyulf had said. But – for me, for the time being at least – this wasn't one of them.

We were looking for wood, taking care to stay close together, when I saw it: the colour of the earth, half-hidden by dirt and dry leaves. Kneeling, I brushed the soil away; lifted it and held it in the palm of my hand. Lyulf's amulet.

He wore it always – had been wearing it last time we'd seen him, in Blade's caravan. Scuffed suede, worn smooth with use and time. It was strangely heavy, and as I weighed it in my fingers I felt something slide and chink inside. The thong was broken. Lyulf's luck. Whatever it was, it had run out.

I showed it to the others by the campfire.

'We'll give it back when we find them,' said Rich.

Jamie gave it a sidelong look and said nothing.

There was a silence; then Blue-bum gave a little chitter that sounded almost embarrassed.

'Ignore him,' grunted Rich. 'It's none of our business.'

'Although it couldn't do any harm . . . and it might

252

give us a clue about what's happened – where they've been taken,' said Kenta.

'Hardly likely to be a clue in Lyulf's talisman,' Rich growled.

'But maybe there is. Maybe he pulled it off deliberately,' Gen said.

Suddenly everyone was looking at me. 'It's private,' I said slowly. 'If it was mine, I wouldn't want whoever found it looking inside. But we're not just anyone; we're his friends. And perhaps . . .' They watched me in silence. The certainty was growing stronger, stronger by the second. 'Perhaps we're meant to know.'

Slowly I loosened the neck of the little bag. The drawstring was tight, the thin leather biting deep into the holes. A long time had passed since Lyulf had opened it. At last it was open. I looked round the circle of faces, checking one last time. I hoped my instinct was right: that I was doing the right thing. I tipped the contents of the bag out onto the palm of my hand.

There, gleaming in the dark, lay the missing golden half of the Sign of Sovereignty, and a silvery arrowhead that glowed with a pale fluorescence like moonlight.

THE EDGE OF THE WORLD

'I t's him.'

'But I thought Richard said the Lost Tribe –'

'It's him.'

'What about the time difference, though? Surely he'd be –'

'It's him.'

'But Adam, how could –'

'Give the guy a break,' said Richard. 'I'd say Adam'd know his own brother.'

My heart had sprouted wings . . . and suddenly the words that had been choked up inside were tumbling from my mouth. 'I know it doesn't make sense, but Rich is right – I *do* know him. I knew him right from the start, deep down in my heart, just like I think he knew me – we just didn't realise it.

'Yes, they put him out to die – but he didn't. As for the time difference . . .' A huge, incredible joy was flooding my mind like sunlight, and with it came Meirion's words, their meaning suddenly clear: '*The twin moons of Karazan follow each their own orbit, one near, one far, tracing their own path through the skies; but*

254

at Sunbalance they rise together as one, silver and gold, a perfect pair balancing the heavens.'

'It ties in with the prophecy too,' Jamie said. *'When man is child and child is man . . .'*

'I've always thought twins had a kind of magic,' said Gen. 'If Lyulf had been some random person, an ordinary brother, he'd have aged in Karazan-years, the same as everyone else; but being a twin was a link so powerful it held him back to Adam's age.'

'The age of the firstborn . . .' murmured Kenta.

'But that'd be awful!' Rich protested. 'Everyone'd think . . .'

I was remembering Temba's words: *'The mind was whole! I knew it with a mother's heart – saw the spirit shine from his eyes, bright as fire. But at a year, he was not able even to crawl upon his hands and knees, just lay and smiled at me.'*

I must have spoken aloud; Kenta was staring at me, solemn-faced. 'That's why he was put out to die. Temba thought he was handicapped because at the age of one he wasn't even sitting up. But he wasn't really one. He was a little baby of only three months old, our time.'

'And there was that thing Blade said, remember?' Rich chipped in. 'When I opened my big mouth and made an idiot of myself . . . she said Lyulf had the skills of a swordsman five times his age . . .'

'Along with the speed and stamina of youth,' Gen finished. 'It was right there in front of us all the time. We just didn't see it.'

And something else made sense. Those anguished words I'd overheard in the firelight: Blade's whispered question: *What are you running from?* And Lyulf's reply: *The evil I battle is mine alone to face or flee, my curse mine alone to carry.*

How much had she known, or guessed?

And how must it have been for my brother to carry the burden of his secret for fifty long years – a curse whose reason he couldn't begin to guess at?

For two days we journeyed across the featureless desert of Limbo. We kept the sun on our right through the morning, stopped in whatever shade we could find when it was overhead, then pushed on till it sank below the left horizon and purple twilight spilled across the land.

For two dark, moonless nights we huddled by the fire, keeping watch in twos, the whispering of the wind merging with the far-off howling of wolves as the night wore on, and weaving its way through our dreams.

More than once I knew there was something – someone – beyond the glow of the fire. If I turned I'd see nothing, but in my mind's eye I could picture them: lithe, dark figures watching, just far enough away to remain hidden, just close enough to keep guard over us. Whatever the dangers of the wildlands, the silent sentinels of the Lost Tribe kept them at bay.

On the third day the wind changed direction, bringing with it something that brought Richard to a standstill, sniffing the air. 'Do you smell what I smell?' he asked with a grin. 'Grass!'

'You can't smell grass!' Jamie objected, then sniffed. 'Though now you mention it . . .'

It was true. After so long surrounded by dust and the occasional stone we could all smell it: a glossy golden succulence with an edge of sweetness that transported me in an instant back to the playing-field on sports day, the newly cut lawn prickling my legs.

By afternoon it was all round us: a billowing sea of grey-green, flocks of tiny birds with strident voices surfing the warm currents of air above. We waded through it, grinning like idiots, pulling long strands and nibbling the pale, tender ends.

'Where there's grass there must be water,' said Gen hopefully. Our bottles were almost empty, and even Rich's magic crystal wouldn't change dust into water.

We walked on further than usual in the hope she'd be right, but the ground was rising steadily instead of falling to a river valley, and soon our steps were dragging and it was almost too dark to see. 'I vote we stop,' said Jamie at last.

'Let's carry on to that next rise,' Kenta suggested. 'Who knows what's on the other side?'

On we plodded, Jamie in the lead, spurred on as always by the thought of dinner and an end to the day's journey. Suddenly he staggered as if he'd been shot and stumbled back with a hoarse cry of alarm, arms windmilling; dropped to his hands and knees and crawled backwards, whimpering.

'Stop right there, everyone!' We didn't need Rich to tell us. We were all rooted to the spot, hearts thumping – all except Gen. She hurried forward, bent double as if there might be an invisible sniper, and crouched beside Jamie. 'What is it, Jamie?' she asked, sharp-voiced with fright and worry.

'It's the edge!' Jamie was warbling. 'The edge of the world!'

'Rubbish!' scoffed Richard, striding up. 'Any excuse to stop, is all –'

He broke off, took a hasty step back and stood, arms folded, staring outwards. 'I'd stay away, guys,' he said over his shoulder. Carefully – *very* carefully – I shuffled up beside him.

Jamie was right: it was the edge of the world. The grassy plain stretched away on either side as far as we could see into the darkness, but ahead . . . ahead there was nothing. It was more than a cliff: two strides ahead the ground fell away as cleanly as if it had been cut with a knife. The grassy plain rolled to its edge – and ended. Below was swimming darkness.

'Maybe in the morning . . .' Kenta began.

'Well,' said Jamie from a safe distance, 'I vote we don't set up camp too close to the edge. What if one of us sleepwalks?'

With that uncomfortable thought in our minds we backtracked a full five minutes, then trampled ourselves a nest in the grass. We shared out a ration of water smaller than we would have liked, and snacked on some dry noodles and cold beef jerky – Jamie voted we didn't light a fire either, with all that grass around, and for once not even Richard argued.

Though no one mentioned it, I knew we were all thinking of that yawning drop and what lay beyond. If what Lyulf and Blade had told us was true, it was the end of the world. But we also knew that past it lay the Realms of the Undead, our friends and the end of our quest – so somehow, in the morning, we were going to have to figure out a way down.

Soon the others' whispers settled into regular breathing and snuffling snores. I tossed and turned, trying to get comfortable on the hard ground, a million miles from sleep. There was something missing, something I'd forgotten. What could it be? Was there something I should have thought of, or done? It hovered on the fringes of my mind, agonisingly close.

I lay back down, scowling up at the clouds. And suddenly it came to me: my thumb! How long had it been? I felt a pang of disloyalty. Hauled it out from under my sleeping bag, and popped it into my mouth. It tasted the same as ever – dirtier, with a kind of spiciness that was a hundred percent Karazan, but otherwise pretty much the way it always had. I settled back, waiting for it to mould to the exact shape of the roof of my mouth. But something wasn't quite right. Different . . . as if my thumb didn't slot into its old position quite the same. I gave it another couple of sucks, partly to be sure I wasn't imagining things, partly for old times' sake. Then I slipped it out and wiped it dry, locked my hands behind my head, and lay staring up at the pale blur of the moon.

I felt almost as if I should apologise to it – though what for, I wasn't sure. But deep down I knew it would understand. And one thing was for sure: it'd still be there, if ever I needed it again.

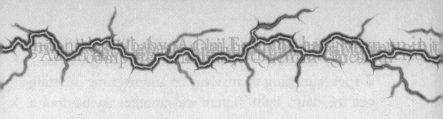

THUNDER IN THE DAWN

I was woken by the sound of thunder. It was just before dawn, when the air has that pearly greyness. But it wasn't thunder: it was an earth-quake. The ground under my cheek was shaking itself apart in a drumming vibration that brought Blue-bum diving headfirst into my sleeping bag. The girls sat up tangle-haired and wild-eyed; Jamie popped out of his sleeping bag like a gopher, chubby cheeks still rosy with sleep.

It was Rich who yelled the warning. 'Hit the deck – *now*!'

In the split second before I dropped to the ground my eyes took a flash-photo my befuddled brain, hazy with dreams and fizzing with adrenaline, refused to process.

Then it broke over us: a tidal wave of thundering giants that shook the earth, riding a hot whirlwind of air with a wild pungency that shot through me in a dizzying mixture of fear, disbelief and wonder.

Though my face was buried in my arms I was aware of their huge bodies stampeding past, massive hooves smashing down all round me like sledgehammers, missing my ears by a hair's-breadth; of great dark shapes launching themselves up and over me, blotting out the dawn light. There was another sound too, a soaring, rushing whoosh. Then as quickly as it had come, it was over.

A muffled voice came from the direction of Jamie's sleeping bag. 'Is it safe to come out now?'

I sat up warily. Before, our little nest had been a hollow in the grass, the tall stalks surrounding us like walls. Now the whole world was trampled flat. I stumbled to my feet and hobbled a few steps, my sleeping bag crumpled round my ankles, gazing after them.

'What was it?' Jamie quavered, his eyes and the tip of his nose peeking out. 'Is it coming back?'

'Horses. It was horses.' I could see them in the distance; they'd wheeled round, still galloping, far away and tiny, scattering, spiralling and regrouping like a flock of birds playing in the breeze.

'Whew!' Jamie was saying shakily. 'How lucky was that! They could've killed us!'

I narrowed my eyes, staring, only vaguely aware of the voices of the others.

'They wouldn't. Horses don't.'

'Well, they nearly did – one jumped right over me!'

'That's exactly it. If a horse sees you're there, it'll do just about anything to avoid standing on you. It happens in horse-racing all the time, with those pile-ups in steeplechases and things . . .'

So Karazeel had been wrong. He hadn't killed all the horses – there were still some left. This one herd at least, safe on the furthest fringes of the world.

I was about to turn away when a movement among the specks caught my eye. Something lifted, wheeled, then dropped again. Birds, massive ones, two of them, soaring above the herd. Chasing each other, coming together, then spinning apart; playing, or . . . fighting? They were too far away to tell.

'Don't worry, Adam, I don't think they'll come back,' Jamie was saying comfortingly. 'Look – the sun's coming up. Let's check out the cliff before breakfast, then work out how to tackle it while we eat. Come on!'

We stood in a solemn line a safe distance from the edge of the precipice and stared down in silence. There wasn't much to say.

The cliff face was perpendicular and smooth as glass. Way, way down was something I thought must be water – the light hadn't reached there yet, and it was too dark to tell. Further from the cliff face it turned patchy and broke up into a deeper darkness that disappeared into distance.

'It's clouds,' Rich croaked. 'Those paler billowy things are clouds. And beyond them, way down – that must be trees: the forest Blade told us about.'

I said nothing. It seemed to me the only way down would be to sprout wings and fly, but it didn't seem helpful to say so.

'Well,' said Gen after a pause, 'there must be a path or something. If that's where the Realms of the Undead are, and the others have been taken there, then there's a way down.'

'Gen's right. We just walk along the top till we find it.' Kenta didn't sound convinced.

'Maybe we're supposed to use Meirion's magic sail as a parachute?' hazarded Jamie.

'I don't know,' said Rich. 'I wouldn't want to be the one to try it. But standing here won't help. Let's eat. The answer's bound to come. It always does.'

But it didn't. We finished our dribble of water and dried apricots in gloomy silence, and all too soon Rich clambered to his feet and said, 'Well, I guess it's walk-along-the-cliff time, guys. How about a vote, Jamie: left or right?'

Then he frowned and tilted his head, listening. Turned, shading his eyes, gazing south. I was on my feet in a flash, heart hammering. I could hear it too. Hoof beats, coming closer.

I could see them now: three of them, two together in tight formation, the other right behind. They were heading straight for us. But there was something about the two bigger ones, something odd . . .

'Adam . . .' Jamie was quavering. I glanced at him. His face was grey and slack with fear.

'Don't worry, Jamie, they won't hurt us. Look at them, they're beautiful!'

264

As I said it, the impossible happened. The rear horse, a powerful white stallion, suddenly spread a massive pair of wings – and flew. My mouth dropped open. He rose in a steep climb, then plummeted like an eagle falling on its prey. As he dropped from the sky he let out a scream of rage.

The other two horses reacted instantly. The smaller one, running ahead, wheeled and raced back the way she'd come, ears flat against her head. I had a clear view of her as she turned: a filly, wingless, a dark dapple-grey with a star on her forehead, her silver tail rippling out behind her like silk. I saw her eyes roll with wild terror; then her haunches bunched and thrust, clods of earth flew, and she was gone.

The other horse spun to face its attacker. As the great stallion fell from the sky he rose to meet it, his own wings outspread, forelegs scything the air. Something about his lightness of foot and the way he held his head, his crazy courage and fierce pride, told me he was hardly more than a colt. The early morning sun gleamed on a coat glossy as a conker and flashed off wingtips blue-black as a starling's; his dark mane and tail flew in the breeze like the spray of a shimmering waterfall. He'd stolen the filly, or tried to – challenged the dominant stallion. And now he would pay.

I half expected the stallion to veer away at the last second, but he didn't. He dive-bombed the colt, smashing into him with a *thwack* that jarred us where we stood. The colt met the blow head-on, but the

265

impact threw him to the ground. Legs flashed as he scrambled to his feet again, but the stallion was on him, hooves slicing like cleavers, yellow teeth snapping like giant castanets.

Somehow the bay colt struggled free, spread his wings and in a single beat was airborne; now it was his turn to scream, a feral shriek with a fury that made my blood race. Then he swooped on the stallion, teeth bared, eyes rolling white.

They met in a confusion of flashing hide and flailing hooves, first one, then the other rearing skywards, necks snaking, teeth slashing and tearing. Suddenly it was over. The stallion wrested himself from the colt's fierce embrace and soared upwards, wheeling like a warplane once over his challenger with widespread wings and a final savage screech of warning before gliding in a lowering swoop after the far-off figure of the grey mare.

The colt galloped after him, nostrils flared. Twice he trumpeted a challenge before his pace broke to a lilting trot, then stumbled to a walk. He gazed into the distance, one foreleg held awkwardly, flanks heaving and head held high. His wings were half-spread, as if he was undecided whether to pursue the stallion or turn back; then at last, with a stretch and a shuffle, he folded them into place at his sides. Slowly, head jerking painfully with each step, he moved away in the direction the others had taken.

'He's hurt,' Kenta whispered. 'Look at him, he's limping.'

'He'll be OK,' said Rich. 'It's all in a day's work to him.'

I walked slowly over to the trampled battleground where the fight had taken place. Where the young horse had walked the golden grass was bent apart to make a V-shaped pathway – and all along one side the stems were slick with blood.

WINGS

'I'm going to help him.'

'Are you crazy, Adam? You can't! He's wild – he'd kill you as soon as look at you!'

'Nah, he's more scared of us than we are of him.' But for once Rich didn't sound very sure.

'The boys are both right,' said Kenta. 'He wouldn't let you near him, Adam, and even if he did, we don't have any healing potion.'

'But we do have something else.' I turned towards my bag, but Blue-bum had beaten me to it. He was already holding it up, leaves withered, pods shrunken and crinkly: the fire-tongue we'd found for Blade.

I found a clean tin mug, snapped off a pod and crushed it between my fingers. It crumbled easily to a fine, slightly gritty powder. 'A few more of these, then a trickle of water and we'll have a paste as good as any antiseptic.' Grinning, I held up my finger, covered in fine red dust. 'Anyone for a taste?'

'Adam, will you be serious?' said Gen. 'What about our quest, and the future of Karazan? What about Lyulf and Blade? She needs that fire-tongue more than anyone. You can't waste time chasing round after a wild horse when what we need to do is find a way down that cliff!'

Without thinking I licked my finger and instantly wished I hadn't. 'OK, guys,' I said, once I could talk again, 'here's a plan: you head off in pairs and hunt in both directions for a way down. I'll stay here and see if I can get near enough to put some of this on the colt's leg. There's plenty left for Blade. If I haven't managed it by lunchtime I'll give up, I promise. I can't just leave him.'

'Well, for goodness' sake be careful,' said Jamie as they headed off, Blue-bum an invisible rustle like a cane-rat in the long grass.

'You too,' I called after them. 'Don't fall over the edge!'

It felt wonderful to be alone under the pale bowl of sky.

I hunkered down and crushed half a dozen more seedpods, whistling between my teeth and trying to remember to keep my fingers out of my mouth; then tipped a few of our remaining drops of water onto the powder, mixing it carefully to the consistency of toothpaste. There was only about a tablespoonful – hopefully it'd be enough.

I rubbed my hands on my breeches and stood, stretching. For the first time I felt a niggle of doubt. Now what? I turned in a slow circle. The grass stretched away all round me, sloping up towards the cliff, and gently down in the direction the horse had disappeared. There was no sign of him anywhere.

The sun was warm on my shoulders. The lightest breeze sighed through the grass, harmonising with the twitter of birds feasting on the lacy grass heads. The sounds wove together to form a song in my mind: the song I'd been whistling moments before. I needed to finger it out on my larigot before I lost it . . . I settled cross-legged with my back facing the cliff. I had heaps of time, and I could keep watch for him while I played. I'd only be a minute. The first clear notes flowed out over the plain . . . and time ceased to exist.

I drifted back from the dream world of the music to the gentlest ruffling current of grass-scented breath on the back of my neck; a warm, whiskery tickle . . . My soul swelled in instant recognition. Hands steady, heart pounding, I played on.

Velvet lips nibbled softly at my hair. A goofy grin split my face. I lowered my larigot and waited. Out of the corner of my eye I saw a hoof the size of a soup-plate brush through the grass in a jerky hobble; another followed it, its edge suspended above the ground. As I watched, a ruby drop grew on its tip, swelled and fell. I sat like a statue.

The colt drifted past me, step by awkward step, head down, tearing at the grass as if he just happened to be passing. But his eye watched me, liquid velvet, luminous with curiosity. He circled slowly, bite by bite, till he was in front of me. Now I could see the narrow white blaze that zigzagged down his nose, shading to a whiskery shell-pink where it met his dark muzzle. He nosed at the grass with lips as sensitive as Blue-bum's paws. His forelock fell over his eyes in a silken cascade; he watched me through it steadily without a hint of fear.

Closer he came, and closer. Now I could feel the faint vibration as he tore at the grass; hear the rhythmic mashing of his teeth as he chewed. The fresh-grass smell mingled with the warm animal perfume of horse.

I was staring at him openly now. His limbs, so fine and strong; his coat, polished mahogany. His angel-wings, as natural a part of him as his swishing tail, folded on either flank, their tips crossing like a swallow's above his gleaming rump. Above the knee of his left foreleg was a single gash deep as an axe-blow, trickling a steady stream of blood.

At last he reached me, nuzzling my face, sharing sweet-scented breath. I blew softly into his nostrils, murmuring to him, kneeling in the cool, fragrant grass; rubbed the satin neck, combing the coarse hair back from his eyes with my fingers; ran my hand over the hot, damp hide under his mane.

Still talking softly, I reached for the mug and scooped the paste onto my finger; reached out and slowly, gently, smeared it deep into the wound. The colt threw up his head and backed away, his skin twitching as if a fly had settled on it. His ears flicked

271

back, then forward; he looked at me and gave his head a vigorous shake, as if he had water in his ears. Then, with a fluttering snort like a long-suffering sigh, he settled back to the serious business of grazing. It was done.

I rose stiffly to my feet, half-expecting him to startle and prance away, but he didn't. I walked over to my pack, wiped the cup clean and replaced it, certain that when I turned back he'd be gone.

He wasn't. He was plodding after me . . . and the limp was almost gone.

I went to him and cradled his head in my arms. He pushed against me, whoofling. As if in a dream I moved beside him, reached up and ran my hand down the smoothness of his back, over the raven-sheen of his wing. And it was then that the idea came to me.

'I've never done this before, any more than you have,' I whispered. 'If you don't want me to, tell me now – while we're still on the ground.'

One moment I was beside him, heart thumping; the next I was astride hot horse, a double handful of wiry mane in both fists.

I'd hoped he might stand still for a second, while I got used to being up there. But as soon as my weight settled I felt fluid power flare through him, every fibre alive with energy. He leapt forward in a rearing lunge, only my grip on his mane stopping me from tumbling off. I hunched and hung on, terror and rapture roaring in my ears, my blood singing. A series of bone-jarring leaps, a smooth surge – and suddenly we were soaring, mighty wind-borne wingbeats bearing us higher, the ground impossibly far below.

Out over the precipice we flew, the clouds a flock of sheep way down; he spread his wings and wheeled a lazy circle, the earth spinning like a globe. Wind whipped through my hair and stung my eyes; dizzy, I clung on and goggled downwards.

How would it feel to touch a cloud? No sooner had the thought begun to form in my mind than the sky tilted and we were spiralling downwards in a wide corkscrew, then levelling hundreds of feet lower to skim through them: not soft and fluffy like I'd thought, but dense drifts of fog that blurred my vision and misted my skin with fine, cool spray. Squinting up I could see the sun, a hazy white glow . . . and suddenly I longed to be high again, to feel its warmth on my skin. Instantly the colt banked and beat upwards with slow, strong strokes, up as high as the cliff and still higher, then turned to glide back in again over the land.

We skimmed low over the others, straggling back dismally along the cliff edge; I caught a flash of pale moon-faces gawking up in disbelief before they were snatched away under the shadow of our wings.

I realised I was laughing: wave after wave of joy, pure and free as air. Somehow, somewhere on that wild roller-coaster ride, I forgot to be afraid. This was our element; I was as safe on his back as a child on a rocking-horse. The air was solid as a cushion under us, bouncy with shape and substance, hills and hollows; my mind flexed with his wings as they lifted and dipped.

When I was astride him it seemed we shared the same soul; a winged centaur, half-boy, half-colt: prince of the wind.

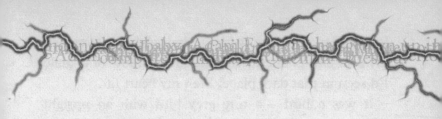

THE VOICES OF MEN

For the last time the colt touched down light as a feather, Jamie spilling off from behind me to land in a heap beside the others. Leaning forward, I wrapped my arms round the muscular neck, now sleek with sweat, and rested my cheek for a moment against the tangled mane. *Thank you*. I didn't say goodbye – I knew I didn't need to. Then I slid to the ground and looked around.

Behind us the endless wall of the cliff stretched up, its top lost in cloud. Ahead loomed the forest, dark and forbidding, the tree trunks grey with damp and lichen. Leaves drooped heavy and lifeless, mottled with decay; the choking dankness of decomposing vegetation hung in the still air. There was no path that I could see, and no sign of life.

I looked at the others. They met my gaze, one by one. Blue-bum clambered up onto my shoulder and twisted his hands into my hair. Together, we entered the forest.

*

It was Gen who saw it first – and when she touched my arm and pointed, with the first shadow of a smile I'd seen in that dark place, I felt my heart lift.

It was a bird – a tiny grey bird with an upright widespread tail like a fan. It was fluttering round us as we picked our way through the trees, sometimes beside us, occasionally behind, most often ahead, treading air like a butterfly, perching for an instant to wait for us, then flitting off again.

'*Birds of the air* . . . It's pointing the way, like Meirion told you,' Kenta whispered.

Sure enough, the undergrowth became less dense, and soon we were moving more easily through the trees. But there was still no hint of sun, no glimpse of sky; instead, the gloom deepened as we walked on, until it seemed that the only source of brightness was the little bird dancing ahead.

Then Jamie, who was leading, stopped dead in his tracks with a squeak of dismay.

'What is it?' asked Gen. 'What's wrong?'

'The bird's gone. It spread its tail and did a little kind of bob, as if it was saying goodbye – then it flew off between those trees and disappeared.'

'Let's go after it,' suggested Rich. 'Maybe it's waiting up ahead.'

In single file, scanning the undergrowth for any sign of the little bird, we followed Jamie in the direction it had gone and then straggled to a halt, staring round us.

We were in a clearing. Trees reared up on every

side, their canopies forming a roof way overhead. The ground was carpeted with fallen leaves, spongy and damp; the air was cool and still, steeped in silence. Still the tiny bird was nowhere . . . but on the far side of the clearing lay a massive fallen tree trunk. On its right the root base reared up in a gnarled tangle like a nest of snakes, furled fern fronds nestling in the exposed hollows. At head-height longer roots merged with the groping tentacles of trees to form a natural archway – with the beginning of a path just visible beyond.

The ruined trunk stretched away to the left, clusters of toadstools sprouting from its damp crevices, to be swallowed by the trees fringing the clearing. At the point where it vanished the rotting wood had collapsed to leave a crumbling stairway choked by underbrush and trailing vines . . . and a second track, half-hidden, leading away into the darkness.

'Look,' Gen said softly. 'The paths Blade told us about. One leading to the Realms of the Undead, the other to *your journey's end*. And those must be the birds that speak with the voices of men.'

They were roosting on the tree trunk, one at the entrance to each path: about the size of pigeons, one black, one white. Their feathers were patchy, showing through to pimpled skin like partly plucked chickens. Their splayed yellow feet were scaly-looking and scabby, but their eyes were bright as jet, watching us unblinkingly.

Rich stepped forward, head tipped to one side.

'Hello,' he said in a bright, enquiring tone completely unlike his normal growl. '*Helloooow?*'

'Shut up, Richard!' hissed Gen. 'These aren't talking parrots!'

But the birds didn't seem to be offended. They shook their wings with a rattle, opened their yellow beaks and cackled, a rising sequence of harsh notes like a mockery of human laughter. It rose to a shrieking crescendo, then trailed away to a clacking giggle, then silence.

We shuffled our feet and huddled closer. 'Now what?' whispered Kenta.

'We ask them which way to go,' muttered Gen, '*without* antagonising them.'

'You do it, Jamie,' Kenta said. 'You're the politest.'

Jamie took a small step forward and cleared his throat. Clasped his hands as if he was about to sing a solo in choir, turned to the black bird on the right and gave a small bow. 'Good day, my feathered friend,' he began. The birds stared at him, their tiny eyes shiny and blank as beads. The thought of them opening their beaks and talking suddenly seemed crazy. But Jamie carried on: 'Are you by any chance the birds that speak with the voices of men?'

As soon as he asked the question the black eyes snapped, and excitement flashed through me. There was no doubt the bird had understood. Its beak gaped open and I caught a glimpse of a thin tongue, oddly stiff-looking and immobile; the feathered throat throbbed. Then it gave a series of strident squawks, hunched its wings, and went back to watching us. It had answered. The only problem was, we hadn't understood.

Was it my imagination, or was there a glint of mockery in its eyes? A knowing smugness, as if it knew all the answers and wasn't telling. 'Hang on a sec,' I said slowly. 'We're missing something. We should have understood him.'

'So why didn't we?' demanded Rich.

'Maybe there's something else we need to do, something we've been told along the way,' hazarded Kenta.

'Or something we should be using, like the teardrop crystal,' said Gen.

Hands shaking, I fumbled for the opening of my talisman and felt inside. There it was: the grey feather I'd found in the Summer Palace. *Something or nothing* . . . As I held it out it seemed to glow in the gloom with its own pale light – and an image of the fan-tailed bird flitted into my mind, bright with the exact same shining paleness as the silvery bars on the feather. 'It's a feather from the finder-bird, the one that led us here! Maybe if we're holding it . . .'

'It's worth a try! Let me have a go.' Reluctantly, I passed the feather to Rich. He turned to the black bird again, holding the feather high like an Olympic torch.

'Richard, I've just thought –' began Jamie.

'Shush, I'm concentrating. *Which path –*'

'No, Rich – wait!' The urgency in Jamie's voice stopped Rich in mid-flow and made us all turn to him, staring. 'Don't you see? There's no point asking him. Even if he answers in proper words, we won't be able to believe him.'

'Jamie's right,' said Gen. 'Blade said one bird always tells lies, and the other always tells the truth.'

'That's easy! We just have to find out which is which.' Rich brandished the feather and turned back to the bird. 'Are you the bird that always tells the truth?' he demanded sternly.

Out of the corner of my eye I half-saw Gen roll her eyes . . . but my attention was fixed on the bird, and I could have sworn it smirked. Then it cocked its head to one side, opened its beak, and spoke. Its voice was raucous and grating, but we could all understand the single word perfectly. 'Yes.'

'There you go!' crowed Rich. 'Now we just ask him –'

'Richard,' said Gen patiently, 'there are a million questions you could have asked, but I'm afraid that wasn't one of them. *Are you the black bird?* would have done, for a start . . . but it doesn't matter; we'll just ask again. And this time, I think you should let Jamie do the talking.'

But it was me who reached out and took the feather gently from Rich's fingers, staring down at it in disbelief. Before, there had been three pale bars at the end, like a tiny rainbow. And now . . . 'Something's happened,' I told the others, my mind racing to make sense of it. 'Two of the silver stripes have disappeared. There's only one left.'

There was a long silence. Then Jamie spoke, his voice strangely flat. 'How many questions have we asked?'

'Two,' said Rich. 'Why? What's that got to do with anything?'

'That's what the bars must be,' said Jamie. 'Three bars, three questions. We couldn't understand the first answer because we weren't holding the feather. We understood the second, but it didn't help us. And that means . . .'

We all knew what it meant. We only had one question left: one question to ask one bird, to find out which path led to the Realms of the Undead. And I had a horrible feeling there'd be no second chances.

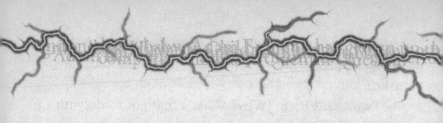

TRUTH AND LIES

'This time, no one asks anything unless we all agree,' Jamie said.

'OK, OK,' grumbled Rich.

There was a long silence before Kenta finally spoke. 'The problem is that there's no point asking anything unless we can believe the answer, or know not to believe it.'

'And we can't use up our last question finding that out,' said Jamie glumly, carefully not looking at Rich.

Maybe there was no way it could be done – not with one question. 'Unless . . .' Suddenly everyone was looking at me. I felt myself flush. 'Unless it doesn't matter which bird we ask.'

Blue-bum had been sitting hunched and still, scraping at the leaves with a pointed stick. I'd thought he was digging for grubs, but now I saw he'd been making little marks, staring at them and scratching his head. Now he was looking up at me with a strange expression on his face, eyes bright.

'Maybe the white bird's the good one, and the black

282

one's bad,' Jamie was saying. 'White and black, good and bad, truth and lies.'

'It's a good thought, but we can't bank on it,' Gen said regretfully.

'What if we ask, *If you were us, which path would you choose . . .*' Rich scowled and shook his head. 'Nah, that wouldn't work either.'

Suddenly Blue-bum jerked bolt upright with a chitter of excitement.

'What, Blue-bum?' yipped Kenta.

Blue-bum was pointing at me and then Rich, then at each of the two birds in turn. 'Was it something I said?' Rich asked doubtfully. 'Or Adam?'

Blue-bum nodded so violently his whole body jigged up and down.

'Well, who?' I said. 'Rich? Me?'

Blue-bum was skipping about in an agony of frustration.

'Or . . . both of them?' said Jamie.

'What *did* you say?' asked Gen.

'I said, *maybe it doesn't matter which bird you ask,* but –'

'And I said, *if you were us* –'

Blue-bum interrupted again, jibbering frantically and practically turning somersaults in his desperate efforts to make us understand.

Finally Kenta grabbed him by the scruff of his neck and sat him firmly on her lap. 'Settle down, Blue-bum – let's take this step by step.' Blue-bum sat very still, watching her face with hopeful button eyes. 'You're

283

saying we can ask either of the birds, it doesn't matter which . . .' Blue-bum nodded once, very definitely. He'd always been super-smart – could he possibly be right? 'Ask either one: *if you were us –*'

Blue-bum shook his head: *no*.

'What then? If you were . . .' Blue-bum pointed to the black bird; then the white one. Looking at them, I felt a surge of hope. Something about the disgruntled way they were squatting made me certain Blue-bum had the answer – and they knew it.

'If you were the *other bird* . . .' I said slowly.

Jamie had been listening with the stuffed-fish expression that meant he was thinking hard-out with every last one of his gazillion brain cells. Now he let out a pent-up breath in an admiring whoosh. 'He's got it,' he said respectfully. 'Way to go, Blue-bum.'

Jamie clambered to his feet, brushing away leaf-mould. 'Here's the answer, courtesy of the one and only blue-bummed brain-box: We ask a bird, either one, *If you were the* other *bird, which path would you say led to the Realms of the Undead?*'

'Huh?' said Rich, looking confused. Then he grinned. 'I'll take your word for it, Jamie. So we go along whichever path they say – done and dusted!'

'Well, actually we don't,' Jamie said. 'We go along the *other* one.'

It took a good five minutes of full-on discussion before everyone was one hundred and ten percent certain Jamie had it right. Then I gave him the feather to hold, and he turned to the black bird. 'At least we know for sure we can understand him,' he whispered, with a quick glance round for agreement.

'If you were the other bird, which path would you tell us led to the Realms of the Undead?' he asked, very slowly and carefully.

'*The path on your right – the gateway of roots,*' squawked the bird sulkily.

'Thank you.' Jamie handed back the feather, his hand trembling slightly, and I tucked it safely away.

'I'm still not sure I get it,' Rich confessed. 'Does that mean he's the bird that tells the truth, or . . .'

'We'll never know, Richard,' said Gen patiently. 'It doesn't matter. The point is, we go down the other path. Come on, everyone. Let's –'

And the black bird spoke again, its voice grating through the still air like a rusty saw. 'Only one mortal may pass.'

'What?' Rich spun to face him, fists clenched. 'What d'you mean? What's a *mortal* – and who are you to say, anyway? I'd like to see you try to stop us –'

'Richard, wait.' A cold hand had gripped my heart; it was squeezing it slowly smaller, till it was wedged like a piece of sharp-edged gravel deep in my chest. 'Gen's wrong. We do know which bird is which – now. The bird of truth is the black one.'

Some paths are made to walk alone . . .

For me, the end of the journey was almost in sight – but for my friends, it was over. The five had done their part – this was one place I couldn't ask them to

285

follow me. I must go alone to the Realms of the Undead in search of my twin, and together we must confront whatever awaited us there.

THE REALMS OF THE UNDEAD

'But what do we do?' asked Rich, more at a loss than I'd ever seen him. 'Wait here?'

'No. You should go home, back to Quested Court. Use the microcomputers Q gave you – he'll have the system fixed by now. Tell him what's happened, and wait for me there. It won't be long. And no goodbyes, OK?'

Kenta clung to me fiercely. 'Be careful.'

Gen gave me a kiss so hard it hurt. 'Be strong.'

Jamie held out a hand. It was as dirty as ever, but dusty and dry, and his grip was firm. 'Be safe.'

That left Rich. 'So long . . . Zephyr.' A handshake turned into a hug that said everything.

I hefted my pack and looked round for the last parting. Once I would have welcomed it, but now it seemed almost hardest of all.

'Look at Blue-bum!' Kenta was trying to laugh. 'He's sulking because he can't come.'

He'd hopped up beside the white bird, which had shuffled grudgingly over to make room for him, and now he was crouching with his back to us, tail trailing mournfully on the ground.

I gave his furry head a ruffle. 'I'll miss you, little guy.'

I walked down the crumbling steps, through the tunnel of leaves and onto the pathway. I didn't look back.

There was a skitter and a scrabble and a sudden rush of air, and something small and lithe skipped up onto my shoulder, gripping a fistful of hair so tight it brought tears to my eyes. Whatever mortal meant, it obviously didn't apply to chatterbots.

The path wound on into the dark forest. The way forward was treacherous and indistinct, every step a struggle: roots caught at my ankles; creepers snagged my legs and arms; twigs snatched at me like grasping fingers, their thorns criss-crossing my face and hands with stinging blood-stitched tracks.

Blue-bum crept into the hood of my cloak and huddled there, and soon I could tell he'd drifted off to sleep. His weight pulled the cloak so tight around my neck it almost throttled me, but it felt good to have him close.

I battled grimly on, doubt and a growing sense of urgency gnawing at my mind. I hadn't allowed myself to question whether I'd find Zenith. But what if even now as I blundered through the forest time was running out? What if I arrived and it was too late? I tried to push the thoughts aside and concentrate on putting one foot in front of the other. I walked on, every footfall, every heartbeat echoing his name.

It was purple twilight when I came to the wall: a jigsaw of dry stone, pitted and crumbling, stained black with mildew. The path ran beside it, choked with brambles and weeds; over it I could see a graveyard, headstones leaning at drunken angles in overgrown grass.

There was a gate, askew on rusted hinges; it creaked open under my hand. I walked soft-footed among the gravestones, trying not to step where I imagined the mounds of the graves might once have been. Now no sign of them was left; even the inscriptions on the stones had disappeared, obscured by lichen and worn away by time – or never there at all.

I'd been in cemeteries before. They had a kind of peace about them, a drifting sorrow like winter rain or slow, soft music. This one was different. There was no church: just row after uneven row of headstones in a desolate field. I walked on through the gathering darkness, not knowing what I was searching for. With nightfall came a fretful wind that wailed and groaned between the gravestones. Blue-bum woke and clung to my neck like a furry scarf, skinny fingers pinching my ear, hot breath in my hair. At last a long, low shape loomed out of the shadows: a tomb, huge and flat-topped. Its lid was a stone slab, resting askew to reveal a gash of gaping emptiness.

I'd found what I was looking for.

I hoisted myself onto the corner, the cold of the

stone seeping into my skin. Swung my legs to dangle into the dark cavity. Took a last deep breath, lowered myself down, feet kicking for purchase . . . and dropped.

I landed awkwardly, my ankle turning on something solid and compact that rolled under my foot. Looking up I could see a slice of gun-metal sky, but here it was pitch dark. The floor of the tomb must be lower than the ground outside; the ledge I'd dropped from was way out of reach. So – no going back. But there never had been.

Fumbling in my bag, I found my torch and flicked it on. Nothing.

Blue-bum's arms were locked in a shivering stranglehold round my neck. 'Hop in the bag,' I whispered. 'It'll be warmer, and you'll feel safe.' *And I'll be able to breathe.* Once he was settled I shuffled forward into the inky blackness. The floor of the crypt disappeared under my foot. Down one step, then another . . . a stairway leading into the depths of the graveyard. I stumbled on. A sweetish smell clogged the air; cobwebs drifted against my skin and stroked my hair with sticky fingers.

At last the ground levelled. I groped my way along the wall: bare earth, hard-packed and damp. In places clumps had fallen leaving hollows where spiders had made nests; my fingers brushed against their bloated bodies and snagged in the weave of their webs. There were other things in the wall too, things I could feel but not see: squashy things that writhed against my skin; many-legged scuttling things; scraps of softness that vanished to nothing in my fingers . . . fragments of something cool and smooth as ivory in the crumbling earth.

It was growing gradually lighter, a sullen orange glow diluting the blackness. The sickly smell thickened and curdled. With it came half-heard sounds: the scuff of a stealthy footfall; the whisper of cloth; a sifting patter of falling earth. The corner of my eye caught movement, a shifting of shadows; but when I spun and focused there was only emptiness and the fading ripples of whispered laughter.

I came to the source of the light: the first in a straggling line of torches giving off a twist of black smoke that caught in my throat. I walked on, the earthen walls giving way to stone, the narrow passage opening to a maze of echoing halls and passageways. It was more than a palace – a vast subterranean city fallen into magnificent ruin, cracked stonework shrouded in cobwebs and dark with crouching shadows, crumbling masonry grinning at me with crooked teeth.

And suddenly there was a figure in front of me where before there had been nothing. Grey against the greyness of the stone, it seemed to suck blackness from the shadows into the empty cowl of its hood. It spoke in the rasping whisper of the Faceless, like the open mouth of a tomb being slid slowly shut.

'The King of Darkness bids you welcome, Living One. He and his kingdom await. Follow me.'

His breath twisted round me, cold and stifling, carrying the stench that haunted my nightmares – the reek of the living grave. A tide of exhaustion and despair washed through me, turning the marrow of my bones to liquid metal.

The King of Darkness – Zeel. It must be. But how, and in what form? I knew I didn't have the strength to face him. Not yet – not now. Not alone.

I had no choice. Lead-footed, I stumbled after the drifting figure, through a labyrinth of passageways and gaping doorways and down a narrow corridor, dark and uneven-floored. Here I could detect the hint of another smell, oddly familiar and somehow reassuring: oily and metallic, overlaid with a tang of leather. Low doors studded with iron and cracked with age were set deep into the wall; I glimpsed a barred grille at the far end, a strange red glow beyond.

A door was unlocked and swung open; I bent and shuffled in, dreading what I would see, hearing it slam shut behind me. I was in a cell lit only by a single lantern and the faint glow of a tiny barred window high in the wall. A still shape lay in a corner on a straw pallet . . . and slouched beside it, staring at me as if he'd seen a ghost, was Zenith.

I gawked back at him. He was here, two paces away, grubby and tousle-haired and every inch alive. It was the moment I'd hardly dared dream of. Hot tears pressed behind my eyes; my throat burned with all the words that waited to be spoken. I stood there dumbly, as shy and tongue-tied as a little child. At last I opened my mouth, with absolutely no idea what was going to come out.

'I brought it – the fire-tongue . . .' I croaked.

'You brought the fire-tongue,' Zenith repeated slowly. 'As easy as that: a stroll across the village green to fetch it from the corner stall. *You brought the fire-tongue.* You did far more than that: you brought yourself, Whistler.'

Suddenly he was on his feet, hands gripping my shoulders, amber eyes blazing. 'What do you owe me or Blade, that you would willingly follow us into the darkness of the underworld and certain death? Yet my heart never doubted you would come.'

'Because your heart knows what your mind does not.'

He stared at me.

I took a breath. 'Lyulf . . . Wolf Flame . . .'

An urgent chitter from Blue-bum interrupted me. He was shoving something in my face – the fire-tongue vine, dry and shrivelled. He was right: that came first. I turned to the motionless shape on the floor. 'Is she . . .'

'I've bound the wound with strips of cloth, but nothing I do will stop the bleeding.' For the first time I noticed he was shirtless, jerkin open over his bare chest. 'Her body is weak as water but her spirit burns strong.'

Gently he drew aside Blade's cloak. Her eyes flickered open and focused on me with wavering

293

wonder. 'Whistler . . . you came.' Her voice was the faintest breath. 'Lyulf promised you would . . .'

I couldn't bear to look at the wreckage of her back. Blue-bum and I busied ourselves preparing the paste while Zenith cleaned the wound and applied the salve, his soothing words masking her whimpers of pain. At last it was done, tidily bandaged with a cleanish dressing – my shirt this time. Blade, exhausted, sank instantly into a deep sleep.

'Now,' said Zenith, 'what lies so heavy on your spirit must be told. Speak.'

I took out his talisman and passed it to him. He shot me a hard glance, and I nodded. 'We opened it. I'm sorry. You were gone, and we thought that whatever it held might be important. And it was.'

I took my own amulet from round my neck, loosened the thong . . . tipped my silver ring out onto my hand. Zenith stared at it for what seemed for-ever. Then his eyes met mine, a thousand questions burning in them.

'I have a tale to tell you . . .' My words were slow and hesitant, as foreign-feeling on my tongue as if they were in some strange language. But as I spoke I heard my voice gather strength and purpose, the rich tap-estry of the past weaving its magic through my mind. '. . . a tale with its beginning more than fifty years ago, and its ending yet to come.' Hardly knowing I was doing it I reached out and took his hand. 'I will tell of your part in it, Zenith, Prince of Karazan – and mine.'

★

'I don't understand how it can possibly be you, or what can have happened to save you – I only know it is,' I finished at last.

For a long time he was silent. I longed for him to look at me, to read whatever was in his eyes, but his gaze was fixed on the floor. When finally he spoke it was in a whisper almost too soft to hear. 'I thought . . . all these years I believed I was cursed, that some evil spell held me back . . .' He shook his head, struggling for words. 'Even in my deepest soul I never dared hope there might be something . . . some good . . . *someone* . . .' Slowly, haltingly, words tore themselves free, tormented fragments of a past never before spoken of: the skeleton of a story I hoped might be fleshed out over the years to come until at last everything was known . . . a tale that is his to tell, not mine.

Even at the end he didn't look at me.

'What about the others?' I asked at last. 'Where are they?'

'The Masked Man was brought here with us, but I have not seen him since. As for Borg and the rest, they released them on the grasslands, along with the glonks. It seems they were not intended to share our fate, whatever that may be. And I think I know –'

'That doesn't matter now. The important thing – the only thing – is Karazan. The prophecy has been fulfilled. *When twain is one and one is twain* . . . At last we are together. And together, somehow, we will overthrow the forces of evil – *I know it.*'

I realised that our hands were still clasped, the

fingers tightly locked. I could feel a current of strength flowing from Zenith's palm to my own; it ran between us like fire, singing in my blood with a wild, strange music. Slowly, I lifted our hands, the lamplight transforming them from flesh and blood into a double fist cast from burnished gold.

At last my brother lifted his head and met my eyes.

'*Together.*'

THE KING OF DARKNESS

There was the rasp of a key in the lock; the door creaked open. Instantly we were on our feet, Zenith instinctively reaching for his sword – but I saw that for the first time since I'd known him, he wasn't wearing it.

The dank reek of the Faceless seeped through the doorway, followed by the croak of a voice. 'The King of Darkness has summoned you. Set your weapon aside and follow me.'

Reluctantly I unbelted my sword and laid it next to Blade, then followed Zenith through the low doorway. Automatically I turned the way I'd come, but a choking cough almost like a laugh stopped me. 'No. This way.'

I turned back, puzzled. In the other direction was a dead end, the iron grille . . . but now the grille was gone. Side by side we followed the cloaked figure to the opening and stepped through into the emptiness beyond. I stopped short, my mind racing.

We were standing at the edge of a vast circular amphitheatre. Ahead and on either side tiered terraces

297

rose into the shadows, darkness pressing down from an unseen roof overhead. Torches were set at intervals round the perimeter, their dim light revealing row upon row of shadowy figures, hunched and intent. Waiting . . .

A glance behind me showed a row of barred windows – the cells where we'd been held. I caught a flash of a small face with a ruff of fur before it ducked out of sight.

In the centre of the floor yawned a circular pit of fiery coals. A haze of blue flames danced above it, heat lapping outwards in a red glow that stained Zenith's skin and stung my cheeks.

At a signal from our guard we moved forward over the stone floor. *Stone, not sawdust* . . . Now I could place that half-familiar smell I'd noticed in the corridor – freshly honed steel, well-oiled scabbards, the supple leather of gauntlets and harness: scents as familiar to me over the past few weeks as glonk dung and burned porridge.

We were in a gladiatorial arena. That was why the gladiators of the wildlands were captured and brought here: to slake the thirst of the Faceless for bloodshed and death. Zenith knew. He'd worked it out in the lonely hours of waiting; been about to tell me, but I'd said it didn't matter. Now I knew it did, as much as life itself . . . or death.

I forced my mind back to here and now – to where we were heading. In one section of the grandstand the perimeter torches were massed to form a frame of light, and in its centre I could make out a dark, motionless shape.

I felt his gaze before I saw him . . . and at once I knew he had changed. Before, I had sensed wickedness, but weakness too – dependence, greed, fear . . . humanity. Now all that was left was evil in its purest form.

We came to a halt below his throne, squinting past the flickering border of light surrounding him. Slowly a black figure took shape out of the darkness, the body oddly bulky and undefined, the head bulbous and misshapen.

'So . . . we meet again.' The voice was strangely distorted, a hollow echo. And suddenly I realised what the grotesque form was. It was armour, the voice muffled by a helmet with a single narrow slit at eye level.

'Look well upon me, little princes. Yes, second-born son of Zane, I know you. Who would not? Zephyr and Zenith: two birds, one trap.

'Well, Zephyr: how the wheel has turned full circle! You believed you had vanquished me, and behold: my forces are more powerful than ever, rooted in the depths of the underworld and fed on darkness. That is what lies within this helm, beneath this black armour. Darkness. Now I am truly immortal – for what can vanquish the dark? Only light from the natural world – and here there is none.

'And what of the kingdom you seek to save? Already the darkness deepens in Karazan; leaves are withering, crops fail. The light fades from men's hearts. What you thought my defeat has turned to victory, Zephyr – a victory greater than ever I imagined. Now all that remains is for you to say your last farewells . . . and meet your end like the princes you claim to be.'

One arm lifted in a clumsy signal, and something spun towards me out of the shadows. Instinctively I lifted my hand and caught it. It was a sword – my sword. Not the real one – the wooden replica Zenith had carved for me.

Still I didn't understand – but Zenith did. 'Wait!' His voice rang out over the silent arena. 'If you wish to see blood spilled, so be it – but let it be mine! Give me a sword of steel, a wooden sword, no sword at all . . . I will welcome the challenge of any with the courage to face me – even you, so-called *king*.'

'Even me? Tempting . . . but I think not. Your reputation goes before you, Wolf Flame. I have no appetite for sport; I desire blood, fear, pain – the simple pleasures of sacrifice and execution. Return him to his cell.'

In moments Zenith was surrounded by grey cloaks. It would have been pointless to resist. They led him past me, close enough to touch. A single glance passed between us, the brush of a hand . . . and something more. Something soft, with a heaviness that shifted and clinked . . . and an urgent whisper: '*Take it . . . use it.*'

It was his talisman; his luck. I hung it round my neck, feeling its weight beside my own. Then I raised my sword and turned to face whatever might come at me from the darkness.

It was already waiting: a figure silhouetted against the red glow of the pit. Tall, cloaked, motionless. I fell instinctively into the guard position, sword poised. Wooden or not, it felt like an extension of my own arm, perfectly balanced and comfortingly familiar.

My opponent moved smoothly forward – and shock jolted through me. After weeks of watching, training, observing, I knew the way he moved and held his sword as well as I knew the shape of my own hand. It was the Masked Man.

Automatically I joined him in the intricate dance of advance and retreat, parry and thrust, my brain spinning with confusion. Did Zeel's amusement lie in pitting friend against friend – brother against brother in a warped corruption of the fellowship of the arena? If so, he would have to do without his pleasure. The two of us had sparred together often enough to stage a display of skill with our eyes closed. If it was swordsmanship he wanted, he could have it; if it was blood he was hoping to see spilled, he'd be disappointed. Nothing and no one could make me harm a brother-in-arms.

Suddenly the Masked Man's sword flashed out in a lightning lunge that ripped my jerkin from neck to hem. Pain lanced through me. I back-pedalled, my chest on fire; glanced down . . . saw a line of blood blossom and well. 'What are you doing?' I hissed. 'Are you crazy? Fake it – we've done it a million times! Play for time . . .'

I circled warily, keeping my distance, trying to gauge the feelings hidden by the leather mask. Had he misjudged the distance in the gloom . . . made a mistake? But the Masked Man didn't make mistakes.

His sword lashed out again in a plunging cut from above, missing my chest by millimetres. I rolled my body sideways, deflecting his blade with a counter-thrust that snagged on my wooden blade, then closing my guard. My heart was thudding so violently I thought I was going to throw up. Cold sweat coated my palm, making my sword-hilt feel greasy and strange. 'What are you *doing*?' I croaked . . . though I already knew. He was fighting – for real.

He was a better swordsman than he'd ever allowed us to see: way better than I could ever hope to be. Seeing that familiar mask in front of me I found myself battling the stubborn belief that he was some-how still a friend, a comrade – though logic told me it wasn't true.

As if to prove it he came in again, driving with a downward thrust that snicked my belt-buckle and missed my thigh by a hair's-breadth. I leapt back with a last desperate appeal: '*We don't have to do this!*'

His reply was a charge that forced me into a running retreat, his blade flashing in a deadly com-bination of cuts and thrusts that would have hacked me to pieces if I hadn't managed to deflect them with my sword. I winced at the catch and tug of the razor-sharp steel slashing into the wood – slowing him a fraction, but doing fatal damage to my weapon in the process.

That's when I realised that to get out of this alive I was going to have to fight on my terms, not his. What was it Zenith had said? *Every strength has a weakness* . . . If it was true, I could guess where the Masked Man's weakness might lie.

I darted forward, taking him by surprise with the suddenness of my attack; feinted with an open thrust to the left to distract him and draw his blade, then ducked inside, brought up one booted foot and kicked him squarely in the groin. He doubled over, his breath wheezing out in an agonised gasp. If I'd been fighting for real I would have finished it then, but I couldn't.

I smashed the pommel of my sword down hard on his head and as he staggered back, I grabbed the binding of his hood and yanked. Before he knew what was happening it was off. I skipped backwards, my trophy in my hand, my heart in my mouth, praying it was all for real and I hadn't made some unforgivable mistake. Slowly he straightened. I don't know what I expected to see in the hellish light of the coals . . . but it wasn't this.

Facing me, murderous with rage, was the melted-wax face of Tallow.

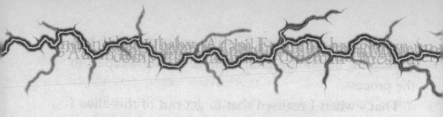

TALLOW

M y mouth dropped open and my sword-arm turned to putty. I stood flat-footed, gaping. 'What . . . how . . .'

He could have run me through then as easily as skewering a kebab. Instead, the melted mouth gaped open in a mockery of mine, and my own voice echoed back at me, pitch-perfect: '*What? How?*' Then the mouth twisted into a smile and he began to circle slowly, sword at the ready, dark eyes fixed on me like a snake's. And now the voice was Shaw's, heart-breakingly familiar: 'Easy as pie, young Adam, that's 'ow. And ter think yer never guessed.'

'But . . .' I was back in my stance, revolving clumsily to keep him in view, my mind still reeling. 'How did you get into Karazan? The computers were all smashed . . .'

'And you think the great Quentin Quested had no back-ups? All it took was a word from me: *Adam's in trouble, Q – you 'ave ter let me go an' 'elp 'im –* and I was on my way with his blessing.'

'But he wasn't there! He was at the hospital with Hannah . . .'

'And who told you that? *Wee 'annah* was in the room next to mine with Q, having her bedtime story. You chose the wrong door, Prince Zephyr, then made the mistake children always do: of trusting, and believing everything you're told. After that it was a simple matter of following, watching and listening.'

So Hannah was OK. With the wave of relief came cold anger and new determination. Tallow was basking in the glow of his own deceit and trickery. I'd keep him talking, play for time . . . and rack my poor befuddled brain for some kind of plan. Because once he tired of bragging, I'd be in serious trouble.

I shook my head, playing dumb, letting my sword-tip dip as if I'd forgotten it. 'But you're a dissembler. You can take any form you like, so why a stupid leather mask?'

He laughed, Shaw's deep chuckle, morphing to Hannah's infectious chortle. I felt my hackles rise and my grip on the sword-hilt tighten. 'There was time for only the most basic disguise . . . and the best concealment of all: silence. And there was much of interest to overhear in the shadows.'

I remembered way back in Karazan, when I'd told the others I had a twin: the feeling that there were listening shapes hidden in the swirling mist . . . that whispered exchange between Lyulf and Blade by the campfire. Tallow must have been skulking in the darkness . . . 'You knew! You figured out who Lyulf was! That's why you disappeared. You told them you'd found us, Zenith and me.'

'Very clever, little prince. Yes, the Faceless are always within call in the wildlands, if you know where to look. When the trap snapped shut you were gone, but I knew you'd follow. And now . . .'

Though I'd been struggling to distance myself from it, the sing-song rhythm of his voice had lulled me into a kind of stupor. His blade flashed once, twice; I felt impact and a wrenching jerk, jumped back . . . and gaped in horror at my sword.

The top half was gone, sliced clean away. Almost in slow motion I saw it spin backwards into the darkness, landing with a clatter on the brink of the pit. Tallow gave a soft hiss of satisfaction, and closed for the kill. If my weapon had seemed pitiful before, now it was worse than useless. I might as well toss the stump into the fire and fight on bare-handed . . .

No! I wouldn't give up – even if he sliced the whole sword to sawdust! I wasn't beaten yet. *Every strength has a weakness*. Zenith and Blade had drummed into us the importance of knowing our opponent and using that knowledge against him. What did I know about Tallow? That form and spirit had been melted and remoulded to the service of evil; that his face bore the scars in the form of the molten wax of a candle . . .

And suddenly the outline of a plan was in my mind – and with it the faintest breath of hope. If I was right, Tallow's weakness had been there under his mask all along. And I could use that weakness against him if I was fast enough, and my plan worked, and I got very lucky. Tallow might not be scared of me, but there was one thing he was afraid of. He had to be.

I backed away towards the pit. He prowled after me, cat and mouse, grinning, in no hurry to end things. I took a deep breath. *Now.* A single quick movement and my cloak was off; a fumble and a twist, and it was wound tightly round my free hand. Not as good as I'd like, but a lot better than nothing – and I needed all the help I could get.

I could feel the heat of the coals on my back as I moved closer, the cloth of my breeches scorching my legs. I kept my eyes fixed on his face, waiting for his eyes to signal an attack – that microscopic tightening Zenith had taught us to watch for. They gleamed back at me, red with blood-lust in the light of the fire. His plan was right there in his eyes: he'd trap me against the rim of the pit and butcher me at leisure. But there was something else too, the slightest hint of uncertainty, a hanging-back . . .

My heart leapt. I'd been right. In one fluid motion I spun and plunged the stub of my sword deep into the pit, using the hand swathed in the thick woollen pad – even in the second it took, bare skin would have blistered in the searing heat. I leapt sideways and up, the stink of singed hair and burned wool in my nostrils . . . and the blazing torch of my sword held high.

Now Tallow stood between me and the fire. He tried to turn with me, but his foot caught on the broken end of my sword and he stumbled and almost fell. His eyes stared from their sockets, wide with horror and denial, his ravaged face contorting as he realised his own trap had been turned on him. Behind him was the furnace, a wavering wall of heat; in front of him I stood, knees trembling and heart knocking wildly, praying the flaming torch thrust in his face would keep him at bay.

'Give up,' I panted. 'Admit you're beaten, and we'll stop this now. Tell Zeel . . . tell him to let us go . . .'

Even as I said the words I knew that here there'd be no *pax*, no easy truce or surrender. There would be only death – for one of us.

Then I took a half-step backwards, staring, sour bile rising in my throat. The face I'd thought was twisting with rage and fear was liquefying, the runnels deepening, drips bulging from the skin like sweat and dribbling down his chin in a grotesque goatee of molten skin.

I staggered back with a cry of horror, hurling my blazing sword away. He lurched after me with a gargle of triumph, sword jabbing awkwardly, then flopping as the strength in the arm that held it drained away. His legs folded as if they were made of jelly and he crumpled to his knees. His cloak billowed behind, floating just out of reach of the dancing aurora of fire – then combusted in a *whoosh* of flame.

I threw my hand up against the searing heat, turned and stumbled into the darkness, my eyes squeezed shut against the pictures playing in white-on-black negative in my mind: a kneeling figure rimmed in flame, arms outstretched, mouth gaping in a soundless scream . . . then crumpling backwards slowly, so slowly, to melt without trace into the ravenous depths of the furnace.

TAKE IT . . . USE IT

I crawled away on hands and knees, dry-retching, gulping air in giant, agonising gasps. All I wanted was to be away from there, away from the horror of what I'd seen and done. Was this victory?

Above my wrenching sobs I heard another sound: a sound I'd heard once before and never wanted to again. Zeel was laughing. When the last demented echoes died I raised my head and stumbled to my feet. Whatever came next I'd meet it standing, face to face.

At last he spoke, the hollow voice wheezing with mirth. 'Well, well – poor Tallow. Who would have guessed you had such a capacity to entertain? Your brother was right: such pleasure is too rare to squander on minions. Go back to your cell; rest; gather your spirit. It has been too long since my sword tasted fresh blood. When next you are summoned, it will be to face the King of Darkness himself in the arena – and this time you may be certain there will be only one outcome.'

I turned and walked as steadily as I could towards

the exit to the cells. I'd nearly reached it when he spoke again. 'Do not forget your sword, little nephew – for without it, however will you fight at all?'

I crossed to where it lay, picked it up and left the stadium without looking back. One glance at the sword had shown me all I needed to know. The hilt was intact, but all that was left of the blade was a stump, blackened and charred, still smouldering and reeking of charcoal.

It didn't matter. Zeel had said nothing could harm him, and for once I believed him. When next we met, he'd have immortality, full armour and a freshly sharpened sword on his side . . . and I'd have nothing.

Worst of all, I didn't even care.

When the door to the cell was opened, I saw to my horror that Zenith, Blade and Blue-bum were gone. It was completely empty except for a single musty blanket, a tin plate holding a stale crust of bread, a bowl of water . . . and my pack, crumpled forlornly in the corner. There was no sign of my sword.

I swung back to the guard, fists clenched. 'The others – where are they?' But the door clanged shut, leaving my question hanging in the cold air. Sinking down onto the hard stone floor, I made a half-hearted effort to gather my courage and focus on what lay ahead . . . maybe even try and find a way out. But I couldn't – not on my own. I'd have given anything for Rich and Jamie, Kenta and Gen, with their grit and

guts and bulldog determination to find an answer . . .
even when there wasn't one, like now.

What was Jamie's great saying? *When in doubt,
eat* . . . with a half-smile I took a sip of water, then a
gulp . . . then I was glugging it down like a camel. I'd
forgotten how thirsty I was, and the water, warm and
metallic-tasting, was washing away the acrid tang of
smoke. But I wouldn't let myself think about that.
I tried a nibble of bread – and next thing I knew it
was finished.

Suddenly I was shivering and exhausted. When
was the last time I'd slept? I'd woken to the drum of
hoof-beats on the high moor. It seemed a lifetime
ago. I wrapped myself in the blanket, trying to ignore
the fusty smell; lay down on the floor and closed
my eyes.

My hand crept to my talisman, feeling for my ring
through the soft suede. Sleep lapped at the fringes of
my mind . . . then I felt something else nestled against
my hand, something unfamiliar. I explored its outline
with my fingers, then remembered. Of course –
Zenith's amulet. His luck. *Take it . . . use it.*

I wrapped my hand round them both and squeezed
my eyes shut. But it was no use – I was wide awake.
Take it . . . use it. Four simple words: round and
round my mind they went, refusing to be ignored.
Well, I *had* used it. I'd worn it, and it had helped. I'd
wear it again . . . keep on wearing it. I'd never take it
off. If Zenith and I couldn't be together, at least our
talismans could. Maybe that would count . . .

I jerked upright. Hands shaking, I took Zenith's talisman from round my neck, then my own. Opened them and tipped the contents out onto the blanket. There lay the two halves of the Sign of Sovereignty, one silver, one gold. Carefully I slotted them together. A twist and a click, and there it was: one ring, heavy, solid, complete.

When twain is one and one is twain . . .

I slipped it on. The last time the two halves were joined had been on my father's hand: King Zane of Karazan. The ring fitted me perfectly. Now I knew for sure I wouldn't sleep – my mind felt clear and super-sharp. I crawled over to my pack and found my larigot; settled myself back-to-the-wall, pulling the blanket over my legs for warmth. As I tucked it in something caught my eye: something that glowed with a pale luminescence in the dark. It must have fallen out of Zenith's amulet along with his ring. I picked it up. I'd seen it before, but I'd been so focused on the revelation of Zenith's identity I'd barely noticed it. Now I held it in my palm and stared at it.

It was the shape of an arrowhead: a deeply angled V-shape made of silver, about the size of my fingernail. Or was it silver? The metal had a strange, almost coppery warmth . . . I gazed down at it, remembering the words Zaronel had written. *This Book of Days was given to me by my father as a parting gift, the quill by my mother. Though it looks at first sight to be a silver arrowhead, it draws out into a finely crafted feather whose magical filaments pull the moonbeams from the night sky onto the page before me.* I had been given our father's larigot, Zenith our mother's magic quill.

There was a tiny protrusion in the angled indent. With the sharp tip held firmly between finger and thumb, I pulled gently. After a momentary resistance it pulled smoothly out into a long shaft. I'd imagined a quill like a feather, but this didn't look anything like a feather. But as soon as it touched the air two flat, shimmering vanes unfurled, one on either side. Now it *was* a feather: the parallel filaments even linked together like a bird's, to make a smooth, unbroken surface. Strangest of all, the entire quill glowed with its own strange light. Moonlight . . . moon-ink! The quill was just like a real pen filled with ink! On the night of Sunbalance, when we'd been born, both the silver and gold moons had been high in the sky, and full. The twin moons. I'd seen them on that same night years later, when they'd lit our way in the desperate race to the portal. The light in the quill was tinged with gold like the moonlight had been last time it was used – that was why the last entries in the diary had that strange, coppery warmth.

Take it . . . use it.

I thought Zenith meant the talisman. But maybe he'd meant the ring. I heard his voice in my mind as clearly as if he was standing beside me: *Every strength has a weakness, and even the creatures of darkest nightmare may be vanquished by the light.*

I sat for what seemed a long time staring at the two gifts, Zenith's from my mother, mine from my father:

the quill in my left hand shining with its strange silver-gold light, the larigot in my right.

And then, finally, I knew what I must do.

Much later I heard a scuffle and a scratch and saw two bright eyes peering at me from between the bars of the window. Before my heart had time to start beating again there was a chitter, a squiggle and a squeeze, and a scrawny armful of chatterbot was giving me a furry hug.

With jibbers and gestures, Blue-bum told me he and Blade and Zenith were safe in a neighbouring cell. Zeel had separated us deliberately. He might not know about the *twain* of the prophecy, but he guessed I'd draw strength from my brother – and that's why he'd decided to keep us apart. But he'd reckoned without Blue-bum. We settled down, sharing the blanket. But still I couldn't sleep.

My mind was full of my plan. I wanted to tell someone, even Blue-bum; to talk it through and convince myself it would really work. I knew it could. But would it? Two vital factors would have to fall precisely into place. And if they didn't . . . I'd find out soon enough. That wasn't what was keeping sleep at bay. It was something else, something looming in my mind like a monster, huge and forbidding: something that had been stalking me like a shadow ever since the moment I realised my true identity. In the mountains above Arraz I'd faced it and given it words, and now it must be faced again.

I was going to have to kill Zeel.

After all that had happened – after my gladiator training, the things I'd seen – after Blade and Tallow – it should have been easier. I felt way older now than I had then; ages old. That should mean I was stronger, tougher, surely? But it didn't. There was a strange new tenderness deep inside me, a longing to turn away from bloodshed and find a different way forward. What had been hard before now seemed impossible; issues that had once been simple were now as complex as a tangled ball of twine.

There were a million reasons why he deserved to die. He had killed my father, stolen the kingdom, brought torture, death and misery to thousands. Now he was planning to kill me – and Zenith, Blade and Blue-bum would be next.

If I didn't kill him, the entire kingdom of Karazan – along with the rest of this world, and others beyond – would almost certainly be doomed. If the task rested with someone else, how easy it would be. To another boy lying awake on the cold stone floor I'd have said without a second's hesitation: *Do it. Kill him.* But this wasn't another boy. It was me.

The question loomed huge and unanswerable in my mind: is it ever right to kill, to take another human life? Maybe if I told Blue-bum, got him to help . . . No. If killing was wrong, getting someone else to do it had to be way worse.

My mind kept coming back to Tallow. That had been an accident . . . sort of. I should be glad he was

316

dead, and I was. But I kept remembering him as Shaw, as the Masked Man, and wondering: was it possible for anyone to be completely evil? This time my mind knew the answer, though my heart didn't want to believe it. *Yes.* But the question still remained: even if it was right, even if it would work . . . *could I bring myself to do it?*

The endless night wore on. Blue-bum was awake, twitching and fidgeting; at last he clambered up and peered into my face with a worried chitter, then stationed himself beside my head, picking through my filthy hair with nimble fingers. 'Stop that monkey-stuff, you darn chatterbot,' I grumbled half-heartedly – but the truth was it felt wonderfully soothing. I gave myself up to his gentle, probing fingers, and gradually felt the tension drain away and my thoughts slide towards oblivion. One last waking thought drifted through my mind: *Hope he's not actually finding anything in there . . .*

And at last I slept, Tallow dancing like a fiery marionette through my dreams.

TWAIN

I was jerked from sleep by a metallic *boom* that shook my cell to its foundations. Another followed it, and another: a giant gong was being beaten in the amphitheatre beyond my window. I sat bolt upright, my heart thudding with adrenaline overload. The last echo died away, leaving the air fragile and trembling.

I clambered shakily to my knees. Blue-bum must have slipped away; there was no sign of him. But someone had come in while I was sleeping. There was a new bowl of water, a new crust of bread; an empty wooden bucket.

Long years of orphanage training had taught me well. I shook out the blanket, planning to leave it tidily folded in one corner – and something fell from its crumpled folds: a tiny greyish cube with a few wispy chatterbot-hairs sticking to it. I knew that Blue-bum had left it for me. Something about it was familiar . . . picking off the hairs, I touched the tip of my tongue to the surface. *Peppermint.* It was the piece of chewing gum I'd shared with him on the boat; I remembered him stashing it away behind his ear. He must have kept it all this time – and now he'd given it back to me.

I used the bucket, drank the water, ate the bread. Then draped the blanket neatly over the bucket, and allowed myself a grim smile. Matron would have approved. I was ready. The ring was on my finger; the two talismans hung over my heart, side by side. My larigot was safely in my pocket.

I looked round the tidy cell. My pack lay in the corner. I picked it up; opened it. There wasn't much inside. Zaronel's diary; the two parchments, tightly rolled. Meirion's magic sail; my microcomputer; my shawl. An empty water bottle. Nothing that would help me now.

And yet . . . whatever happened, I doubted I'd be coming back. After a moment's thought I pulled out my shawl and slipped the charred sword hilt in with the rest of the stuff, then shrugged the pack onto my back, feeling it settle into its familiar place between my shoulder blades. I folded the shawl into a triangle, then over and over into a flat strip, like a wide bandanna, then tied it round my waist. It felt good – firm and warm, like a hug. Best of all, it helped stop the quaking.

There was nothing left to do. I sat down with my back to the wall, staring at the door and chewing my gum. And waited.

At last the key squealed in the lock and the door opened. Two of the Faceless stood outside. For the last time I ducked under the low doorframe and into the passage; glanced along the wall at the row of closed doors. There was no way of telling which was Zenith and Blade and Blue-bum's. I walked slowly towards the open gateway. The only sound was my footfalls on the stone, measured and slow as the beating of my heart.

I stopped just inside the amphitheatre. Everything was the same as before: the dim grey shapes clogging the terraces, the central fire, the bare stone floor. But now the dark air seemed to tremble with something new: a tension that ran like an electric current round the galleries and flickered like invisible sheet lightning above us in the still air.

I flicked a glance sideways and up, knowing he'd be there. Just above me, on the narrow stone sill outside his window, crouched Blue-bum.

I turned away, my whole being focused on the creature that stood before me. He was waiting between me and the pit of fire. Even at this distance he towered over me like a giant, a mountain of metal blocking the light. Standing in the cold spill of his shadow I could feel the force of evil pulsing outwards in invisible waves . . . at the same time the darkness behind the black helm sucked at me like a vacuum, draining my strength and filling me with confusion and uncertainty. A sour, burned smell hung in the air: the smell of victory – or guilt? I longed for certainty, for forgiveness in advance of what I planned to do. A wave of dizziness swept over me; I took a stumbling step sideways to stop myself falling . . . and I was out of his shadow, and my head cleared.

I closed my mind, straightened my back, locked my knees so they wouldn't wobble. Took a deep breath and stood watching him, waiting.

'Well, Zephyr: going on a journey? Indeed you are – a one-way journey.' The helmeted head tipped back and once again hollow laughter rang out over the arena, making my flesh crawl. Round and round the curved walls it rolled like a great steel ball, endless and unstoppable, till at last it ground down to a rasping chuckle and then silence.

He took a slow step forward. The armour gave his movements a stilted awkwardness that reminded me of a robot, or some clumsy mechanical toy. I could almost hear the stone floor creaking under his weight. Now I could see the thickness of the steel, the joints and flanges and rivets. There were no chinks; only the narrow eye-slit gaped, dark and empty. One gauntleted hand held a black sword, unsheathed, reflections of the firelight dripping from its blade.

I took a deep breath and spoke, willing my voice to be steadfast and strong. 'Before we begin, I have one request.'

'A last request? How touching.'

'My gladiator name is Whistler . . .' I slid my hand into my pocket and carefully withdrew my larigot, holding it up so he could glimpse its silvery gleam.

He gave a soft hiss: a low, menacing sound that made my skin crawl. 'Zane's larigot! Curse him and all who carry it – and curse that which you wear on your hand!' I was wrong, he wasn't slow and cumbersome. Without warning he lunged forward in another giant stride. His sword swung in a whistling arc that missed me by millimetres as I sprang back, brushing my face with a gust of air that reeked of cold metal and emptiness, and catching in my throat like a sob. My heart gave a painful hobble, but I kept my voice steady.

'I would like to play a final song, to bring me courage.'

'A final song? Your funeral dirge: a lament for one about to die . . . why not? The thought pleases me. But my sword's bloodlust must soon be sated. Let the tune not be too sweet, nor too long.'

'It won't be sweet – and you'll wish it was longer.'

As I raised my larigot to my lips time seemed to slow. I saw my hands were trembling; saw how the heat from my fingers printed misty crescents on the bright silver. I positioned my fingers over the holes . . . and suddenly everything I'd felt, seen, smelled, flew together in my mind like a bright flock of birds. The hollow echo of the voice . . . the empty laughter . . . the metallic non-smell. The nothingness behind the helm.

It won't be killing . . . because he's already dead. He isn't human. He was – once. But now he is darkness – only darkness. He said so himself. Darkness and a voice: the force of evil.

And finally I knew without doubt that what I was

about to do was right. I fixed my eyes on the slit in the black helm, took a last deep breath, closed my lips over the smooth silver – and blew.

Blew a single, discordant shriek that split the air like the wild call of a sea-bird – a blood-curdling primeval battle-cry.

Blew a single, ferocious blast that propelled Zenith's quill from its hiding place at the heart of my larigot like a dart from a blow-pipe, an arrow whose wings unfurled as it flew. It carried its own pale light with it like a shooting-star: the silver-gold light of the twin moons. The two shining vanes carried the quill straight and true towards its target. As the discordant note died I could almost hear the whisper of its wings through the air, though they were silent as an owl's. *When twain is one and one is twain . . .*

Straight and true the arrow flew, on and on through the dark air.

To me its journey seemed to take forever, as if I could have stepped forward and plucked it from the air with my bare hand at any moment I chose. But in reality it was as swift as thought. The great armoured head never had time to turn away. Through the slit in the black helm the bright arrow flew, and into the bottomless darkness beyond. And even then, as a dazzling radiance blossomed and grew within the helm, the giant figure stood as if turned to stone.

A great weariness settled over me. It was done. My knees buckled and I fell forward onto the stone floor; knelt there, watching. As blinding brightness welled from its eye-slot into the thick murk of the arena, the creature gave a single wordless shriek of rage. The hand holding the sword lifted, drew back – threw.

I couldn't have moved if I'd wanted to. But I felt nothing more than a wondering curiosity as the black sword hurtled towards me through the dark air like a javelin, its speed both swift and slow, as if it was suspended in some strange dream-time I wasn't part of and didn't understand.

I only knew that it was over – the dark force of Zeel was vanquished, finally and forever. I had completed my quest. And whatever happened next just didn't seem to matter . . . didn't seem to matter at all.

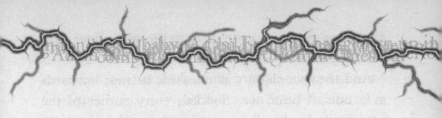

JOURNEY'S END

From above me came a chitter as urgent as machine-gun fire – and then something was falling, dropping like a furry hailstone faster, way faster than the black javelin forging so slowly through the dense air. I caught a momentary flash of blue, a glimpse of a face clenched tight and eyes squeezed shut.

In that last fraction of a second time flicked forward into super-fast – and it was too late. Too late for me to do anything except cry a single, choking sound without words and launch myself in a desperate dive towards him.

I didn't even get close.

There was a flat smack, as if some invisible watcher had clapped his hands just once. Blue-bum thudded into me, turning as he fell, something long and black and shining sticking out of the centre of his back.

In the same instant the moonlight burst the black armour apart. It blew to pieces with a crack that tore the air like an explosion, chunks of metal flying in all directions and raining down onto the stone floor with a ringing clatter.

And the moonlight was released. It leapt outwards in a tide of brilliance, flooding every corner of the arena with dazzling light, surging like a tidal wave over the terraces where the Faceless clustered, obliterating them as if they'd never existed. For a second a pale haze like sea-mist drifted in the air; then even that was gone.

But all I cared about was Blue-bum. Ears ringing, squinting against the dazzle, I struggled to my knees, his limp body cradled in my arms. The fierce determination had vanished from his little face, leaving a look of faint surprise. A vast hilt bound with oily-looking leather reared like some grotesque ornament from his skinny chest. I wanted to cuddle him close, but the cold steel skewering his tiny body stopped me. Instead I held him with a terrible gentleness as if he might break, terrified of hurting him, though in my heart I knew nothing could hurt him now.

His button eyes met mine, his monkey-mouth moving as if he was trying to say something, or even smile. But as I watched the brightness of his eyes began to fade, as if they were looking far, far beyond my face at something only they could see. I held him, saying nothing, my tears falling through the brightness onto his soft fur like rain through sunshine, until the last light died from his eyes.

On every side the radiance grew. Bright and unstoppable as a full moon rising it pushed back the shadows, squeezing into cracks and crevices and banishing the dark. A shuddering vibration was growing, as if the hugeness of the light was too great to be contained even by the bounds of the underworld.

And still I gazed at Blue-bum. As I watched, the sword-hilt embedded in his chest began to change, its elaborate carvings vanishing like the ridges on a barley-sugar being sucked smooth. Beneath his small, still body I could feel the sword itself dwindling, shrinking, its dead weight lightening to nothing. For a second my heart lifted with wild hope . . . but his shuttered face and blank eyes told me it was too late.

All round us every manifestation of darkness was cracking, crumbling, shattering into a mosaic of bright-edged fragments swallowed to nothing, vanquished by the brilliance of the light.

I sank to the ground, closed my eyes against the dazzle and cuddled the body of Blue-bum close at last as the Realms of the Undead fell to ruin around me.

It could have been seconds or hours later that I felt a hand on my shoulder and opened my eyes. The face of my brother swam into focus, grimy and creased with concern. Blue-bum's body, cold and lifeless, was still cradled in my arms.

I was sitting in a clearing in a forest, dappled sunlight sifting through shifting leaves. Fine, soft grass carpeted the ground; birds twittered and chirped in the branches above. There was another sound too, a rhythmic munching . . . slowly, numb and dream-drenched as a sleepwalker, I turned my head towards it.

The winged colt lifted his head and met my eyes with a thoughtful, measuring stare, then plodded across to nudge me with his nose and breathe grass-scented breath into my hair.

On the far side of the clearing a great tree trunk lay, patterned with dappled sunlight. There was no sign of the two birds who had once stood sentinel there. On one side of the fallen trunk a braided arch of roots and vines opened to a tunnel beckoning with shifting sunbeams; on its other side a dense, impenetrable tangle of undergrowth held no trace that any path had ever been there. I laid Blue-bum's body down on the soft earth and covered it with my cloak.

Zenith reached out his arms. We held each other, heads bowed. I felt the slow, steady beating of his heart in time with my own; his strength soaking into me. On the ground Blade lay watching us, eyes huge and shadowed but luminous with life. I managed to smile at her. 'Blade. Welcome back.'

Beside her was my pack; next to that, my sword. I buckled it into place with clumsy fingers. 'Whistler – what happened?' Blade was asking. 'We heard voices, and suddenly the world was shaking apart around us . . . then everything was brightness, and when it cleared . . .'

'. . . we found ourselves here.' Zenith shrugged and smiled. 'Whatever passed between you and Zeel, it seems you have completed our quest, my brother.'

'It has been completed.' I slipped off his amulet and handed it back to him. 'Thanks to this – and you. Our parents' gifts . . . the answer – or part of the answer.'

He frowned. 'What do you mean?'

'*When twain is one and one is twain* . . . at first I thought I had to find a way of combining my larigot and your quill to defeat Zeel. Symbols of you and me, I suppose Jamie would say. And then I realised it was more: the light of the twin moons, gold and silver, together as one. But you'd already worked it out – tried to tell me, in the few seconds you had. *Take it, use it*, you said. It took me a while to realise what you meant, but . . .'

He was looking at me oddly, his mouth twisted into a half-smile. 'I meant nothing. I said that, yes, but I didn't mean anything by it – or no more than the words themselves. All I could do was give you the only thing I had: my talisman. I had no idea if it would help, or how. What you made of it was yours alone. And as for luck – in this life we make our own, just as you have done.'

We rested a while in the leafy stillness, talking quietly, breathing the fresh, sweet air and listening to the song of the birds and the soft sighing of the wind in the leaves. The colt grazed peacefully nearby.

I felt the cool essence of the surrounding forest soak into my soul like balm. The glade was the same, yet utterly changed. The wild, spicy smell and soft patterning of leaf and shadow reminded me of Shadowwood, and I had a growing certainty that our journey's end was closer than we thought; that through the arch and round a few bends we might come across a distant view of the ochre walls, turrets and pinnacles I already thought of as home.

Blade was still far too weak to walk. We tried to lift her onto the colt's back, but he tossed his head and circled his hindquarters away, clearly not comfortable with the idea. 'Perhaps if you rode him, and carried Blade in front of you . . .' Zenith suggested at last.

I shouldered my pack for the last time and turned with a heavy heart to the shrouded form of Blue-bum. He would come with us on this final journey, to be buried with every honour beside the singing fountains of the Summer Palace.

I bent to gather the small body into my arms – and stopped, staring. Before, my cloak had swamped the tiny chatterbot. But now, it barely covered what lay beneath. Hardly daring to breathe, I reached out a hand and drew the cloth away from his face.

I saw a tangle of filthy hair and a skin grey with grime; a straight nose with a faint sprinkling that could have been either freckles or dirt; level sandy-coloured brows over eyes closed in what looked like peaceful sleep. A jaw that had squared and strengthened; a quirk almost like laughter in one corner of the wide mouth . . .

As I stared down at him his eyelids flickered and opened. Brown eyes met mine for a puzzled second, then flicked down to the long boy-body under the cloak and cleared to instant understanding. He'd always been smart.

Not me, though. I goggled down at him, a bewildered grin spreading itself over my face, my mind reeling as I battled to figure it out. What had Evor said? *There is one way he can be restored to his original form, but from what we have come to know of William Weaver, it might as well not exist.*

He'd been wrong. This wasn't William Weaver – the Weevil I'd once known. It was someone new, someone who had done without hesitation what Evor thought he never would: willingly given his life for a friend.

A faint flush was appearing beneath the dirt on his face. When he spoke, his voice was slightly croaky, as if it hadn't been used for a while. 'Adam . . . Zephyr . . . there's something I've been wanting to say to you for ages.'

I opened my mouth to tell him I already knew what it was – and it was OK, he didn't even have to say it. But then I closed it again. I knew that this was what he'd tried to tell me in the amphitheatre; what I'd seen in his eyes countless times along our journey. And I realised he needed to say it, so we could leave it behind and move on together.

'I . . . I'm sorry. For everything I did – but especially . . .' the blush deepened, his voice dropping to a whisper, 'for your gladiator project. I'm ashamed to think I could have done that to you – to anyone.'

'Apology accepted,' I told him. 'We've all done stuff we regret – me as much as anyone. But I've done a lot of thinking, and I wouldn't change any of it. I've figured you can use bad things kind of like stepping stones when you cross a river: as long as you move past them and they help you go forward, it turns them from bad to good – sort of like magic. And now I've got something to say to *you*: two things. First: thank you – for everything. And second: we'd be honoured if you'd agree to stay and help us put things right in Karazan – wouldn't we, Zenith?'

'Yes, of course,' said Zenith, looking confused. 'And since he's staying, can you please explain who he is? Or who he *was*, before . . .' he paused delicately.

'That doesn't matter,' I said with a grin. 'To us, he'll always be Blue-bum.'

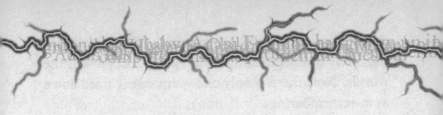

EPILOGUE

The colt banks and turns, the wind whipping through my hair and my eyes watering as I stare downwards. The whole of Karazan revolves below me in a slow circle: purple smudges of forest, their outlines already familiar; silver strands of rivers whose courses thread my dreams. Gliding low, I feel the colt's legs gather into the first stride of a canter-on-air that catches and settles into a drumming rhythm as we land, steadies to a trot and then a walk.

The early morning is grey and damp, only the lightest breeze stirring the mist that veils the surface of Lake Stillwater. Water birds call across the silence, their plaintive notes questions hanging unanswered in the still air. The Dark Citadel floats on the mist like a phantom; above it, the dawn streaks the sky with gold. The colt drops his head and drinks, then nuzzles me, dribbling icy water down my front.

I shrug off my pack: weather-beaten and stained, the seams beginning to fray. There's only one thing inside. My hand finds it easily, though it feels smaller than I remember. The microcomputer. Not long ago there were five of these computers, all loaded with the VRE Interface that was the passport between the worlds. Now there is only one – this one. I stare down at it, remembering . . .

Q had removed the software from the others and destroyed the code that took him so long to write. 'You and your brother are the only ones with the right of passage between this world and Karazan,' he told me the last time we spoke at Quested Court. 'In times past, the door between the worlds has been the salvation of them both. But that may not always be so. The key – and the decision on whether and how to use it – should be in your hands alone.'

In his eyes I'd seen wisdom, warning, love, regret . . . and unshed tears for something I didn't understand.

Now I weigh the tiny computer in my hand. It feels strangely heavy for something so small, as if an entire world is really contained inside its plastic casing. And I suppose it is, in a way. If I press the keys now, I'll be there.

ALT CONTROL Q.

I think of that world and everything it contains. Richard, Jamie, Kenta, Gen. Silver sports cars and skyscrapers; television and hamburgers. Pollution, overpopulation and corruption; greed and starvation. My friend Cameron . . . and Matron.

I think of Q, of Hannah, of Tiger Lily and Bluebell. I think of Karazan: of what it is now and what I dream it will become. I think of the door between the worlds.

Would it be better for it to be open, closed . . . or locked forever?

I'm already so used to wearing the twisted crown I barely feel it. Zenith and I each have one, his the original gold part and mine the silver, each with a newly forged piece added to complete it, as with the Sign of Sovereignty we both wear. Now suddenly my crown feels heavy and cold.

I think of Usherwood's crisp words to us both after the coronation, in her self-appointed role of governess and adviser-in-chief: 'Remember, both of you: no one ever said it would be fun being King of Karazan. There will be right choices and wrong ones – and the right ones will often be the hardest to make.'

I draw back my hand, hesitate for one final second . . . and throw. The microcomputer soars away in a long arc, out, out, out over the water; then down to vanish without a sound into the mist blanketing the lake. Closing my eyes I imagine it sinking down, rocking slightly as it drifts through the green water into the darkening depths and wavering weed, then settling at last in the silty mud of the bottom. Perhaps a few tiny bubbles rise, the last breath of a world lost forever . . . perhaps not.

It's a long time before the first faint ripples appear, chasing each other with little lapping chuckles onto the beach. Slowly, then faster, then slowly again and slower still . . . until at last, like faraway laughter, they dwindle to nothing.

★

The colt follows me into the fragrant gloom of the stables. A soft whicker greets us, a pale face appearing over the door of the stall beside his. She and the colt touch noses; then he clops on into his stable, wanting breakfast. I give Starlight's neck a gentle rub and smile at the tiny face peering inquisitively from the safety of her flank. Her smudged star and the colt's blaze have combined in their foal to form a perfect shooting star and give her a name that chose itself: Wish.

All round me the palace is stirring to life. I smell breakfast – and suddenly I'm ravenous. I run up the stairs two at a time, heading for the morning room where we have most of our meals. But before I even reach the door I hear an impatient squeal. 'Adam! Is that you? Come and see what's happened!'

'I have told you before, young lady, the King's name is not Adam but Zephyr. *King* Zephyr, to commoners like you.'

'You're a commoner too, Usherwood, don't forget. Anyhow, Adam's the King of Karazan and *he* says I can still call him Adam.'

I can't help smiling as I shoulder my way in and the familiar scene opens out in front of me. Sun streaming through a wide casement opening to a distant view of the sea. My mother in her rocking chair, murmuring to herself as she counts the stitches in her knitting, while her new husband Zagros stokes the fire. Zenith slouched in a chair, grinning at me through a mouthful of toast and honey.

Two men at a table, locked in silent combat over

the chess set between them. One has long grey hair, deep smile lines and a studied expression of seriousness; the other, a raggedy scarecrow with smeared spectacles, shakes his head distractedly. 'Why, I do believe you might be right, Meirion,' he's saying. 'Checkmate indeed – however did that happen?'

Only three of us are missing: Blue-bum – now officially Sir William Bluebottom, Blue for short, Blade and Kai; they'll be joining us after breakfast for the first meeting of the newly formed Knights of the New Dawn. When Zen and I dreamed up that name, even Usherwood had been impressed.

Now old Usherwood's doing her best to frown severely at the little figure in pink and grey Eeyore pyjamas tugging at my hand.

Obediently, I follow her over to the huge carved dresser where the brocade table linen is kept. Everyone in the room is watching us now, even Meirion with his sightless eyes. They're smiling. Starting to smile myself without knowing why, I watch as Hannah kneels and opens the door. There's a strange sound coming from inside.

I bend and peer in.

There in the darkness is Tiger Lily. She's made herself a nest among the tablecloths and napkins and is lying in it with her back to us, purring thunderously. She looks up when the door opens and narrows her golden eyes at me smugly. Impossibly, the volume of the purring increases. As usual, I'm lost. 'What . . .'

'Shhhh. Look,' Hannah is whispering. She reaches

in with careful hands, scoops something up and holds it out for me to see. It even looks small in Hannah's little hands: the tiniest pastel-coloured kitten – all velvet tummy, scrunched face and pincushion claws. 'There are four of them.'

I gaze down at Hannah's bright face, at the tiny kitten cradled in her hands. And then, for no reason at all, Meirion's words of long ago come into my mind: *For you, Child of the Wind, your destiny lies where you least look for it – the beginning will be the end, and every end a new beginning.*

I see Hannah's name as an endless circle, with no end and no beginning:

She laughs up at me, and the future shines from her eyes.